I0818144

MISFORTUNE

(AND GOUDA)

(A European Voyage Cozy Mystery —Book Four)

BLAKE PIERCE

Blake Pierce

Blake Pierce is the USA Today bestselling author of the RILEY PAGE mystery series, which includes seventeen books. Blake Pierce is also the author of the MACKENZIE WHITE mystery series, comprising fourteen books; of the AVERY BLACK mystery series, comprising six books; of the KERI LOCKE mystery series, comprising five books; of the MAKING OF RILEY PAIGE mystery series, comprising six books; of the KATE WISE mystery series, comprising seven books; of the CHLOE FINE psychological suspense mystery, comprising six books; of the JESSE HUNT psychological suspense thriller series, comprising nineteen books; of the AU PAIR psychological suspense thriller series, comprising three books; of the ZOE PRIME mystery series, comprising six books; of the ADELE SHARP mystery series, comprising thirteen books; of the EUROPEAN VOYAGE cozy mystery series, comprising six books (and counting); of the new LAURA FROST FBI suspense thriller, comprising three books (and counting); of the new ELLA DARK FBI suspense thriller, comprising six books (and counting); of the A YEAR IN EUROPE cozy mystery series, comprising nine books); of the AVA GOLD mystery series, comprising three books (and counting); and of the RACHEL GIFT mystery series, comprising three books (and counting).

An avid reader and lifelong fan of the mystery and thriller genres, Blake loves to hear from you, so please feel free to visit www.blakepierceauthor.com to learn more and stay in touch.

ISBN: 978-1-0943-9108-3

BOOKS BY BLAKE PIERCE

RACHEL GIFT MYSTERY SERIES
HER LAST WISH (Book #1)
HER LAST CHANCE (Book #2)
HER LAST HOPE (Book #3)

AVA GOLD MYSTERY SERIES
CITY OF PREY (Book #1)
CITY OF FEAR (Book #2)
CITY OF BONES (Book #3)

A YEAR IN EUROPE
A MURDER IN PARIS (Book #1)
DEATH IN FLORENCE (Book #2)
VENGEANCE IN VIENNA (Book #3)

ELLA DARK FBI SUSPENSE THRILLER
GIRL, ALONE (Book #1)
GIRL, TAKEN (Book #2)
GIRL, HUNTED (Book #3)
GIRL, SILENCED (Book #4)
GIRL, VANISHED (Book 5)
GIRL ERASED (Book #6)

LAURA FROST FBI SUSPENSE THRILLER
ALREADY GONE (Book #1)
ALREADY SEEN (Book #2)
ALREADY TRAPPED (Book #3)

EUROPEAN VOYAGE COZY MYSTERY SERIES
MURDER (AND BAKLAVA) (Book #1)
DEATH (AND APPLE STRUDEL) (Book #2)
CRIME (AND LAGER) (Book #3)
MISFORTUNE (AND GOUDA) (Book #4)
CALAMITY (AND A DANISH) (Book #5)
MAYHEM (AND HERRING) (Book #6)

ADELE SHARP MYSTERY SERIES
LEFT TO DIE (Book #1)
LEFT TO RUN (Book #2)
LEFT TO HIDE (Book #3)
LEFT TO KILL (Book #4)
LEFT TO MURDER (Book #5)
LEFT TO ENVY (Book #6)
LEFT TO LAPSE (Book #7)
LEFT TO VANISH (Book #8)
LEFT TO HUNT (Book #9)
LEFT TO FEAR (Book #10)

THE AU PAIR SERIES
ALMOST GONE (Book#1)
ALMOST LOST (Book #2)
ALMOST DEAD (Book #3)

ZOE PRIME MYSTERY SERIES
FACE OF DEATH (Book#1)
FACE OF MURDER (Book #2)
FACE OF FEAR (Book #3)
FACE OF MADNESS (Book #4)
FACE OF FURY (Book #5)
FACE OF DARKNESS (Book #6)

A JESSIE HUNT PSYCHOLOGICAL SUSPENSE SERIES
THE PERFECT WIFE (Book #1)
THE PERFECT BLOCK (Book #2)
THE PERFECT HOUSE (Book #3)
THE PERFECT SMILE (Book #4)
THE PERFECT LIE (Book #5)
THE PERFECT LOOK (Book #6)
THE PERFECT AFFAIR (Book #7)
THE PERFECT ALIBI (Book #8)
THE PERFECT NEIGHBOR (Book #9)
THE PERFECT DISGUISE (Book #10)
THE PERFECT SECRET (Book #11)
THE PERFECT FAÇADE (Book #12)
THE PERFECT IMPRESSION (Book #13)

THE PERFECT DECEIT (Book #14)
THE PERFECT MISTRESS (Book #15)
THE PERFECT IMAGE (Book #16)
THE PERFECT VEIL (Book #17)
THE PERFECT INDISCRETION (Book #18)
THE PERFECT RUMOR (Book #19)

CHLOE FINE PSYCHOLOGICAL SUSPENSE SERIES
NEXT DOOR (Book #1)
A NEIGHBOR'S LIE (Book #2)
CUL DE SAC (Book #3)
SILENT NEIGHBOR (Book #4)
HOMECOMING (Book #5)
TINTED WINDOWS (Book #6)

KATE WISE MYSTERY SERIES
IF SHE KNEW (Book #1)
IF SHE SAW (Book #2)
IF SHE RAN (Book #3)
IF SHE HID (Book #4)
IF SHE FLED (Book #5)
IF SHE FEARED (Book #6)
IF SHE HEARD (Book #7)

THE MAKING OF RILEY PAIGE SERIES
WATCHING (Book #1)
WAITING (Book #2)
LURING (Book #3)
TAKING (Book #4)
STALKING (Book #5)
KILLING (Book #6)

RILEY PAIGE MYSTERY SERIES
ONCE GONE (Book #1)
ONCE TAKEN (Book #2)
ONCE CRAVED (Book #3)
ONCE LURED (Book #4)
ONCE HUNTED (Book #5)
ONCE PINED (Book #6)
ONCE FORSAKEN (Book #7)

ONCE COLD (Book #8)
ONCE STALKED (Book #9)
ONCE LOST (Book #10)
ONCE BURIED (Book #11)
ONCE BOUND (Book #12)
ONCE TRAPPED (Book #13)
ONCE DORMANT (Book #14)
ONCE SHUNNED (Book #15)
ONCE MISSED (Book #16)
ONCE CHOSEN (Book #17)

MACKENZIE WHITE MYSTERY SERIES
BEFORE HE KILLS (Book #1)
BEFORE HE SEES (Book #2)
BEFORE HE COVETS (Book #3)
BEFORE HE TAKES (Book #4)
BEFORE HE NEEDS (Book #5)
BEFORE HE FEELS (Book #6)
BEFORE HE SINS (Book #7)
BEFORE HE HUNTS (Book #8)
BEFORE HE PREYS (Book #9)
BEFORE HE LONGS (Book #10)
BEFORE HE LAPSES (Book #11)
BEFORE HE ENVIES (Book #12)
BEFORE HE STALKS (Book #13)
BEFORE HE HARMS (Book #14)

AVERY BLACK MYSTERY SERIES
CAUSE TO KILL (Book #1)
CAUSE TO RUN (Book #2)
CAUSE TO HIDE (Book #3)
CAUSE TO FEAR (Book #4)
CAUSE TO SAVE (Book #5)
CAUSE TO DREAD (Book #6)

KERI LOCKE MYSTERY SERIES
A TRACE OF DEATH (Book #1)
A TRACE OF MUDER (Book #2)
A TRACE OF VICE (Book #3)
A TRACE OF CRIME (Book #4)

A TRACE OF HOPE (Book #5)

CHAPTER ONE

London stifled a yelp of alarm. She'd almost spilled a tray of drinks when the worried-looking steward came dashing up to her. She was helping out in the lounge of the riverboat *Nachtmusik*, which was not her usual job. But as the ship's social director, and as a dedicated employee of Epoch World Cruise Lines, she often volunteered to fill in wherever help was needed—and help was obviously needed here today.

"I'm sorry to trouble you, Ms. Rose," he said. "But do you know where I can find Emil Waldmüller?"

Recovering her balance and making sure the drinks were still in place, London glanced at the clock above the bar.

"Judging from the time," she told the anxious steward, "he must be up on the *Rondo* deck getting ready to—"

"He's not there," the steward said in reply. "People are gathered up there, waiting to hear him. The ship is almost within sight of the *Mäuseturm*—'Mouse Tower'—but Herr Waldmüller hasn't shown up yet."

That was a surprise to London. It wasn't like her German colleague to be late for anything, ever.

She knew that Emil, the ship's historian, was scheduled to point out sights along the Rhine Gorge as they passed through it, sharing his considerable knowledge with an eager group of listeners. Surely he would show up soon. And besides, right now London had more than a dozen drinks to serve.

"Don't worry," she assured the steward, "Herr Waldmüller would never miss a lecture. He probably got held up for a few moments. He'll be there—if he isn't there already."

The steward nodded uncertainly and headed back out of the lounge.

London felt a flash of worry as she tottered with her tray toward her first table, weaving among the people who were coming and going.

Emil—late for a lecture? she thought.

She was sure he wouldn't miss the assignment altogether. He was probably already up there on the open-air *Rondo* deck starting his talk right now.

Meanwhile, she needed to get these drinks safely to the passengers who had ordered them. Her customers were seated at the various tables and clusters of sofas and chairs in the large room, or were playing games in the mini-casino off at one side.

It had been a long time since London had worked in a bar, and she'd forgotten how hectic it could be. She had to remember which drinks on her tray went to which tables, not losing track of which customers had ordered the deceptively strong Long Island Iced Teas, or the vodka-based Moscow Mules in their chilled copper mugs, or the bottles of lager and stout, or the glasses of wine, or the whiskeys-and-water. Her mind clicked away frantically as she made her way around one of the attractive potted plants that were part of the décor, navigating with the care of a tightrope walker to keep the tray level and the drinks from spilling.

Feeling harried by it all, London wondered if her often-tousled auburn hair still held anything resembling the neat style she combed it into before she'd started this.

Well, she told herself, *it never stays in place very long. Surely the passengers are used to that by now.*

London was busy serving drinks this afternoon because the *Nachtmusik* had been traveling all day and would still be in transit all night. With no opportunity to go ashore, more passengers than usual were crowded into the spacious lounge. Besides that, drinks were being served at half price as part of a bundle of perks, bargains, and vouchers that had been put into effect to mollify the passengers. The cruise was now two full days behind schedule, due to the weird fact that people kept winding up dead whenever the *Nachtmusik* pulled into port, and the local police always delayed their scheduled departures while investigations were going on.

London hoped with all her heart that the cruise's run of bad luck was over.

In any case, she actually hadn't heard many passengers complain about the delays.

But they sure are taking advantage of these drinks, London thought.

Many of the customers seemed to be speculating about their upcoming visit to Amsterdam.

Those who had ordered the Long Island Iced Teas were discussing Amsterdam's historical sights.

"All my life I've wanted to visit Anne Frank House."

"And I want to visit De Waag *on Nieuwmarkt square—the ancient city."*

Then at the table where London served the Moscow Mules, people were talking about something else altogether.

"I can't wait to visit the Artis Royal Zoo."

"Yes, they're said to have the most amazing tortoises."

When London set down a couple of glasses of wine at another table, she heard two women talking about shopping.

"They say you can buy wonderful clothes on the Nine Little Streets."

"And all kinds of accessories, I hear."

At the table with the whiskeys-and-water, the talk was about art.

"I've read that the painting 'Sunflowers' is on display in the Van Gogh Museum."

"Yes, and so is 'Almond Blossom.'"

London had visited Amsterdam as a child, although she remembered little about it. She knew that she must have seen many of those sights accompanied by her mother. Now she felt her breath catch in her throat as she thought of that address she had found back in Germany.

65 Poppenhuisstraat, Amsterdam

Could that note really mean that Mom might be in Amsterdam again, even after all these years?

Pay attention to your job, London told herself firmly.

Moving around to see who needed service next, she was a bit taken aback by the conversation she heard at the table with the lager and stout.

"Is it true that Amsterdam has a perfectly legal Red Light District?"

"Yes, and it has shops where you can buy and smoke cannabis!"

"Lots of things are legal in Amsterdam."

What those customers were saying was perfectly true, of course. Amsterdam was home to a number of well-regulated activities that were illegal in most other places. It was the cheeky tone, the slight snickers of delight, that she heard in these voices that set off mini-alarms for her. The folks at that table looked less mature to her than most of the other passengers. The group of 100 they had on board for this trip was largely made up of retirees and second-honeymooners and the like.

Of course, many of these same people had participated wholeheartedly in the beer festival at their last stop in Bamberg, Germany. London could feel herself cringe as she remembered that it was she who had briefly tangled with the law there. Except for the one passenger who had gotten involved in the investigation, the rest has suffered nothing worse than a hangover.

On the other hand, might Amsterdam offer unusual opportunities for embarrassing escapades?

London momentarily wondered whether she or somebody else in authority—Captain Hays, maybe—should make an announcement advising passengers to avoid such activities, or at least on how to behave if they did engage in them. But she quickly decided it wouldn't be a good idea.

They're adults, after all.

It was neither her nor the captain's job to be a policeman or a parent.

Her tray was finally empty, but that didn't mean that she was about to get a break.

"Another lager," a passenger called from a nearby group, and she was off again, memorizing which drinks were to be served at which tables. London didn't have enough time (or enough free hands) to jot the orders down on paper. She simply had to keep moving while maintaining a high level of alertness.

Finally, she returned to the bar to recite her orders to her friend Elsie Sloan, who was in charge of the Amadeus Lounge. She and the tall woman with bleached blond hair had become friends on ocean-going ships in years past and had been delighted to meet up again on the riverboat *Nachtmusik.* As always, London was amazed by Elsie's prowess as she absorbed London's entire list while mixing drinks without pause and still barking Bronx-accented orders to her bar assistants.

While she stood waiting, London saw a head of smooth dark hair approaching through the crowd. Amy Blassingame was also filling in as a temporary server today. The ship's concierge was a few years younger, a bit shorter and sturdier than London, and seemed to be moving through the crowd with greater ease. Looking unruffled, Amy arrived at the bar with her own empty tray and recited her own litany of drink orders to Elsie.

"I need a gin and tonic and a Bloody Mary for table six, a Black Russian and a strawberry daiquiri for table nine, two bottles of stout for table 15, and two straight-up scotches for table 10 … or is it table 12? No, I think maybe it was nine."

Elsie tossed London an eye-rolling glance of annoyance, then said to Amy, "You just told me you needed a Black Russian and a strawberry daiquiri at table nine."

"Oh, that's right," Amy said, beginning to sound flustered. "Now I remember. The scotches are for table 10."

"Are you sure of that?" Elsie asked skeptically.

"Positive," Amy said in a shaky voice that sounded anything but positive.

As London and Amy stood waiting for their drinks to be poured, the steward came rushing back toward her.

"Ms. Rose, I'm awfully sorry to bother you again, but Herr Waldmüller still hasn't shown up for his lecture."

London's jaw dropped with surprise.

She looked at Amy and asked, "Do you know where Emil is?"

Amy frowned and replied grouchily.

"How would I know? Why are you asking me?"

London felt another wave of surprise at Amy's tone.

She almost said, *Well, you two were an item, the last I heard. Yesterday.*

Back when the *Nachtmusik* had been leaving Bamberg, London had caught the normally straightlaced Amy and Emil making out like teenagers in the ship's library. They'd been trying to keep their little romance a secret, but they hadn't done a very good job of it.

What's going on with them now? she wondered.

Meanwhile, the steward fidgeted anxiously.

"We're sailing within sight of the *Mäuseturm* right now," he said. "And the group is really looking forward to hearing Herr Waldmüller tell them all about it."

He leaned forward and tried to keep his voice low.

"I … I can't do the lecture … They all keep staring at me … Don't make me go back up there …"

"Don't you worry," Amy told the panicky man. "London will take care of it for you."

London's mouth dropped open with surprise.

I'll take care of it? she thought.

CHAPTER TWO

London's head swam with confusion. She hadn't had a chance to decide where she was most needed—right here serving drinks, or up on the *Rondo* deck filling in for Emil. And now Amy had taken the liberty of volunteering for her.

London stopped herself from snapping at Amy about that. She had to admit, it was a perfectly sensible solution because, next to Emil, she knew more about the places they were visiting than anyone else in the crew.

But she felt far from secure about her ability to entertain the passengers about the more than dozen castles they would be passing. She hadn't visited this area before in person—and besides, it was a choice she'd rather have made for herself.

"I suppose I could," London said. Then she asked Elsie, "But don't you need me here?"

"I think my guys and I are getting things under control now. Go ahead, it sounds like you're needed more up there."

"Oh, thank you," the anxious steward sputtered. "I'll go tell them you're on the way."

As the man hurried off, Elsie said to Amy, "You can go help London."

London's mouth dropped open again.

"How is Amy supposed to help me?" she wanted to ask.

She couldn't think of anything useful Amy could do to help her cover for Emil's absence.

Then she caught the mischievous expression on Elsie's ruddy face. Elsie was just looking for an excuse to get rid of Amy, whose efforts at helping in the lounge were proving to be a lot more trouble than they were worth.

"Are you sure you don't need me?" Amy asked Elsie.

London saw that Elsie could barely keep from laughing.

"Oh, we'll get by somehow, Amy," Elsie said.

"OK, then," Amy said, sounding relieved to be released from her current duties. "Let's go, London."

As they headed away, they passed the door of the ship's library that was situated at one end of the lounge. Since that was Emil's usual post, London stopped to see if the historian might be there.

Trotting past London, Amy turned to call back to her.

"What are you doing?"

"Looking for Emil," London said.

"Why?"

"Well, I just thought maybe—"

"If he were in the library, the steward would surely have found him. Come, we've got to hurry!"

London saw at a glance that Amy was right. Emil was not in the library. The book-filled room was empty, as was the large table where Emil sometimes worked or seated passengers gathered for his lectures.

As they continued out of the lounge, through the reception area, and toward the stairs, Amy added, "Honestly, I don't know how Emil ever got this job. You just can't depend on him for anything."

London felt a bit jarred again. It seemed a peculiar thing for Amy to say. London hadn't always gotten along with Emil. In fact, they'd been pretty seriously at odds more than once. But he did have one quality that London always respected. He was absolutely dependable.

Or at least he has been until now, she thought.

She wondered—had something happened to him? Ought she to be worried about him? She could have him paged, but she thought that might make matters worse. She was sure that the historian hadn't forgotten his lecture and would be horribly embarrassed if his absence was announced over the PA system. Something was wrong, and she would just have to sort it all out later.

And by now, the steward would have announced that she was taking over the job.

But why she did get the distinct feeling that Amy was anxious *not* to find Emil?

She and Amy were trotting up the spiral stairs when they ran into Sir Reggie, London's little Yorkshire Terrier, coming down. The dog yapped at London anxiously, as if to say, *"Come quick! We've got a problem up there!"*

Sometimes Sir Reggie seemed to understand whatever was going on aboard the *Nachtmusik* better than most people did.

She and Amy and Sir Reggie continued up the stairs together. When they burst out onto the open upper deck, London let out a gasp of awe at their surroundings. The staggeringly majestic Rhine Gorge was even more spectacular than she'd expected.

The river swelled wide and far, shining as blue as the vast, late afternoon sky with its columns of heavenly white clouds. On either side of the river towered steep, mountainous banks dotted with villages, vineyards, and castles. The other boats on the river looked tiny in the midst of such grandeur. Even the *Nachtmusik* seemed like some kind of toy, and its passengers like tiny little dolls.

London had stop for a moment to catch her breath. It was an especially staggering sight after having spent the last couple of hours on the deck below, working in the crowded Amadeus Lounge. It suddenly seemed a shame that so many passengers were missing this spectacle in order to enjoy half-priced drinks.

She felt an urge to rush back down to the lounge and tell everybody to come right up here and not miss another moment of this view. But, of course, she couldn't do that. And anyway, there were quite a few other passengers already up here enjoying the spectacle—including the group up ahead of her near the prow who were waiting to hear Emil's lecture.

A wave of anxiety hit London as she strode toward the group of a dozen or so passengers who were looking expectantly toward her.

What am I going to tell them? she wondered.

She'd read quite a bit about the *Mäuseturm,* so she had plenty of information to share with them. But she knew that passengers had come to expect more from Emil's lectures than bare facts. He was always ready to put on something of a performance.

And that's what I've got to do, London realized.

As a clever storytelling tactic took shape in her head, a voice called out from the group.

"London, is Herr Waldmüller ill?"

Another passenger said, "We were expecting him to tell us about the tower."

"He's fine," she replied. "Um, something just came up."

Following her newly developed plan, she strode through the group toward the prow, followed by Amy and Sir Reggie. Sure enough, standing along the river up ahead was one of the quaintest castles she had ever seen. Crowned with bright red battlements, the building was narrow and perpendicular and fronted by a single cigarette-shaped tower. It was built upon a slender, rocky little island in the middle of the Rhine.

She looked down at Sir Reggie and said, "What do you see up ahead, boy?"

Playing his part perfectly, the dog ran up to the rail and barked at the sight of the tower.

"Oh, no!" London said. "Do you think we're in trouble, boy?"

Sir Reggie just kept barking, which was exactly what London wanted. People in the group chuckled expectantly at whatever London might be up to. She glanced around at the familiar faces.

Standing right next to her were Gus and Honey Jarrett, a middle-aged couple London had gotten to know well during the last few days. Gus had a pair of binoculars hanging from his neck.

"Gus, could I borrow your binoculars?" London asked.

"Uh …" Gus said with surprise.

"Of course you can, London," Honey said with a snap of her chewing gum. "Gus, be a good hubby and lend London your binoculars."

With an obedient shrug, Gus handed London his binoculars.

As London looked through them, the castle appeared even more picturesque than before, with its off-white stone walls, its coat-of-arms, and its Gothic windows.

London breathed a mock sigh of relief.

"Oh, thank goodness," she said, still looking through the binoculars. "I don't see any soldiers or archers or crossbowmen over there in the Mouse Tower. I was afraid we were going to be attacked with spears and arrows. But I forgot, the evil archbishop who used to cause that kind of trouble has been dead for more than a thousand years—since 970 AD, I believe."

London smiled and handed the binoculars back to Gus Jarrett.

"Sorry for the false alarm, everybody," she said. "Keep on enjoying the view."

As she pretended to start walking away, she heard exclamations of eager protest.

"Hey, aren't you going to tell us about the castle?"

"What about the spears and arrows?"

"Who was the evil archbishop?"

"Why do they call it the Mouse Tower?"

London's smile turned mischievous.

"Well, if you're really interested …"

"Of course we're interested!" Honey said as she nudged Gus into letting other people take turns looking at the tower through the binoculars.

"OK, then," London said. "But keep in mind, this is a legend. How much of it is true is up to you to decide."

London leaned on the railing overlooking the river.

"Way back in the tenth century, this whole countryside was ruled by Hatto II, the evil Archbishop of Mainz. Hatto made river traffic along this part of the Rhine very dangerous. He stationed archers and crossbowmen over in that tower to rain down spears and arrows on any boats that didn't pay a hefty fee to pass by. He got rich that way. He was very greedy."

"It sounds like he was also very mean," Honey said.

"Oh, meaner than you can imagine," London said. "He treated his subjects very cruelly. When a famine came and all the peasants were starving, Hatto's own barns were filled up with enough grain to feed everybody. But he refused to share it. Instead, he played a heartless, vicious trick. He told the peasants to wait inside an empty barn for him to bring them all the food they needed. Then he locked them inside and set the barn on fire."

"Oh, my!" one of the passengers gasped.

London continued, "He laughed with glee as the peasants were burned alive. 'Listen to those mice squeal!' he gloated aloud to his servants. But as he headed away from the fire, a whole army of mice started to follow him. Soon they climbed all over him and began to bite him. He climbed into his boat and tried to get away to his tower on the island. But thousands upon thousands of the mice just kept swimming after him."

"What happened then?" another passenger said in a breathless voice.

"He ran to his tower and locked himself inside. But the mice ate right through the wooden doors and chased Archbishop Hatto all the way to the roof, where they ate him alive. And ever since then, it's been called *Mäuseturm*—the 'Mouse Tower.'"

A murmur of appreciative wonder passed through the group.

"A tale well told," one of the passengers said.

London's smile widened as a small round of applause broke out. Even Sir Reggie barked with approval.

London knew that Emil would have told the same story if he'd been here. Although Emil was quite a storyteller, London couldn't help wondering if he'd have told it with quite the same style.

The only person in the group who didn't seem to have been paying rapt attention was Amy Blassingame, who was now in possession of the binoculars. She'd been idly looking around through the binoculars and was now amusing herself by aiming them at people's faces, which of course must have looked enormous.

Suddenly Amy gasped with alarm and hastily shoved the binoculars back into Gus Jarrett's hands. Without a word, the short, sturdy concierge whirled and dashed away from the group.

What's wrong now? London wondered.

CHAPTER THREE

London struggled to keep her mind—and the attention of her audience—on the intriguing *Mäuseturm* as their riverboat moved on past the tower. She didn't want the passengers to take notice of Amy's odd behavior. But even as London managed to keep talking, she couldn't help but see that the suddenly erratic concierge was ducking behind a magazine rack near a row of deck chairs.

Is she hiding or something? London wondered.

She didn't pause to try to figure it out.

"Anyway, that's how the legend goes," she told the group of listeners. "Whether it's true or not, the tower you're looking at is different from the one that stood there in the tenth century. It's been built and rebuilt many times and put to all kinds of different uses. But the story has been told over and over again by all kinds of writers and poets, for example …"

London was interrupted by a German-accented voice.

They have whetted their teeth against the stones,
And now they pick the bishop's bones;
They gnawed the flesh from every limb,
For they were sent to punish him!

It was Emil, of course. He came strolling out of the cubicle that housed the elevator and stairs, smiling as though he wasn't even late for what was supposed to be his own lecture.

London breathed a sigh of relief. She'd never been happier to see the tall, intelligent historian than she was right now. Wherever Emil had been when she had come up here to substitute for him, at least he was here now and could take over. There would be a lot more to talk about as the *Nachtmusik* moved through the scenic gorge, and she wasn't at all sure she was up to the task. Besides, she was worried about how things might be going back down in the crowded lounge.

In his most charming professorial manner, Emil added, "Those lines are from a poem by the Romantic-era poet Robert Southey—'God's

Judgment on a Wicked Bishop,' the poem is called. So the legend of how the evil archbishop was devoured by thousands of mice even found its way to England, and into English poetry."

London stepped aside, expecting Emil to take her place and resume the lecture.

Instead, Emil glanced around nervously for a moment.

Then his smile stiffened.

"Carry on, Fräulein Rose," he said, with a nod. "You are doing very well.

With that, he turned and marched back toward the stairs.

What on earth ... ? London wondered.

She glimpsed Amy's dark helmet of hair poking out from behind the magazine rack and then disappearing out of sight again.

What's going on with those two?

Was Emil hiding from Amy?

Or was Amy hiding from Emil?

Or were they both hiding from somebody else altogether?

And why?

All London knew was that she didn't have time to worry about any of that right now. Emil had again left her with the task of describing the sights along the Rhine Gorge. She had to get back to work.

It now seemed that Emil was going to skip his scheduled lecture altogether, which of course was completely unlike him.

But it was happening.

She turned to the group of passengers and began describing the next castle that was coming into view high on a hillside above the river. As she talked, she wondered how soon she would be able to bring this lecture to an end.

*

Dusk began to fall, and tiny lights blinked on in homes, castles, and villages along the banks of the Rhine. Even brighter lights gleamed from boats passing upstream and downstream, casting shimmering reflections on the water.

London was exhausted from describing the castles and vineyards and settlements along the Rhine Gorge. She didn't have Emil's vast historical knowledge, so her task wasn't easy. From time to time, she did a quick search on her cellphone for information to fill in whatever details she didn't happen to know off the top of her head. But Emil hadn't returned, and she had seen Amy slip away long ago. Sir Reggie had climbed up on a nearby canvas desk chair and gone to sleep.

But the *Nachtmusik* had still been passing by remarkable sights, Emil had not returned, and London had managed to keep talking. She was bringing up an article about the next feature along the river when the buxom Honey Garrett called out.

"Hey, look! There's a really big ship coming right at us!"

Honey was peering through her husband Gus's binoculars. The colorful middle-aged couple was on their honeymoon, and they seemed to be having a great time on the riverboat tour. On a day like this, Honey's dyed red hair appeared to actually glow in the sunlight.

Gus grabbed the binoculars from his wife and looked for himself.

"Holy smoke, that thing is huge!" Gus said. "It looks way too big for river travel—big enough to sail on the ocean. And if somebody doesn't change course, it's liable to plow right into us!"

A few other passengers stared ahead and murmured with alarm.

With a reassuring laugh, London said, "Don't worry, there's not going to be a collision. Gus, Honey, please pass the binoculars around so others can have a look."

The next person to look through the binoculars spoke up.

"Why, that's not a ship at all. It looks like some kind of a building rising right out of the water."

London referred to the article she'd found on her cellphone.

"It's called Pfalzgrafenstein Castle, and it takes up almost the entire little island where it was built. The tall tower in the middle looks like the bridge of a huge ship, doesn't it? And the part of its surrounding wall facing us certainly looks like a prow. When the French author Victor Hugo first saw the castle, he described it as 'a ship of stone, eternally afloat upon the Rhine, and eternally lying at anchor.'"

London paused to make sure that everybody was getting a turn looking through the binoculars.

"The castle was built during the 14th century as a toll-collecting station. You see, there used to be a dangerous cataract in the river to the left of the island, so ships couldn't pass that way. They had to pass through the narrower channel on the right. A chain was stretched between the castle and the village on the shore, so boats couldn't pass without paying a toll."

"Did the castle belong to another evil archbishop?" one of the passengers asked jokingly.

London laughed and replied, "No, but the toll collectors there were strict and not very nice. Boaters who couldn't pay their fees were locked up in the castle's dungeon. I don't know how they ever got out. I guess somebody had to pay their fees for them."

"Or maybe some of them never did get out," Honey added sadly.

London noticed a couple of her listeners fidgeting and yawning, although most of them still seemed interested in what she had to say. She also felt her own voice becoming a bit hoarse.

"Well, it's getting pretty late," she told them. "And it's time for me to wrap things up, I hope everybody has enjoyed my rambling little lecture."

The group gave her another generous round of applause and then began to break up and start to leave.

"Great job," Honey Jarrett said loudly as she and Gus made their past London. Gus just nodded, but at least he was smiling.

"Thank you so much," another woman said on her way to the elevators.

Finally, London waved at the last departing passenger, and looked at Sir Reggie, still sleeping on the chair.

"So what do you think, pal?" she asked. "Did I carry that off as well as Emil would have?"

Sir Reggie yawned and covered his eyes with his paws.

"Everybody's a critic," London chuckled, picking up the tired little animal and carrying him toward the stairs. "Well, I certainly have a new respect for how tough Emil's job can be. I just wish I knew where he was and why he skipped his lecture. Do you have any idea?"

Sir Reggie yawned again.

"I didn't think so," London said. "Let's check and see how things are going in the lounge."

London carried Reggie down a flight of stairs to the *Menuetto* deck, where he gently wiggled loose and began to trot alongside her again. They went into the Amadeus Lounge, which was still swarming with business.

Elsie, still working behind the bar, didn't look happy. And London quickly saw why. When Amy had skipped out on her lecture, she had apparently come back here to help out again.

The concierge was at the drinks station, reciting orders to Elsie.

"… and I need a White Russian and a Margarita for table five, and a

Tom Collins and a bottle of stout for table eight, and a pitcher of beer with three glasses for table 10, and two screwdrivers for table five …"

Rolling her eyes at London, Elsie interrupted Amy.

"You just said you needed a White Russian and a Margarita for table five."

"Did I say that? Well … I guess they need two screwdrivers too."

Elsie sighed tiredly and pointed toward the table in question. She said, "There are only two people sitting at table five."

"Are there? Oh, that's right. I meant the screwdrivers were for table five and the White Russian and the Margarita are for table six."

"There's only one customer seated at table six," Elsie said, pointing again.

"Is there? Well, maybe he's really thirsty."

Elsie rolled her eyes again.

"I don't think that's it, Amy," she said.

Amy looked truly flustered now.

"I guess I need to go back and ask again," Amy muttered.

Elsie gently tugged the list out of Amy's hand.

"Oh, you don't need to do that," she said. "Things are slowing down here, so you should enjoy the rest of your evening. Just let me keep this list, and my team and I will take things from here."

"Are you sure?" Amy asked.

"Quite sure."

"Well," Amy said, "I hope I've been of some help."

"Uhm-hmm," Elsie said with a polite but noncommittal nod.

Elsie shook her head at London as Amy headed on out of the lounge.

"Thank goodness she's going," Elsie said when Amy was out of earshot. "If she'd rechecked the orders, she'd only have made a bunch of new mistakes. Do me a favor, London. The next time the bar gets clobbered with business like it did today, make sure the River Troll *doesn't* help me out."

"How am I supposed to do that?" London asked with a laugh.

"I don't know. Tie her up and lock her in her room, maybe. Meanwhile, do you think you could straighten out this little mess?"

"I'll see what I can do," London said. "But don't let her ever hear you call her by that name."

With Sir Reggie trotting attentively beside her, London quickly circulated among Amy's tables and asked some customers to repeat their orders. It turned out that the White Russian and the Margarita were for table three. The sole customer at table six actually wanted a very dry vodka martini. Amy had been right about the screwdrivers, though. They really were for table five.

London returned and recited the corrections to Elsie, who continued mixing the drinks. Meanwhile, London's stomach was starting to rumble with hunger.

"Could you give me some chips to snack on while I work?" London asked.

"No," Elsie said, shaking the martini.

London's eyes widened with surprise.

"Uh … why not?" she asked.

"Because I took the liberty of ordering a sandwich for you from the kitchen."

"You didn't need to do that. I won't have time to eat it."

"Yes, you will. A lull is starting to settle in. I'll put you on break for a few minutes. I'll use force if need be. How long has it been since you've eaten anything?"

"Well, since lunch, I guess, but—"

"Then you need your energy. You look exhausted."

"I guess I kind of am," London admitted.

"I take it Emil never showed up for his lecture," Elsie said.

"Well, he did, but then he scurried away right when he saw that I was covering for him."

"What's with that guy lately?"

"Let me know when you figure it out," London said. "He and Amy are both behaving pretty oddly."

Elsie finished making the drinks, and London headed off among the tables with the newly loaded tray. Sir Reggie stayed right at her side, skillfully managing to never get underfoot as she served the drinks and delighting customers just by his presence.

London soon managed to get the right drinks to the right customers. As she mentally prepared herself to circulate among the tables taking new orders, her eyes fell upon an especially dour-looking customer sitting alone at a table.

The little old man was hunched over his drink staring morosely into space.

London wondered, what could be wrong? The last time she'd seen this passenger, he was having a great time.

She looked down at Sir Reggie and shook her head.

"An unhappy customer," she said to the dog. "This is unacceptable. Come on, let's get to work."

CHAPTER FOUR

As London approached his table, the hunched, hawk-nosed, squinty-eyed man didn't look up from his glass. His expression and posture worried London. Tonight, Stanley Tedrow looked very much the same as when she'd first encountered him, holed up alone in his stateroom. He'd been so intent on writing his novel that he'd taken all meals in his room and completely ignored the first two stops on the tour.

But he'd made a complaint to the captain about her barking dog.

Then it had been Mr. Tedrow's idea for London to have a doggie door installed into her stateroom door, so Sir Reggie could come and go as he pleased. That had solved the barking problem. And London had thought the problem of this passenger's lonely cruise had been solved when she'd seen him hanging out with Bob Turner, the *Nachtmusik's* so-called "security chief." He had seemed to be enjoying himself, but now he clearly was not.

Even so, she wondered …

Maybe I shouldn't bother him.

One lesson she'd learned in the service industry is that not everybody wanted to be cheered up. Sometimes the best thing she could do in her line of work was to leave people alone.

But somehow, she couldn't quite do that with Mr. Tedrow. His enjoyment of the cruise had been something of a personal "project" for London.

Of course, she knew one perfectly professional way to try to start a conversation.

"Are you ready for another drink, Mr. Tedrow?" she asked.

"Huh?" Mr. Tedrow said, looking up blankly.

Before London could repeat her question, Sir Reggie let out a friendly yap.

Mr. Tedrow's squinty eyes opened a bit more widely.

"Oh, hi there, Sir Reggie," he said to the dog in a friendly voice. "Have a seat, why don'tcha, pal?"

Sir Reggie jumped up into a chair.

For a moment, London didn't know what to do. Mr. Tedrow's invitation was to Sir Reggie, not her. So far, Mr. Tedrow didn't seem to have quite noticed she was even there. She wondered if maybe she shouldn't just leave Sir Reggie here to keep Mr. Tedrow company while she continued on her own way. For all she knew, her popular and beloved little Yorkie might do the man more good than she could.

"What are you drinking?" London asked.

"Seltzer water with a slice of lime," Mr. Tedrow said as if he were talking to himself.

London wasn't surprised that he was drinking something non-alcoholic. Like many of the other passengers, Mr. Tedrow had consumed quite a lot of beer during their two days at a festival in Bamberg. A lot of them seemed to be compensating for their overindulgence.

"Are you ready for another?" London asked.

"No, I'm fine with this one," Mr. Tedrow said.

A silence fell. Mr. Tedrow was yet to make eye contact with London.

"How's the writing going, Mr. Tedrow?" she asked.

"The writing?" he said, glancing at Sir Reggie as if the dog had asked the question. "Oh, fine. Just fine."

Then he stared at the tabletop again.

London's worry sharpened.

She got the feeling that nothing was "just fine" with Mr. Tedrow right now. But what was she going to do about it? *Was* there anything she could do about it?

London was especially concerned to find Mr. Tedrow sitting by himself like this. Although Bob Turner was hardly much of a detective, he'd taken it upon himself to help Mr. Tedrow by teaching him all the secrets of his supposed investigative prowess.

Mr. Tedrow had seemed to be enjoying those lessons and had taken copious notes for his book. So why was he alone here tonight?

"How's Bob?" London asked cautiously.

"Hmm? Bob? Oh, he's fine. Just fine."

"What has he been up to?"

"He's been in bed in his room."

London's eyes crinkled with surprise.

"You mean—all day long?" she asked.

"Pretty much," Mr. Tedrow said. "Nighttime too."

"Why?"

"He's not feeling so great," Mr. Tedrow said.

London ignored the fact that Mr. Tedrow had just said Bob was "fine" a few seconds ago. The man's brain seemed to be a bit foggy at the moment. Consistency was probably more than she should expect from him.

"What's wrong with him?" London asked.

"He's got a cold, I guess," Mr. Tedrow said. "I think it's just the sniffles. He's decided to stay in his room, he doesn't want anybody else to catch it."

London now found herself worrying about Bob as well as Mr. Tedrow. This was the first she'd heard that he'd been under the weather.

"Has Bob visited the ship's medic?" London asked. She felt her cheeks grow warm when she asked the question. Many of the officers on this ship had more than one job, and the Australian chef, Bryce Yeaton, doubled as medic when needed. London's relationship with Bryce had been definitely veering toward the romantic.

"Not that I know of," Tedrow replied dourly. "I don't think he wants to. He figures if he just stays in his room, he'll get better and nobody will catch whatever it is he's got."

Mr. Tedrow's gaze kept shifting from the tabletop to Sir Reggie, as if London weren't actually still standing there and he was carrying on a rather absent-minded conversation with the dog.

Something's wrong here, London thought.

But how was she going to find out what it was? She knew from experience that Mr. Tedrow could be awfully hard to talk to. Besides, she wasn't absolutely sure that whatever was going on was any of her business. Still, she felt obliged to do her best to draw him out.

"So do you want to tell me about the book?" she asked.

"Book? What book?"

"The book you're writing."

"Oh. That book. Naw, I think I'd better not talk about it. I don't want to spoil it for you."

Mr. Tedrow then stood up from the table and spoke directly to Sir Reggie.

"Well, I'd better be going, I guess. It was good seeing you, pal."

Without another word, he left the lounge.

London looked at Sir Reggie, who was still sitting in his chair.

"What do you think is going on with him?" she asked the dog. "Do you know anything I don't know?"

Sir Reggie let out one of his indecisive little whines.

"Well, I don't guess there's anything we can do about it," London said. "At least not at the moment."

London glanced toward the bar and saw that her sandwich had just arrived. She figured she'd better eat it before the lull ended and business picked up again. She was pretty sure she still had a busy night ahead.

*

After a couple more hours, the lounge's business started to slow down in earnest. London finished serving another tray full of drinks, then circulated among the tables and took orders for a few more, and finally went back to the bar and recited the list of orders by memory to Elsie.

"OK, great, I've got it," Elsie said. "You go now. My team and I can take it from here. You should rest."

"Are you sure?" London asked.

"Sure, I'm sure. You'd be sure too if you could see yourself. You don't exactly look spruce and chipper and perky."

"Thanks for the compliment," London said with a sigh.

"Hey, what kind of friend would I be if I didn't tell you the truth? Call it tough love, sweetie. Don't worry, you'll look perfectly gorgeous again after a good night's sleep. Meanwhile, you need to get off your feet."

"Yeah, I guess I'm pretty tired at that," London said.

"Thanks for all your help," Elsie said. "This isn't even supposed to be your kind of gig. You went beyond the call of duty, and I'm grateful."

"Glad to help out," London said, taking off her server's apron and setting it on the bar. "I'll see you tomorrow."

As she walked out of the lounge, she noticed that Sir Reggie was no longer tagging along at her feet. She wondered how long it had been since he'd decided to call it a night and headed back to their stateroom. She'd been too busy and distracted to notice his departure.

She walked on into the reception area, which happened to be completely empty. She stopped and stood for a moment, just enjoying the sudden quiet and letting her exhaustion start to sink in.

She felt too tired to walk all the way down two flights of stairs to the *Allegro* deck. As she went toward the elevator, an idea occurred to her.

It would be nice to see Bryce, she thought.

She flashed back to the night before last, when they'd shared their first and, so far, only kiss up on the *Rondo* deck while the *Nachtmusik* sailed past the lighted banks of the Main River on its way away from Bamberg.

She and Bryce had both been constantly busy since then—certainly too busy to share such a sweet moment again, and too busy to seriously talk about what had happened. But they'd been smiling at each other warmly and affectionately whenever they ran into each other, however brief those moments were. Bryce's smile had been enough to assure London that their kiss hadn't been a dream, and not a one-time thing either.

Now that things were calming down aboard the boat, maybe she could catch him in the Habsburg Restaurant. Although neither she nor Bryce seemed ready to take their fledgling romance to the next level, maybe they could go up to the *Rondo* deck for another romantic little moment. It could be very pleasant up there on the top deck late at night.

But as London looked at her reflection in the shiny steel elevator doors, she wavered. Elsie hadn't been kidding when she'd said London didn't look "spruce and chipper and perky." Her hair was a mess, and there were bags under her reddish-looking eyes. On the other hand, she wondered …

Is Bryce likely to look his best right now?

After all, he had probably put in as long and hard a day as she had. And if whatever was going on between them was the least bit real, it surely didn't matter whether either one of them looked less than perfect.

Looking at her reflection, she hastily pulled a comb through her hair and pushed the elevator button. She took the elevator down one short floor to the *Adagio* deck, then walked straight into the Habsburg restaurant.

Her heart sank when she saw that it was completely deserted. The place was dimly lit, and all the chairs were turned upside down onto the tabletops. London glanced at her watch and realized she'd forgotten that the lounge stayed open later into the night than the restaurant. The restaurant had been closed for about half an hour now. Bryce had probably returned to his own stateroom.

London briefly considered giving Bryce a call to ask if he'd like to meet her in the lounge or on the *Rondo* deck.

But then her mouth opened into huge, weary yawn.

It's best to call it a night, she decided.

She took the elevator down to the *Allegro* deck and went to her room. Sure enough, she saw a telltale dog-shaped lump under the bed covers. Sir Reggie was already asleep there. And a few minutes later, London lay curled up next to him, fast asleep as well.

London stood on the bank of a canal, which was flanked by quaint, narrow old buildings. It was nearing sunset, so the color-streaked sky reflected playfully on the water. Small boats moved back and forth along the canal.

They appeared to be motorboats, leaving small trails of foamy, bubbling ripples behind them. Eerily, though, the boats made no sound—nor were there any city noises on either side of the canal. The only sound to be heard was a breeze that whistled over the rooftops and across the water.

London rubbed her eyes and wondered ...

Where am I?

And how did I get here?

As if in reply, a soft, whispering voice wafted over the canal.

"You're in Amsterdam."

London gasped as she recognized a voice that she hadn't heard for years and years.

"Mom?" she said in a trembling voice.

There was no reply.

"Mom, are you here somewhere?" London asked.

"That's what you want to know, isn't it?" the voice replied enigmatically.

Now London saw a woman standing in one of the boats. Although the woman was silhouetted against the sunset, London was sure she recognized the halo of red hair and a face that was shaped much like her own.

"Mom!" London gasped. "It really is you!"

"Are you sure?" the same voice asked, although it seemed to come from elsewhere.

Now London saw yet another silhouetted figure in another boat.

"I could be anywhere," the voice said.

Then there was another figure in another boat.

"I could be here."

Then there was yet another figure in yet another boat.

"Or here."

Soon London saw dozens of boats with exactly the same figure standing in them. And now their voices echoed in a whispery chorus.

"I could be anywhere."

"Mom!" London shouted.

The sun set quickly now, as if in a time-lapse film. London kept shouting as the city and the canal and the boats and the figures were all plunged into darkness.

CHAPTER FIVE

"Woof!"

London's eyes snapped open at the sound.

Just inches away, two big brown eyes were staring at her. The fuzzy teddy-bear-like face looked worried.

"Did I cry out in my sleep?" she asked Sir Reggie.

Her Yorkshire Terrier let out an affirmative little whine.

London began to recall scattered images—the glow of a sunset on the water of a canal, quaint buildings on both of the canal's banks, and boats in the water, each of them with a similar standing, silhouetted woman's figure. She also remembered how she'd called out to the woman.

"Mom?"

Yes, she remembered most of the dream now. She sighed deeply and sat upright in the bed.

"It's nothing to worry about, boy," she said, scratching the little dog's head. "I just had one of my 'Mom' dreams. You know. I have them all the time."

Even so, she realized she was trembling all over. This one had unsettled her more than the dreams normally did.

Her mother had been on London's mind a lot since she'd arrived in Europe. Many years ago, when she and her older sister Tia were still children, Mom had disappeared while traveling in Europe. There had been no sign of foul play, but no one had heard from her since. Growing up, London had appreciated their father's dedication to raising his daughters well, and she thought that both she and Tia had come through that early trauma rather well. But it had affected them in different ways.

Tia had settled into a conventional, secure life with a husband and three children, while London had become averse to rooting herself in any single place. But London spent time with her sister whenever she was in the States and kept in communication with her father wherever he continued to travel as a flight attendant.

She had long ago accepted the likelihood that she'd never see Mom again. But then, during the tour's stay in Salzburg, she'd spoken with a woman who had known Mom briefly—but recently. The woman had told London that Mom was still in Europe, working as an itinerant language tutor.

Since then, London had been struggling with a desire to track Mom down, to ask her why she had walked away from her husband and two children, to find out what her life had been like since then. She knew perfectly well that it was almost certainly a hopeless quest—even if she had time to pursue it. And spare time was one thing that her job aboard the *Nachtmusik* didn't allow much of.

Still, London couldn't help thinking she saw telltale clues to Mom's whereabouts here and there. The night before last, standing alone on the *Rondo* deck, she had tried searching for information about Mom on her cellphone, hoping to find some sign of her in the Netherlands. And maybe, just maybe, she had found something—a webpage with three enigmatic lines of text.

London reached over to the end table beside her bed for the sheet of paper where she'd written down those brief notes.

The first line consisted of just two Dutch words: *"Reis Lust."* Combined as a single word, they meant "wanderlust." Back in Regensburg, London had found a posted ad for an English tutor named Fern Weh and realized that *fernweh* was the German word for wanderlust—a word that London strongly if maybe not quite rationally associated with Mom. Now her recent research had led her to the Dutch equivalent. Could it be that Mom was using those aliases as she traveled around and put notices up about her tutoring?

The next line in London's notes read *"elke Europese taal,"* which translated meant "any European language."

Was the website an advertisement for a multilingual language tutor—someone like Mom?

If so, it seemed strange that there was no phone number or email address—nothing except a street address:

65 Poppenhuisstraat, Amsterdam

London groaned a little as she sat on the bed holding the paper in one hand and scratching Sir Reggie's little head with the other.

"I don't know, pal," she said to the dog, perusing the words. "Sometimes I'm starting to wonder if maybe I'm losing my mind.

Looking for Mom is crazy. How can I not know that? I mean, she must have reasons of her own for disappearing for all these years. She obviously doesn't want to be found. So why can't I leave well enough alone?"

Sir Reggie made no reply.

"Well, I definitely must be out of my mind if I think the website had anything to do with Mom," she said to her dog. "I mean, what are the chances of that? Why do I even think there might be a connection?"

Sir Reggie remained silent.

"I've got to face reality," she said. "I've got a job to do. We're only going to be in Amsterdam for part of a day, and I'm sure not going to waste part of it tracking down this address."

She wadded up the sheet of paper and tossed it into the wastebasket. Resisting the urge to reach into the wastebasket and take it out again, she looked at the clock on the end table.

She'd woken up a little earlier than she'd planned, which wasn't a bad thing. It gave her a bit of extra time to eat breakfast in the ship's Habsburg Restaurant before she went about her busy day. And she hoped staying busy would help distract her from this foolish obsession with her long-missing mother.

She got up from the bed and opened the curtains over her narrow window.

The *Nachtmusik* was traveling through the Amsterdam-Rhine canal, the last leg of their journey into the Netherlands capital. The landscape outside her window was completely flat now, totally unlike the gorge that they had passed through yesterday.

Going through canal locks was always slow, so they wouldn't be in Amsterdam for hours yet. Then they would have the afternoon and evening to tour before leaving again.

London took a clean uniform out of her closet, went into the bathroom, and got dressed and ready for her day. She ran her comb one last time through her short springy auburn hair, checked her bright blue eyes in the mirror, and decided that she appeared adequate for the day.

When she came back into the bedroom, London saw that Sir Reggie was still stretched lazily over the bed, his eyes barely open.

"Oh, don't bother to get up, pal," she said with a note of good-natured irony. "I'll take care of your breakfast."

London always had plenty of doggie supplies in her closet. She had inherited the Yorkie when his previous owner had fallen victim to foul play when the ship had stopped in Gyor. The unfortunate elderly woman had left plenty of dog food for the trip, a variety of collars and leashes, and even a self-cleaning potty that the dog already knew how to use. London had only added a couple of doggie toys to the collection.

By the time she had poured food and fresh water for Sir Reggie, he'd fallen fast asleep again.

Poor little guy, she thought.

He'd spent most of yesterday dashing around at her feet, faithfully trying to keep up with her during an especially hectic workday. London herself still felt tired and achy, even after a good night's sleep. It was hardly any wonder that Sir Reggie was as exhausted as she was.

Petting him gently, she murmured, "You just take some time off, pal. I can get along without your help. Sleep as long as you need. You deserve it."

She gathered up a stack of flyers with information about their visit to Amsterdam and put them in her handbag. While virtually all of the passengers had access to the same bundle of information on their cellphones, London knew from experience that some of them preferred to have that kind information in pamphlet form.

Then she headed out of her room and took the elevator up to the *Adagio* deck. As soon as she stepped into the Habsburg Restaurant, a lovely large dining hall with tables elegantly set with white tablecloths and silver, she saw that a line of passengers was already waiting to be seated. And there was no sign of the hostess who always took care of seating during the mealtime rushes.

Then London remembered that the regular hostess had requested the morning shift off because she was nursing a head cold. The ship's concierge had been supposed to fill in for her. On a small riverboat like this, they all had to cover for one another from time to time, but Amy was nowhere in sight.

Where's Amy? London wondered.

Had the ship's concierge gone AWOL?

CHAPTER SIX

Am I wrong? London wondered.

Although Amy didn't have the most pleasant personality in the crew, she was usually dependable. Maybe the concierge hadn't expected to work the hostess shift this morning.

But no—London distinctly remembered their conversation about it. And she had made a note of the assignment in her schedule for today.

She checked her watch again. Amy was supposed to have been at this post ten minutes ago.

What could be going on with her?

She hastily typed Amy a text message on her cellphone:

You're needed in the Habsburg Restaurant.

Then London took over the hostess job herself.

"I'm sorry for the delay," she said to a waiting couple who were looking a little impatient.

"We'd like that table by the window."

When London began to lead them to the place she thought they had specified, the man interrupted.

"Not that window," he said sharply. "The one where we always sit, overlooking the water."

London smiled and changed course. Of course, the regular hostess would probably have known which table they meant, and this couple probably didn't usually have to wait so long for their breakfast. It was no wonder they were a little prickly this morning.

"The chef has some nice specials this morning," she said, handing them their menus along with a tour flyer. Then she glanced around and saw that a line of other passengers waiting to be seated had formed. It didn't look like she was going to get a chance to sit down and eat breakfast herself.

Then, just as London was getting ready to seat Honey and Gus Jarrett, Amy burst through the door and rushed toward her.

"I just got your message," Amy said to London breathlessly.

"What's the matter?"

Fortunately, the Jarretts went ahead, seated themselves at the nearest table, and began to peruse the breakfast selections. Gus was focused on the food, but London saw that Honey was peeking at them over the top of her menu, looking amused.

She drew Amy away from the tables.

"You're needed for hostessing," she said.

"Really?" Amy said, looking around a bit nervously. "I don't see why. It looks like you've got things under control."

London squinted at Amy curiously.

"You're scheduled to fill in here this morning," she said.

"Am I?"

"Yes."

"Well, this is awkward," Amy said with a shrug, "But I've got other things I need to be doing. Just take over for me this time, OK?"

London was dumbfounded for a moment. Yesterday, Amy had volunteered London to fill in for Emil to lecture about historical sights in the Rhine Gorge. That had been reasonable, since it was something that only London was equipped to do. But now Amy was trying to push London into taking her hostessing assignment.

She sternly reminded herself that she was Amy's boss, not the other way around.

"Amy, this is your job today," London said firmly.

Amy's dark brown eyes widened.

"London, I'm surprised at you," she said in a hurt voice. "It's not like you to quibble about such things."

"I'm not exactly quibbling, Amy."

"OK, then," Amy said huffily. "Give me those menus."

London took a menu for herself and handed the rest to Amy. Then she found a seat alone at a small table. As she sat watching Amy began to seat customers, London realized that the concierge kept glancing nervously all around. Then the image of Amy peeking out from behind the magazine rack flickered through London's mind.

What's going on with her?

London's confused thoughts were interrupted by a familiar voice.

"Good afternoon, charming lady."

When she looked up, London pushed aside her concerns with Amy. She only hoped she wasn't blushing.

Bryce Yeaton had come to her table. The classically trained

Australian chef always struck her as especially dashing in his white floppy hat and a double-breasted white tunic. But he was handsome in any case, with sparkling gray eyes, strong dimpled chin, and carefully maintained stubble of beard.

"I don't believe we've met, madam" he added, impishly playing the role of a total stranger.

I guess I'll just play along, London thought, smiling back.

"I think not, sir. Odd, isn't it? I'm London Rose, and I'm the *Nachtmusik's* social director."

"Indeed? I'm Bryce Yeaton, and I'm the ship's head chef."

His smile widened as he added, "I also happen to be a mind reader."

"Really?" London said with a chuckle.

"Oh, yes. Allow me to demonstrate. I can tell you exactly what you plan to order for breakfast this morning. Would that impress you?"

"I suppose it would," London said, laughing some more at their little charade.

Bryce pressed his forefingers to his temples and squinted for a moment in mock concentration.

"Let's see … It's coming to me … you want … a lobster frittata … no, lemon poppy seed pancakes … no, Danish waffles with cardamom and ginger … no, cream-and-strawberry-filled crepes …"

Then he snapped his fingers.

"I've got it! Eggs Benedict!"

"I'm astonished!" London said, laughing and clapping.

Of course, there was nothing astonishing about this little make-believe performance. Bryce knew perfectly well that Eggs Benedict was London's favorite breakfast—especially when it was made in his own inimitable style. She'd never been able to pin down exactly what made Bryce's version of the rich and buttery Hollandaise sauce so special, but she found it a delicious way to start a day.

"I will go to the kitchen prepare it at once, charming lady," Bryce said.

He took London's hand and lifted it to his lips and kissed it.

London laughed at his exaggerated show of gallantry. Then she felt herself blush.

Oh, dear, she realized. *We're surrounded by people.*

Bryce blushed too as he seemed to realize the same thing.

As she gently drew her hand away, she and Bryce glanced around at the seated customers. Sure enough, a few of them had noticed the playful gesture. Some were gaping with surprise, while others—including Honey Jarrett—smiled with what seemed like approval.

"Oops," Bryce said.

"Yes, oops," London replied with a nervous chuckle.

"I guess I'd better get back to work," Bryce said.

As he turned to go, London reminded herself that he was also the ship's medic.

"Bryce, wait just a minute. Are you aware that we've got a sick passenger?"

"It's the first I've heard of it," Bryce said.

"It's Bob Turner," London said. "Mr. Tedrow mentioned it to me yesterday. It's only the sniffles, he said, but he's confined himself to his room, and … well, it worries me a little."

"I'll check up on him after the breakfast rush," Bryce said.

"I'd appreciate that."

As Bryce headed back to the kitchen, London could still feel his kiss on her fingers. It wasn't exactly the kind of kiss she longed for, but it would have to do until she and Bryce could share a more private moment.

Whenever that turns out to be, she thought sadly.

As a waiter came by to serve London some coffee, she glimpsed Emil standing in the restaurant entrance, apparently with the intention of eating breakfast himself. But then he glanced around the room, frowned, and ducked back out again.

Because he spotted Amy, London realized. And yesterday he had apparently cut off the talk he was giving for the same reason.

She was glad that the concierge was chatting with customers at a table and didn't seem to have noticed the historian. At least, there was no dodging into hiding this time.

What's going on between those two? London wondered. *This is getting ridiculous.*

On one hand, she supposed it wasn't any of her business. On the other hand, it was starting to affect both of their work.

This could get to be a real problem, she thought.

She only wished she had some idea what to do about it.

*

"We're here, Sir Reggie," she said. "We're in Amsterdam."

It was just a few hours later, and London stood with Sir Reggie in the open air of the *Rondo* deck, watching from the rail as the *Nachtmusik's* crew went about their docking procedures. A short while ago the boat had passed the point where the Amsterdam-Rhine Canal converged with other waterways into this major water highway through the city. Then the *Nachtmusik* had bypassed the crowded River Cruise Port where larger riverboats were lined up three-thick along the piers.

She was glad that the smaller, more maneuverable *Nachtmusik* had been able to pull in near the *Westerdok.* Here the passengers would have easy access to city streets and to smaller boats that traveled the fascinating web of canals.

London picked up her doggie companion and told him, "The thing I keep wondering is …"

She hesitated before she finished her sentence.

"Have I been here before? Did Dad or Mom or both of them bring me here for a visit when I was little?"

As young children, London and her sister had spent a lot of time moving around Europe with their flight-attendant parents. But after they'd reached school age, the family had put more permanent roots down in Connecticut. Of course, London remembered some of her early travels, but other memories were vague.

Sir Reggie let out a critical-sounding little growl.

"You're right, I guess. Why should it matter? What difference does it make?"

Anyway, she didn't feel any sense of *déjà vu.* The view from the deck certainly didn't look familiar, with its shores lined with industrial facilities, historical buildings, and some examples of incredible modern architecture.

"And yet," she said to Sir Reggie, "I can't help but wonder. I wish I knew why."

As if in reply, that mysterious address popped into her mind.

65 Poppenhuisstraat, Amsterdam

London groaned aloud, remembering when she'd wadded up that piece of paper and thrown it away last night.

Out of sight, but not out of mind, she realized.

Her brain wasn't like a wastebasket, after all. She couldn't just empty it of thoughts she wanted to get rid of. She had an unusually good memory, which served her well at tasks like waiting bar tables and other aspects of her job aboard the *Nachtmusik*. But at times like now, it seemed more like a curse.

"It's no use pretending I don't care about that address," she said to Sir Reggie. "I just can't help myself. I'm going to have to check it out. I'll do it the first chance I get so I can focus on my job for the rest of the day."

Now that the docking was completed, London carried Sir Reggie down the stairs from the *Rondo* deck to the reception area, where passengers were already beginning to disembark. Sir Reggie nudged her purse—his signal for her to put him on a leash so he could go along with her.

"I'm sorry, not this time," she said, giving the dog a little kiss on the top of the head. "In a little while I'll be visiting a big museum full of famous artworks, and they wouldn't let you in."

She set the disappointed dog down and said, "You stay here and watch over things while I'm gone."

Sir Reggie ducked his head, but obediently turned and trotted away.

London joined the passengers going down the gangway and onto a narrow dock that stretched alongside the boat.

When they all reached the shore, she began to circulate among the passengers, passing out more flyers and answering more questions.

Letitia Hartzer and Audrey Bolton, two women London had gotten to know during the Nachtmusik's previous stops, came up to her.

"Is it true you're not taking us on our usual city tour?" Audrey asked with a note of slight disappointment.

"No—not the whole city, anyway," London explained. "Nobody expressed any interest in large group tours this time. Anyhow, Amsterdam lends itself better to smaller groups and individual exploration. But everybody is welcome to meet up in two hours for a tour of the Rijksmuseum."

"Will you be leading that tour?" Letitia asked.

"No, that will be Herr Waldmüller," London said.

At least I hope so, she thought anxiously.

If Emil was a no-show, she wasn't at all sure she was up to the task of covering for him at the Rijksmuseum.

Handing flyers to both women, London added, "You'll find all the information you need right here about places to visit and how to get there—especially boat transport along the canals."

"Oh, the canals!" Letitia said, clasping her hands together. "They sound so charming!"

"Like Venice, Italy!" Audrey added.

London said, "Yes, Amsterdam is sometimes called the 'Venice of the North.'"

Then an elderly couple she'd gotten to know and like during the voyage came up to her—Agnes and Walter Shick.

"I hear we can see great fields of blooming tulips here in Amsterdam," Agnes said.

"I'm afraid we missed the season for those," London said. "The huge tulip fields bloom in the spring. But you'll still see some greenhouse tulips in the flower stalls."

Walter said, "I suppose the best way around town is by boat."

"Yes, or on foot," London said, handing each of them flyers. "Or maybe you'd prefer to rent bicycles." Handing them copies of the flyer, she added, "You'll find information about that right here."

"Oh, that sounds like fun!" Agnes said. "I haven't been on a bicycle for years."

In fact, there was lots of pedaling traffic in the bicycle lanes that ran alongside the pedestrian path next to the water. Although the Shicks were in their seventies, they wouldn't be out of place here where riders of all ages were gliding by.

As she continued walking, London pulled up a map and pinpointed the address that was nagging at her mind.

65 Poppenhuisstraat, Amsterdam

She saw that it didn't look very far away. She felt sure she could go there by boat or on foot and then head straight to the Rijksmuseum and be there in time for the tour.

But what was she expecting to find at the address?

Probably nothing, she told herself.

Or maybe something very important.

All she knew was that she just had to try. If she left Amsterdam without finding out what—or who—was at that address, she might never forgive herself.

She felt her face break into a smile when she spotted a familiar face up ahead. As the other passengers continued on their ways, Bryce Yeaton waved and walked toward her.

“So, we meet again, charming lady,” he said, resuming his gallant little act from earlier in the Habsburg Restaurant.

“So it would seem,” London said with a smile.

“I wonder if you’ve got any plans for the next couple of hours,” he said. “Before our tour of the Rijksmuseum, I mean.”

London’s heart sank a little. This seemed like exactly the opportunity she and Bryce had both longed for—a chance to spend some time together on their own. But now she had other plans.

Then she wondered—why shouldn’t she just tell Bryce outright about her obsession with finding her mother? Opening up to him about it might do her good. And why not ask Bryce to come along on this peculiar errand? His company might be more than helpful.

Taking his offered arm, she was about to start explaining everything to him.

But then she was interrupted by a German-accented voice calling loudly from nearby.

“Hallo-o-o, you two! Come and join me!”

CHAPTER SEVEN

London glanced at Bryce in consternation. She had been about to tell him something important about her childhood, about her mother leaving. They had been about to grab a chance to spend some time together.

But now here was Emil, calling to them from a boat in the nearby canal. Could they just walk away and leave him?

"I have hired a very nice boat, as you can see!" Emil yelled. "Come on, let us go exploring, the three of us!"

The historian was standing in a red and white canal boat with an inboard motor. Although the boat looked large enough for ten or more people, Emil was alone except for a smiling, red-bearded man wearing a nautical cap who stood at the wheel.

Both men were looking expectantly at London and Bryce.

"Couldn't we just say no?" Bryce asked London in a quiet voice.

"Maybe, but …"

London hesitated. As much as she wanted to go find that address … as much as she wanted to spend some time with Bryce …

She didn't want to hurt Emil's feelings by rejecting his invitation, especially now that he seemed to be in better spirits than she'd seen him lately. And besides that, she thought it was probably not a good idea to let the historian go sailing around the canals of Amsterdam all by himself. Not if she wanted be sure he'd show up for his Rijksmuseum tour.

"I'm afraid we'd better go along," London told Bryce.

Bryce shrugged a bit sadly, and they both climbed down a flight of concrete steps.

As they got into the boat, London asked Bryce, "Did you check on Bob?"

"I gave him a call, anyway," Bryce said. "He said he didn't want me to come to his room. He said he was afraid I'd catch whatever he had. Kind of an odd thing to say to a ship's medic. But he says it isn't serious."

Emil gallantly directed them to padded seats and sat down facing them.

The engine made a surprisingly gentle sound as the boat pulled away from the embankment—more like a purr than a machine-like growl.

Emil gestured toward the man at the wheel in the stern of the boat.

"London, Bryce, I would like to introduce you to *Kapitein* Claes Stoepker."

"I am at your service," the man said in Dutch-accented English with a tip of his cap.

Emil said, "*Kapitein* Claes is the owner of this fine little ship with a fine little name—the *Jonge Gouda.*

Bryce smiled and translated, "The 'Young Gouda,' eh?"

Emil tilted his head, apparently slightly startled that Bryce knew at least a smattering of Dutch.

"Very good, my friend," Emil said with a slightly condescending smile.

London now observed that the *Jonge Gouda* was rather charmingly painted to resemble a block of cheese, with a bright red hull and a yellow prow.

Emil continued, "The *kapitein* says that he knows Amsterdam like—eh, like the 'back of his fist' is how you put in English, I think."

Although Emil's English was quite superb, London knew that he sometimes tripped over little idioms like this.

"'The back of his hand,'" Bryce said.

Emil smile clouded just a little at being corrected. London gave Bryce a little nudge with her elbow, hoping he'd take it as a warning to be careful not to question Emil's oversized sense of his own authority.

"Yes, like the back of his hand," Emil said. "He and the *Jonge Gouda* are at our service for next few hours."

London felt a prickle of worry.

"Uh, Emil," she said, "you're supposed to conduct a tour of your own in a couple of hours."

"Really?" Emil said, then snapped his fingers. "Oh, yes. We're meeting some of our passengers at the Rijksmuseum, are we not? Thank you so much for reminding me. It almost slipped my mind."

London's jaw fell slightly at Emil's apparent forgetfulness. She clearly had made the right decision to come aboard and keep her eye on him.

But what's going on with him? she wondered.

London was sure it must be something between him and Amy. They had seemed so enamored of each other at their last port of call, but now they were both behaving like flighty teenagers. Sooner or later, Emil and Amy were going to have to deal with whatever it was face to face.

As the boat whirred its way across the *Westerdok* channel, London again asked herself that nagging question.

Have I been here before?

This view from the boat didn't look the least bit familiar. Modern commercial boats smaller than the *Nachtmusik* were docked along the banks, and glassy buildings constructed from jagged, jutting rectangles flanked the broad waterway. London guessed that much of this construction must have been completed during the years that had passed since she might have visited with her family.

The *Jonge Gouda* passed under a deep, tunnel-like overpass while a high-speed passenger train roared above their heads. When the boat emerged from the shadows into the sunlight again, a very different scene awaited London.

She gasped aloud at the sight of quaint Dutch-style buildings with ornate facades and gables flanking the water. As they moved into one of the canals that networked throughout Amsterdam, for a moment she thought she heard a child's voice—a little girl expressing her amazement at the scene.

"What a pretty river!"

She also imagined she heard a woman reply with a musical laugh.

"Not exactly a river, sweetie. It's called a canal. There are lots of them in Amsterdam. They're like streets."

Now London knew that she really had been here before. She'd come here with Mom back when she was maybe six or seven years old. Her older sister, Tia, had been here too. Tia would have been nine or ten years old.

Her childhood enchantment came back to her in a rush. Again, she was delighted by how the whole scene seemed to be dancing happily all around her. Both the shore and the water bustled with movement.

All kinds of boats moved effortlessly through the water. Some were little motorboats even smaller than the one they were in right now. The largest were long touring boats with awnings and canopies over their outdoor decks. Boats of all kinds of shapes and sizes traveled the canal, but they were all short and stubby enough to pass beneath a low arched bridge with room to spare.

The banks, lined with trees and lush bushes and flowers, were alive with pedestrians, cyclists, small cars, and sidewalk cafes.

Just as she had been all those years ago, London was especially delighted by the stationary boats docked along each of the canal's stone banks.

Seeming to follow her gaze, *Kapitein* Claes spoke to her in excellent English.

"I see that you are interested in the houseboats."

"Yes, very much," London said.

"Woonarks, we call them in Dutch," Claes said. "I believe in English it means 'house ark.'"

"What can you tell us about them?" Bryce asked.

"Oh, whatever you could possibly want to know," man said with the chuckle. "I know every inch of this canal ..." He finished his sentence with a sly wink. "Like the back of my hand, I think is how you just put it."

Pointing to the nearest vessel, he said, "That one used to be a seagoing freighter, back around 1910. Years ago, before I was born I am sure, it was stripped of its engine and fuel tank and other functioning features in order to remodel it into a comfortable home. The cargo hold is now a living room, and the wheelhouse has been turned into an office."

Pointing to another boat, he said, "That one used to be a fishing trawler. When the weather was bad, fishermen used to fix their nets under that covered bow. Now that area has been turned into a cozy little guest room."

Pointing to another, he said, "And that one was once a steam tugboat. Although it has been here for years, it is very up-to-date. Look, it even has solar panels for power. You will find all the necessities of life on these boats."

As they passed by other houseboats, London was even more charmed by them. *Kapitein* Claes waved at some of the inhabitants, and they waved back. Some of them were taking in the sun on spacious decks. Children were jumping from the sides of some boats into the canal for a swim. As Claes had said, some of them had clearly once been in use as practical work boats. Others were just large floating box-like structures that would obviously never navigate open waters.

"What a marvelous way to live," Bryce said. Then with a playful nudge, he added to London, "How would you feel about retiring here?"

London's eyes widened.

Was Bryce thinking about a future for them together? From his broad grin, she guessed he wasn't considering anything so serious.

Anyway, it's fun to think about, she thought.

She nodded and replied, "It would very nice, I think. I wish we had time to—"

London was a bit shocked when Emil interrupted her with a chuckle.

He said, *"Kapitein,* maybe you should tell these two why moving here might not be so easy."

Kapitein Claes frowned a little.

"Times have changed, I fear. After World War II, houseboats were popular because they were cheap as well as comfortable. A lot of struggling artists once lived in them. Now you have to be quite rich to be able to afford one."

"Are the boats really that expensive?" Bryce asked.

"Oh, not the boats, really," *Kapitein* Claes explained. "An old boat that has not yet been renovated can be very cheap to buy. But the *berths*—the spaces for the boats along the banks—are what are really expensive. They alone can cost as much as a half million dollars these days."

"Oh, my!" London said.

Bryce laughed and added, "I'm afraid that's always going to be a bit out of my price range."

"The boats themselves are changing as well," Claes said, pointing and frowning at a larger, newer-looking boat with multiple levels and terraces. "I am not very fond of boats of that type. Look closely and you will see that it was never a water-going vessel. It was just designed to look that way."

Pointing to another modern craft, he added, "And that one is built on pontoons. It doesn't even *look* like it was ever supposed to sail. A lot of the newer boats are like this—luxurious, I suppose, but lacking in character."

Shaking his head, he added, "Times must change everywhere, I suppose. Amsterdam is no exception."

I guess gentrification is a happening all over, London thought with a sigh.

The *Jonge Gouda* passed through a busy intersection where their canal crossed another waterway, then continued under two more low bridges. On the shore to the boat's port side, London saw a group of people standing in line outside a modest Dutch-style building that looked much like all the others around it.

Unexpected emotions flooded London at the sight of that building. Tears stung her eyes, although she had no idea why.

"I want to stop there," she cried.

CHAPTER EIGHT

As *Kapitein* Claes steered his boat toward the water's edge, London wondered what had come over her at the sight of that building. She didn't even know what it was, but seeing it had triggered some memory.

Or if not an actual memory, at least a strong feeling of familiarity.

"Yes," Claes said, "you really must visit *Anne Frank Huis*—the Anne Frank House. One cannot come to Amsterdam without stopping there."

Emil added with a nod, "I completely agree."

"But I hope you have reservations," Claes added. "It is very popular."

"I do," Emil replied. "In fact, I made a dozen reservations and passed most of them on to our passengers. As it happens, I have three left."

"Just the right number," Bryce commented.

"Yes, I had this in mind when I flagged down the two of you to accompany me."

When the *Jonge Gouda* came to a stop at the embankment, Bryce climbed out and offered London his hand to help her join him.

Kapitein Claes asked Emil, "You may wish to stay here for a while. Do you want me to wait for you in the meantime?"

Emil looked at his watch.

"No, you need not inconvenience yourself," he said to Claes, "You have been very helpful." After handing the boatman a hefty-looking tip, Emil joined them on the walkway that bordered the canal.

Claes thanked Emil with a tip of his hat, then pulled his red and yellow boat away from the shore and continued on his way.

"We are within easy walking distance of the Rijksmuseum," Emil explained to London and Bryce. "We can spend some time here at the Anne Frank House and still get to the museum in time for our tour. Of course, even with reservations, one must wait in line. But the line is not as long today as it sometimes is."

"Have you been here before?" Bryce asked Emil as the three of them joined the line.

"Oh, yes," Emil said in a somber voice. "Many times. One cannot come to this place too often. It has so much to tell us."

"This will be my first visit," Bryce said. "What about you, London?"

"I came here once," London said. "But I was very young."

Too little to understand, she thought. Of course, she had long since read Anne Frank's diary, so she knew the girl's story.

They stood in a line that took them past the original wooden front door of the house into the adjacent modern building. London recognized a few faces of *Nachtmusik* passengers in the group as they passed through an entry gate and continued on their way toward the original house. Although some background information was posted on the walls, Emil told them more after they went up one flight of stairs.

"Otto Frank's spice company offices were all around us," Emil said. "It was a bustling workplace during the day. Only a few of the employees knew the secret of the house—that Jewish people were hidden from view on the upper floors. Earlier they had fled Germany where the Holocaust was raging and came to the Netherlands. But the Nazis invaded the Netherlands in 1942, and then they hid away on the top floors of this building."

The group walked up another flight of very steep stairs, where they came upon a large, heavy bookcase sitting askew. An opening in the wall was visible behind it.

"This leads into a part of the original building that can't be seen from the street," Emil explained. "A family friend built this bookcase, especially, to cover the entrance. It is hinged like a door so it can open and close."

London felt a flash of recognition. She remembered being fascinated by this secret passageway when she was here as a child.

The group followed Emil into the dimly lit rooms where the Frank family hid.

Bryce remarked, "I can't imagine a family of four staying hidden here. I understand that it was for two years."

Emil replied, "Oh, Otto Frank and his family were not the only people hiding here during that time. There was another whole family—Hermann van Pels and his wife Auguste and his son Peter. Another man named Fritz Pfeffer joined them, so there were eight people hiding here overall."

This secret annex suddenly felt extremely crowded, even claustrophobic, to London.

Emil said, "Any noises up here could easily be heard on the floor below. The eight people had to keep extremely quiet—at least throughout the day during the company's business hours. At night they could actually come out of the secret annex into the main building. Those nights were the only time they had access to hot water."

As the group moved among the other visitors, they quickly found themselves in a room with old pictures on the wall.

Pointing to the old pictures on the walls, Emil continued, "Anne pasted these pictures and postcards here herself. In a way, her collection shows how she matured during those two years. The early photographs are of then-famous movie stars. So as you can see, at first she was a typical star-struck 13-year-old. But as she became more interested in the fine arts, she put up images like this one of a Greek sculpture."

The group looked into the room where Otto, his wife, and his other daughter had slept. Then they continued up the stairs to see the kitchen, the living room, and the room where the van Pels family stayed.

Finally they arrived at the foot of another steep staircase, which was blocked from entry by glass. Through a strategically placed mirror, they could catch a partial view of the upstairs attic, which appeared to be brighter than the rest of the annex.

Emil commented, "In the mirror you can see the only window that was never covered over. Anne used to stand there looking out at the chestnut tree, which you can also see still standing outside. That was the only glimpse of the outdoors she ever had during those years."

"Anne wrote about that tree in her diary, didn't she?" London asked.

"Indeed, she did," Emil said. Then he shut his eyes and recited by heart:

"From my favorite spot on the floor I look up at the blue sky and the bare chestnut tree, on whose branches little raindrops shine, appearing like silver, and at the seagulls and other birds as they glide on the wind."

The group of people was very quiet as Emil led them back down the way they'd come. Finally, they turned into a room with an altar-like black display case at one end.

"This is where Anne's diary is kept," Emil said, pointing to the book's open pages filled with the young girl's handwriting. "The case is temperature controlled to protect the pages from fading with age."

With a sigh, he added, "Anne loved her diary. All during those terrible years, she dreamed of becoming a writer and journalist and sharing her thoughts with the world. Those dreams came to an end in August 1944, when she and her companions were captured by the Nazis. She died at the Bergen-Belsen concentration camp, probably early in 1945."

Now London remembered standing in this very room when Mom had read those words aloud to her daughters.

Then Mom had said, *"Maybe someday when you're older you'll understand all this."*

Then, Mom had added …

"When you do, please explain it to me."

London's throat tightened with emotion.

Sorry, Mom, she thought. *I still don't understand how this could have happened. I don't think anybody ever will.*

As she followed Emil out of thc Anne Frank House, London felt overwhelmed by the weight of things she didn't understand—many of them regarding her own mother who had once brought her to this place. Somehow she couldn't put together her memory of that caring woman with the thought of the person who had disappeared from her life.

Seeming to sense her mood, Bryce gave her hand a quick squeeze. Then they walked along quietly as the historian led the way along a street that bordered the canal. As they passed narrow houses, cheerful shops, flower gardens, and waterfront cafes, London's spirits began to lift. She realized how fortunate she was to have a rich and rewarding life.

As they entered a broad street near the Rijksmuseum, she turned to Emil to thank him for the information he had given them on their tour.

But at that moment, the historian let out a gasp and dashed away from them.

CHAPTER NINE

Bryce's jaw dropped as Emil scurried away down the street.

"Where's he off to?" he asked London.

"I don't know," London said. "But we'd better not lose him."

She was still worried that he might disappear before he could give his scheduled lecture at the Rijksmuseum. She hadn't prepared to substitute for him.

London and Bryce broke into a trot, following after the escaping historian. Fortunately, he didn't go very far. He stopped in front of a corner shop with a sign that read Meyer Fijne Kunst.

Meyer Fine Art, London thought, translating the name from Dutch.

As she and Bryce came nearer the storefront, they could see that windows on either side of the corner entrance were filled with paintings and sculptures.

Emil stood staring at a piece that was strikingly different from all the rest.

Resting on an easel was a large, flat ceramic plaque, about two feet high. Painted on it entirely in blue was a landscape featuring a windmill on a riverbank, a cloudy sky, and two small boats sailing nearby.

"Exquisite," Emil proclaimed as London and Bryce joined him at the window.

"Yes, it is," London agreed, although she still didn't quite understand why Emil was so strongly drawn to this plaque that he had dashed over here to gaze at it.

"What is it?" Bryce asked.

"You do not know?" Emil replied with a haughty grin.

"Well, there's not a label on it," Bryce said.

"No, nor do you see any labels on the other artworks either," Emil said. "That tells you something about the excellence of the gallery. It caters to people who know what they are looking at, who do not need to be told."

Bryce's slight grumble expressed a bit of annoyance at Emil's show of superiority.

London sighed. Earlier in the tour, when she had been getting a lot of attention from both Emil and Bryce, she had understood why the two sometimes got competitive about their knowledge of one thing or another. Fortunately, Bryce always stepped back before an actual argument broke out.

She had actually been relieved when Emil recently paired off with Amy, although their behavior had been so weird lately that it wasn't clear where that relationship stood anymore.

At least, she thought, *Emil is acting more like himself again.*

"It's very nice," London told him, looking at her watch. "Now we'd better be on our way to the Rijksmuseum."

"Not just yet, please," Emil said. "Please, I have not for many years seen a large piece like this done with such skill."

"It reminds me of Blue Willow china," London observed. "My sister has some at home."

"Oh, yes, Blue Willow," Emil said with a disdainful chuckle. "I have seen pictures of it. An English pattern, I believe, although it is meant to look Chinese. Very popular in America, is it not? Well, there is a distant connection, I suppose. Both Blue Willow and this superb piece were inspired by decorative porcelain imported from China in the 17th century. However Blue Willow is but a poor relation in my opinion. It soon became a mass-produced motif that turned up absolutely everywhere."

London was glad Tia couldn't hear Emil's words. Her sister was very proud of her blue-tinted china with its East Asian landscape featuring a footbridge, a pavilion, a pair of flying swallows, and of course a willow tree. The images were supposed to tell a story, which London had heard Tia relate to her children—something about a mandarin's daughter falling in love with a commoner against her father's command. After their tragic deaths, the two lovers were transformed into swallows.

Or something like that, London thought.

This much larger piece in this window told no such story. In fact, it looked very much like scenes painted on framed canvases displayed in the same window.

Emil pointed at the elaborate border decorated with flowers and leaves and topped with a shell-shaped carving.

"Can either of you identify the style of the border?" Emil asked.

Stifling a sigh, London glanced worriedly at her watch again.

Now he's quizzing us.

If he started playing the role of the learned academic, London feared they would never get away from here. He had a lecture to give elsewhere, after all.

"It's very elaborate," Bryce said, looking at it closely. "Somewhat like the architecture we see around Amsterdam—including this building. My guess is that it's Baroque."

With a snort of glee, Emil said, "A mistake—but an easy one to make. It is another style even more noted for its intricacy."

Bryce didn't look happy to be corrected. London spoke up quickly, hoping to settle the matter right away.

"It's Rococo—a 17th-style that evolved out of Baroque," she said. "You can tell by all the asymmetrical curlicues."

"Very good," Emil said.

"Now we'd really better being going," London added.

"Oh, but we must not rush," Emil said with a wag of his finger. "This is charming old Amsterdam, after all, not a city of turmoil and frenzy. I believe your English term for this kind of mellow place is 'laid out.'"

Laid back, London thought, but stopped herself from correcting him.

Then to her alarm, Emil walked on into the gallery.

"Come on, we've got to get him out of there," London said to Bryce.

They followed Emil inside the gallery, which was full of paintings, sculptures, and furniture of various periods—although London noticed a lack of anything modern.

"Mostly 18th and 19th century," Emil muttered, gazing at the paintings of ice skaters, windmills, and families lined up on the wall.

A severe-looking man was standing as if at attention. His head was shaved and he wore what looked rather like a butler's uniform. But his stiff posture and a microphone on his shoulder suggested he might also serve as some kind of security guard.

"Pardon me, sir," Emil said to him in Dutch, "but could you tell me the provenance of that ceramic piece in the window?"

"Provenance?" the man asked with a tilt of an eyebrow.

"Yes, I would like to know exactly where it was made and by whom."

The man frowned darkly.

"I can assure you that every item in this gallery is quite authentic," he said.

"I do not doubt it," Emil said. "All I am asking for is … well, a bit more information about this particular piece."

The man stared at Emil, and Emil stared right back at him. Then the man spoke into his microphone.

"Meneer Meyer, there is a gentleman here with whom you may wish to speak."

Then the man tilted his head at Emil and said, "I am sure that the gallery owner will join you shortly."

Shortly? London thought anxiously.

How shortly is shortly?

"Emil, listen to me—" London said.

"Yes, yes, I know, I have a lecture to give. I have not forgotten. Honestly, London, it is hardly like you to nag. I assure you we will be at the Rijksmuseum with time to spare."

London was really beginning to doubt that, but she didn't figure there was any changing Emil's mind.

While they waited for the mysterious *Meneer*—Mr.—Meyer, Emil peered closely at one of the paintings.

"But what have we here? A much earlier work by Esaias van de Velde, unless I am very much mistaken."

London looked and saw a painting of a bleak winter scene with bare trees, a run-down cottage, a muddy-looking road, and warmly bundled peasants.

"Indeed, it is by van de Velde," a nearby voice said in Dutch. "A new acquisition of ours. Esaias was, of course, a cousin of Jan van de Velde, who was quite famous for his etchings and engravings."

London turned and saw a hefty gentleman with wavy, steel-gray hair, wearing a pale blue silk shirt and a crooked bow tie and a vest with a silver watch chain.

Emil replied in Dutch with a nod of approval.

"You have an interesting collection, Meneer … ?"

"Meyer, Axel Meyer," he said, answering Emil's unspoken query. "This gallery has been in my family for five generations. You seem to have discerning tastes, Meneer …"

"Waldmüller. Emil Waldmüller. And these are my, eh, colleagues, London Rose and Bryce Yeaton."

London and Bryce exchanged frowns at the tone with which he said the word "colleagues."

He doesn't sound exactly proud to be seen in our company, she thought.

With a wry twinkle in his eye, Meneer Meyer replied in Emil's own language.

"Ah, then you are German, judging from your name … and your accent."

It was Emil's turn to frown a little. Although London wasn't sufficiently fluent in either language to recognize accents, it was clear that Meyer was making a somewhat snooty point to Emil.

Emil cleared his throat and spoke somewhat defensively again in Dutch.

"I would like to know more about the ceramic piece on display in your window."

With a sly expression, Meyer went back to speaking in his native Dutch.

"Ah, yes—our *Delfts Blauw* piece."

Meyer walked toward the plaque and turned the easel so they all could look at it.

"A 19th-century original, of course," Meyer said.

"I don't doubt it," Emil said. "An excellent work of faience."

With a somewhat condescending nod, Emil added to London and Bryce, "Faience, as perhaps you know, refers to a fine type of tin-glazed pottery. The exquisite hand painting was done in *Delfts Blauw*—a shade of blue specially made in the Dutch city of Delft, where this type of earthenware was produced."

Fingering the edge of the plaque, Emil added, "If I am not mistaken, this particular piece was made in the 1890s."

"Indeed, it was," Meyer said. "You seem to be quite knowledgeable in such matters. Would you be interested in making this purchase?"

"Perhaps," Emil said, "It is signed by its maker, I assume."

"Absolutely," Meyer said. "I will show you."

Meyer gently picked up the plaque and carried it over to a table, where he placed it face down. There was a signature on the back written in exquisite blue script.

"How much will you sell it for?" Emil asked.

Meyer's smile turned a bit more supercilious. London remembered what Emil had said about the lack of signs and labels in this gallery.

"It caters to people who know what they're looking at, who do not need to be told."

And now London thought Meyer almost seemed to be silently saying, *"If you have to ask ..."*

With a tilt of his head, he asked Emil, "I am curious, sir—what is your profession?"

"I am a historian," Emil said.

"Indeed?" Meyer said. "With what institution are you affiliated? One of the major German universities? Heidelberg, perhaps? The University of Bonn? Goethe University in Frankfurt?"

Emil looked briefly crestfallen at what struck even London as an impertinent query. Of course, Meyer was only trying to get some idea of Emil's income. But Emil drew himself up and replied with as much pride and self-assurance as he could muster.

"My colleagues and I serve aboard a fine European river tour boat. Perhaps you've heard of it—the *Nachtmusik.*"

"Alas, it is not familiar to me," Meyer said, sounding distinctly unimpressed.

Meyer picked up the plaque and placed it back on the easel.

Then he said, "Well, it was nice to talk with you. I wish you and your colleagues a good visit to our lovely city."

As the gallery owner turned to walk away, Emil spoke up.

"Just a moment, sir. I would be willing to pay 2500 florins for the *Delfts Blauw* piece."

London's eyes widened as she estimated the amount in U.S. currency to be around 1400 dollars.

Can Emil really afford that? she wondered.

She certainly considered it well out of her own price range.

For the first time, Meyer actually chuckled.

"Oh, I hardly think so, sir," he said.

Emil blurted, "Might you accept 2750 florins?"

Meyer frowned slightly.

"I'm not in the business of haggling, *Herr* Waldmüller," he said. "This is not an auction house. And now if you will excuse me ..."

Without another word, Axel Meyer disappeared back into his office.

The sentry took up his post again, pointedly ignoring the visitors.

Emil turned pale.

"I cannot believe this," he murmured, staring after the departed gallery owner.

London took Emil firmly by the arm and started hustling him out of the gallery.

"I'm sorry it didn't work out for you, Emil," she said. "But we've got to get to the Rijksmuseum right now."

As they left the gallery and walked along toward the museum, a pair of voices called out in unison—"hi." London looked around to see a familiar gray-haired couple peddling by on a tandem bike.

Walter Shick, who was in front, waved and called, "We're on our way to the museum."

As they sailed on past, Agnes called out from the second seat, "We'll meet you there."

"See," London told Emil, "I told you that our passengers will be waiting for us to arrive."

Fortunately the museum was already in sight, just a block away. London was beginning to believe that they might just make it in time to meet the passengers who would surely be waiting for them at that massive palace-like edifice with its ornamental facade.

"I cannot believe this," Emil said again.

Relieved that they were finally on their way to their destination, London replied, "I can't believe it either, Emil. Were you really ready to pay well over a thousand dollars for that plaque? I mean, I understand that it's very beautiful."

"I would have managed it," Emil said. "Oh, it would have been tight, but I could have pulled that much or more out of my savings."

"But why?" London asked.

"You don't understand," Emil said. "I have wanted an authentic *Delfts Blauw* ever since I was a little boy."

London couldn't help but smile as she tried to imagine what kind of little boy would be obsessed with fine Delft pottery.

Emil was always one of a kind, she thought.

She really did feel sorry that he hadn't been able to make the purchase.

Bryce patted him on the back and said, "Tough luck, old fellow. Better luck next time, eh?"

Emil nodded disconsolately.

As they approached the Rijksmuseum, London saw some familiar figures grouped near the entrance—the passengers who had signed up for Emil's tour.

Just as a few of those people caught sight of London, Bryce, and Emil, the historian gasped aloud.

“What a fool I was!” he cried.

To London’s alarm, Emil whirled and started back the way they’d come.

CHAPTER TEN

"Wait a minute," London cried. "Emil, where are you going?"

She hurried to catch up with the briskly striding historian.

"Where do you think I am going?" Emil replied, without slowing down. "I have to offer him a better price. I must have been out of my mind offering 2500 florins, or even 2750. I am quite sure he will sell it for 3500 florins."

"Emil, that's about 2000 dollars!"

"Do you think I do not know the exchange rate? I am sure I can afford it somehow."

"Not if you lose your job, you can't."

"Now, London, there is no call for that kind of talk. We are part of a team, are we not? And we look out for each other—'watch each other's backs' I think is how you Americans put it. Could you not fill in for me this once?"

"I filled in for you yesterday," London said.

"And you did a superb job of it," Emil said. "I am sure you will do just as well today. You can give a tour of the Rijksmuseum with no trouble at all. I promise to make it up to you."

With that, Emil speeded up and trotted away.

For a moment London just stood there staring after him. Then with an exasperated sigh, she turned around and walked back toward Bryce.

"It's no use," she said. "I don't know what's gotten into him, but there's no reasoning with him. I'll have to conduct the tour myself."

"Do you think you can do it?" Bryce said.

"I hope so," London said. "I don't know if we can get a museum guide on such short notice."

Although the truth was, she didn't feel the least bit confident, but she knew she had to get the tour started right now. They were nearing the huge building that spread across the far side of a flower-adorned plaza. Its two towers flanked a grand arched entranceway and wings wrapped the plaza on both sides. Like much of Amsterdam, the building combined several historical styles into an impressive structure.

A group with familiar faces was standing in the plaza, waiting for them.

Were any of them watching that little scene with Emil? she wondered.

Her question was soon answered.

A long-limbed, middle-aged woman with a shock of curly hair came striding out of the group. Pointing down the street, she demanded, "Where is Herr Waldmüller off to?"

"Hi Audrey," London replied. "Um … he had an errand to run."

At least that's partly true, she thought.

Even though they had become friends during some recent adventures, London knew that Audrey Bolton had a tendency to become quite irritable if she believed that anything was amiss.

And her new friend looked rather cross right now.

"But he's supposed to conduct our tour of this museum," Audrey complained, looking at her watch. "We've all been waiting here for several minutes. I thought Germans were supposed to be punctual—and dependable."

I always thought so too, London thought.

"I'll be filling in for him," she said instead.

"Well, that's hardly fair, is it?" Audrey complained sharply. "I heard about how you had to cover for him yesterday when we were sailing by the Mouse Tower. It sounds like he's getting to be downright irresponsible. I've got a notion to complain to the captain about it."

"I'd rather you didn't," London said.

"Why not?" Audrey said.

That's a good question, London thought.

She wasn't sure why not, except that she didn't want Emil to get into serious trouble before she could figure out what was going on with him—and with Amy as well. It worried her that word of Emil's odd behavior was already getting around. The *Nachtmusik's* rumor mill was grinding away as usual. And that couldn't be good.

"Let's just get this tour going," London said. "Please," she added.

To her relief, Audrey shrugged and stepped back among the others. London saw that Agnes and Walter Shick were parking their tandem bike in a nearby bike rack and coming to join them. Honey and Gus Jarrett were there, and so was the large and formidable Letitia Hartzer.

Bryce took a few steps forward and stood with the others, facing London with an attentive look on his face.

London put on her best professional smile. Fortunately, she had a fair amount of knowledge about the building itself, even if she didn't know as much as Emil did about the works exhibited there.

"Welcome to the world-famous Rijksmuseum," she said. "I hope you enjoy today's visit."

As they came near the arched entryway, Walter Shick gasped in amazement.

"Why, I can see daylight through there," he said. "'Light at the end of the tunnel,' so to speak."

"It *is* like a tunnel, isn't it?" Agnes said. "It goes all the way through the building."

"That's right," London said. "This building was completed in 1885 as a place to house the Netherland's greatest cultural treasures. But it was also designed to be a literal *gate* into the city. Today you see cyclists and pedestrians walking through here. A hundred years ago you would have also seen people in carriages and on horseback."

"How appropriate," Letitia Hartzer remarked. "Almost symbolic."

"Yes," London said. "It was as if the city's very entryway was meant to transport you through the culture and history of the Netherlands."

London led her little band of tourists into the tunnel, then through an entryway into a startling burst of interior sunlight shining down from on high onto a vast expanse of gray stone floor.

"This is an atrium," London explained as she paid their admission. "It's one of a pair of what used to be open courtyards. The spectacular, high steel and glass ceiling was added in recent years."

The passengers murmured with interest in the blend of styles.

Meanwhile, London was uneasily trying to decide where she should take the group next. She was glad to see that they had arrived right at an oval-shaped information desk that featured an array of brochures.

I guess I'll have to learn myself as I go along, she thought.

Bryce picked up a folded map and handed it to her. As she nervously perused it, London realized that she was getting expectant stares from her other companions.

Maybe I should just admit I'm not as prepared as I should be.

But she was rescued by a Dutch-accented voice.

"Can I help you?"

London turned and saw a tall, short-haired woman approaching the group.

Holding out her hand to London, she said, "I am Helga van den

Heuvel, a docent here at the Rijksmuseum."

London managed not to breathe an audible sigh of relief as she shook the woman's hand.

"My name is London Rose, and I'm the social director aboard an American tour boat visiting Amsterdam."

Blushing a little, she added quietly, "And I'm afraid I'm a little out of my depth trying to conduct a tour through this great museum."

The woman laughed sympathetically.

"You need not trouble yourself. I am here to help out."

"Oh, thank you, Mevrouw van den Heuvel," London said, using the Dutch word for "miss."

"Call me Helga, please."

Turning to the group, Helga said, "As I suppose you know, the Rijksmuseum is home to Dutch art from every era, dating all the way back to the 12th century. Would anybody like to make a request as to where to begin?"

Honey Jarrett raised her hand shyly.

"Have you got any Van Goghs?" she said.

London couldn't help but smile. She figured Honey was simply mentioning the first and perhaps only Dutch artist she could think of. Even so, it was a perfectly good suggestion.

With a tilt of her head, Helga replied, "Not as many as we'd like—certainly not as many as the Van Gogh Museum here in Amsterdam, which has the largest collection in the world. But we've got a few excellent pieces if you would care to see them."

The group spoke with eager approval.

"Very well then," Helga said. "Follow me."

London nudged up against Bryce as they all headed out of the atrium.

"Now *that* was a stroke of luck," she whispered to him.

"I suppose," Bryce said with a wink. "But I was kind of looking forward to seeing you try to wing it."

"Very funny," London replied with a chuckle.

As they continued on their way, she admired Helga's confident, ultra-professional posture and poise. The docent was sleek, athletic-looking, and so tall that London thought at first glance she must be wearing very high-heeled shoes.

But no, the woman was wearing flat, soft-soled shoes with her pantsuit—a sensible outfit for someone who had to spend all day walking.

Helga said, "It is just possible that we are following in Vincent's footsteps right now. He came to this museum quite often and found a lot of inspiration here—as I hope to show you shortly."

She led them straight to the section where the Van Gogh works were exhibited.

"We have a small selection of his works, as you can see," Helga explained. "And mostly drawings, with only a few paintings. But this is enough to give you an idea of how Vincent developed as an artist during his short career."

She pointed to a painting of cottages under an overcast sky.

"For example, he painted *Farming Village at Twilight* in 1884, when he was still learning his craft. The painting is done in a very muted, realistic style, nothing at all like his works from just a few years later."

Then Helga pointed out a much more familiar image—a portrait of the artist himself with an intense gaze, wearing a felt hat.

Helga said, "You have probably seen photos of this painting. It is said that he painted lots of self-portraits because he couldn't afford models! In fact, he was extremely poor during much of his sad life. He depended on his brother Theo for money."

She pointed to details in the painting.

"Here you can see his mature style in its expressive glory, with pure, vibrant colors and bold brush strokes. In fact, he sometimes didn't bother to use a brush, just squeezed paint directly out of its tube onto the canvas. You can see how his face seems to vibrate with the kind of life that he brought to all of his later works."

London felt a lump of emotion form in her throat as she realized something.

I saw this painting with Mom.

And she remembered Mom quoting Vincent's own words to London and her sister as they'd looked at this very painting.

"I want to give the wretched a brotherly message."

Helga turned and looked at London with surprise.

"Oh, dear," London said, blushing. "I hadn't meant to say that aloud."

But Helga smiled with apparent approval.

"I'm glad you did," she said. "Sending a brotherly message was what Vincent was trying to do with all his work. He was trying to bring comfort to humanity. Before he became a painter, he actually tried preaching and missionary work. That didn't work out very well. He wound up giving everything he had to the poor! He eventually realized that he could achieve his spiritual goals through art."

Helga stepped away from the painting and asked the group, "Can I answer any questions?"

"Yeah," Honey said. "Did Van Gogh ever get to see any of his paintings exhibited right here in this museum?"

"Oh, no, far from it," Helga said. "He was virtually unknown all his life. Out of some 800 paintings and 700 drawings, he only managed to sell one artwork. Of course, today he is one of the most famous artists who ever lived. Some of his works sell for millions of dollars."

Honey's husband Gus raised his hand and asked, "Is it true he cut off his ear?"

She must get asked this a lot, London thought.

"Well, that's how the story goes, isn't it?" Helga said in a patient tone. "He supposedly got into an argument with his friend, the painter Paul Gauguin, and tried to attack him with a razor. When Gauguin got away from him, he cut off most of his own left ear and gave it to a young woman in a brothel. That's what you've always heard, isn't it?"

"Pretty much," Gus said.

"It probably didn't happen quite like that," Helga said. "In 2008 a pair of art researchers went through police records. They came to the conclusion that Gauguin himself probably attacked Van Gogh with a sword and caused the injury. Whatever else happened between the two men that day, it ended their friendship."

Helga added, "There are all sorts of legends about Van Gogh. You should be careful what you believe about him. But what is true is that he was a brilliant and troubled soul. He was very lonely, and he may have suffered from epilepsy or schizophrenia or both. It's also true that he wound up taking his own life—a tragic end for a man who brought so much beauty into the world."

Then Helga smiled and said, "Let's be on our way, shall we? There is much more to see."

As the group started following Helga out of the exhibition hall, London looked back and noticed that one passenger was lagging behind. It was Cyrus Bannister, and he was peering closely at a painting of tulips. In fact, his nose was almost up against the canvas.

"Are you coming?" London asked.

Cyrus stepped back from the painting with a startled look.

"Yes, of course," he said. "Absolutely."

As London and Cyrus followed after the group, London asked him, "Did you notice something interesting about that painting?"

"No," Cyrus said. "Nothing interesting."

He cleared his throat and added, "Except, of course, that it's a masterpiece."

Something about Cyrus's tone suggested to London that he wasn't telling her everything he was thinking. Always dark-clad and typically rather dour, Cyrus was a peculiar sort of man, and not always an especially pleasant one. He did, however, seem to be knowledgeable about many things, ranging from classical music to dog training.

She couldn't help but wonder what had caught his attention.

As they continued on their way, Helga approached London and asked, "How much time do you still have for your tour?"

London looked at her watch and said, "Enough time to visit the Hall of Honor and Rembrandt's *The Night Watch,* I think. Oh, and to spend a little time in the gift shop."

"The gift shop is right on our way," Helga said.

The group seemed enthusiastic as Helga led them inside the little shop. It had a charming variety of items, including tote bags, scarves, jewelry, greeting cards, ceramic vases and plant holders, t-shirts, and souvenir mugs. There were even some little "action figures" of artists like Van Gogh and Rembrandt, and crochet dolls representing characters that appeared in some of the museum's great artworks.

London was pleased to see smiles on the passengers' faces as they browsed.

But then something worrisome caught her eye.

Letitia Hartzer was fingering a souvenir pen shaped and painted like one of the ceramic vases on display in the room where they'd last been. The pen was attached by a little chain to an equally decorative base.

And Letitia's interest seemed to be more than that of an innocent buyer.

Oh, no, London thought. *Not this again.*

CHAPTER ELEVEN

London held her breath anxiously.

Letitia Hartzer was one of her favorite passengers, but the woman had a personality flaw that had led to trouble in the past.

She was a small-scale kleptomaniac.

Early in the tour, London had found Letitia's stateroom virtually decorated with stolen items, mostly inexpensive little knickknacks. London had made sure that all those items were returned to their rightful owners and Letitia had also promised that she would never steal anything again.

But now there she was, fingering just the kind of pretty object that she had shoplifted at earlier stops on their tour and even purloined from the *Nachtmusik* itself.

Should I stop her right now? London wondered.

Maybe not, she told herself.

She resisted the urge to pounce. Of course, letting Letitia actually steal something was out of the question. But it did look like the woman was at the very least struggling with her temptation.

As London stood there wavering, Letitia picked the pen up by the base. For a moment, she seemed to be holding her own breath. Then she smiled. And in a completely non-furtive manner, she carried the pen over to the cashier and properly bought it.

While she was paying for her pen, Leticia caught London's gaze and her smile widened.

As the group left the gift shop, London patted Letitia on the back and whispered to her.

"You did good just now."

Letitia laughed quietly.

"Thanks," she said. "It's not a bad idea to keep an eye on me, though."

"I'll keep doing that," London said.

She turned her attention back to the docent who was leading their tour of the Rijksmuseum. Helga ushered the group up a flight of stairs into a magnificent hall with a high arched roof. The walls were covered with elaborate decorations and murals, and sunlight streamed in through grand stained-glass windows.

"This is the Great Hall," Helga explained. "The paintings and the windows show scenes from Dutch history and portraits of Dutch artists, writers, and architects."

As the group approached a set of glass doors, Helga paused and spoke in a reverent tone.

"I want you to prepare to see one of the greatest exhibit halls in the world—the Rijksmuseum's Gallery of Honor. Here you will see a collection of paintings from the 17th century, the Dutch Golden Age, when Amsterdam was one of the world's busiest and most important centers of trade, learning, philosophy, art, and military power."

Helga opened a door, and the group entered a stunning hallway flanked by alcoves filled with masterpieces. At the far end of the hall was a little room with walls of glass.

Although London was sure that she had been here long ago with her sister and her parents, this didn't look at all familiar to her.

Helga explained, "Our most famous painting by possibly the most famous of all artists—Rembrandt van Rijn's monumental *The Night Watch*—is undergoing restoration. You will still be able to get a look at it, but it's important to get a whole sense of 17th-century Dutch art before you take in that amazing picture. Let's look at some of the smaller masterworks all around us."

The group began to visit alcove after alcove, viewing works by such masters as Jan Steen and Frans Hals. Two works by Johannes Vermeer, a milkmaid pouring milk into a bowl and a pregnant woman reading a letter, created an amazing feeling of real sunlight.

Helga explained as they went, "As you can see, these aren't images of kings and queens and aristocrats, nor of mythological heroes. In the 17th century, the Dutch middle class was gaining wealth and power. Many of these paintings were bought by people who weren't interested in the exotic or the noble. They were more interested in life as it was going on around them."

Helga drew the group's attention to a painting of food on a table.

"You can even learn about how Dutch people ate from paintings like this one—*Still Life with Turkey Pie* by Pieter Claeas. Here the painter celebrates the bounty of a Dutch dinner table with its oysters, grapes, olives, and a turkey. The turkey pie itself is enough to tell you that the family who ate at this table was quite wealthy. The pie would have been spiced with cinnamon, mace, cloves, and ginger—spices from the east that were as dear in their way as gold."

London was struck by the painting's extreme realism, more vivid than any photograph could be.

Helga pointed out one detail, "Do you see this lemon, with a spiraling rind that has been carefully peeled away? This is a common image in Dutch still lifes—a symbolic reminder of how life is fleeting and temporary. With this, the artist reminded this painting's owners to be humble."

Fleeting and temporary, London thought.

The partially peeled lemon reminded her of Mom, and of a happy and adventurous days long gone.

Moving on to a different alcove Helga said, "Sometimes Dutch painters celebrated things that might strike us as extremely ordinary and mundane." Pointing to a canvas, she added, "For example, take a close look at this picture by Pieter de Hooch. What do you see there?"

London and the others bunched in around the painting, which showed the interior of a perfectly ordinary home of the time.

"I see a woman at home holding a little girl in her arms," Agnes Shick said. "The girl is her daughter, I guess."

"I see a little family dog," Bryce said.

Others noted paintings on the walls, pillows on a cubbyhole bed, plain drapes, a laundry basket, drab wallpaper, sunlight pouring in through an open window with a wooden shutter, and a laundry basket.

"And that looks like a wooden chair," Gus said, "except it there's no real seat to it."

Cyrus Bannister let out a knowing laugh.

"That's because it's actually a little indoor toilet," Cyrus said.

"That's right," Helga said with a chuckle. "A *kakstoel,* it was called in Dutch back then. Imagine, putting a bathroom seat in a painting like this! No subject was too ordinary or every-day or mundane for the people who bought this painting. But what about the woman and the little girl. What do you think they're doing, exactly?"

London and the others looked more closely at the seated woman, whose daughter's face was snuggled against her side.

"She's doing something with her daughter's hair," Letitia observed.

"Braiding it maybe?" Audrey suggested.

Honey let out a squeal of realization.

"Oh, *I* know what she's doing! She's checking her daughter's hair for lice!"

The others let out exclamations of surprise.

"That's right," Helga said. "Which explains the painting's title—*A Mother's Duty.*"

Although London was having trouble remembering what she might have seen here before, she felt a flash of *déjà vu* as they came in sight of Rembrandt's famous—and enormous—*Syndics of the Drapers' Guild.* That painting showed six black-clad, prosperous Dutch businessmen gathered closely together around a table.

When she, Mom, and Tia had seen this painting years ago, London had felt a childish urge to apologize to those men.

"I'm sorry to bother you," she'd felt like saying. *"I can see you're busy."*

London got the same uncanny feeling right now. The men had been poring over a record book, but their gaze appeared to have suddenly turned to the viewer, as if they'd been interrupted in their work.

Helga said, "I mentioned a while ago that Van Gogh came to this museum to view great paintings, especially by Rembrandt. He admired this one very much."

Cyrus Bannister quietly interrupted in a knowledgeable voice.

"But this one wasn't Van Gogh's *favorite* Rembrandt."

Helga looked a bit surprised by Cyrus's comment, but not the least bit displeased.

"You are quite correct," she said to him. "Let's go look at his favorite right now."

They walked a short distance to see a painting of a man and a young woman rendered in bright, glowing colors.

Helga said, "In Van Gogh's day, this painting was known as *The Jewish Bride.* Scholars hadn't yet figured out that the man and the woman were characters from the Bible—the patriarch Isaac and his wife Rebecca. Even so, the painting had a tremendous effect on Van Gogh."

Smiling at Cyrus, Helga added, "Would you care to elaborate, sir? You seem to have some knowledge of this work."

Cyrus nodded and said, "Vincent wrote about this painting in a letter to his brother Theo. He called it an 'intimate, infinitely sympathetic picture, painted with a glowing hand.' He said that this artwork proved Rembrandt to be more than just a painter. He could actually 'make poetry' out of images."

Helga nodded, obviously rather impressed, then spoke again to everybody.

"I'm sure you all remember Van Gogh's thick brushstrokes, his heavy use of paint. He learned at least some of that technique from this painting." Pointing to the couple's clothing, she said, "You can see that Rembrandt did much the same thing right here with layers of paint."

Cyrus nodded again and said, "I believe Rembrandt deliberately scratched the thick globs of paint with the butt end of his paintbrush to achieve such a glowing effect."

"You are quite correct, sir," Helga said. "And now I believe we are ready to see the greatest work in this hall full of masterpieces. Come with me to the Night Watch Gallery. It will be a fitting way to end your tour."

As the group continued on their way, London looked at Cyrus Bannister curiously. His expression, as usual, was hard to read. She'd already been aware that he knew a lot about art. But now she realized something more.

He can actually quote Van Gogh by heart.

Which made London think about that strange moment a little while ago, when she'd found him staring at the Van Gogh painting of tulips, with his nose almost up against the canvas.

When she'd asked him if he'd noticed something interesting, he'd said that he hadn't.

"Except, of course, that it's a masterpiece."

Now London wondered again …

What wasn't he telling me?

CHAPTER TWELVE

London was still watching Cyrus Bannister closely as the group walked toward the far end of the Gallery of Honor. It was clear that he knew a lot more than she did about fine art. And for a man who exhibited disdain for so many matters, he did seem unusually interested in the works they were seeing now. Even so, his stern demeanor gave her no clue to his feelings about any of them, not even the huge painting inside an enormous glass enclosure in front of them. Was his interest strictly intellectual?

With no answers to her questions, London turned her own attention to the grand painting inside that glass room. Rembrandt's *The Night Watch* was a staggering sight, peopled with 17th-century characters arranged in a gigantic composition. Many of the characters were carrying muskets, swords, and other weapons.

As London took in the spectacle, she could almost hear a voice speaking to her.

"You mustn't touch, sweetie."

It was what Mom had said when London had first seen this masterwork, standing right in front of it and reaching toward it with her little fingers.

London remembered how startled she'd been by those words. She actually hadn't meant to *touch* the painting. It was more as though she'd felt as though she could walk *into* the painting, into a wonderful world of exciting characters that stretched out far beyond her reach.

Of course, she wasn't nearly as close to the painting right now, and there was a sheet of glass separating her from it. Three people were inside the glass enclosure. Two women and a man, all wearing black, uniform-like jackets were mounted on a hydraulic platform that reminded London of scaffolding used by window washers on skyscrapers. At the moment, they were operating what looked like some kind of a high-tech digital scanning device while looking at images in a computer monitor.

London said to Helga, "I'd heard that *The Night Watch* was being restored. I hadn't realized the restoration was still going on."

"Oh, it will keep going on for years," Helga said. "We call it 'Operation Night Watch,' and it's the most ambitious restoration and research project ever carried out on this masterpiece. Rather than keep the painting out of view, the museum decided to invite the public to witness the whole process from beginning to end. It is even being livestreamed, so people all over the world can watch it in real time."

Helga said to the group, "*The Night Watch* is the pride of the Rijksmuseum. It was completed by Rembrandt in 1642 after three years of work. It was commissioned by a company of *Kloveniers*—civic militia guards—for a sort of group portrait. Thirty-four characters wound up in the painting, as you can see."

Pointing through the glass, Helga continued.

"It is a painting of many mysteries, legends, and misunderstandings. For one thing, Rembrandt never called it *The Night Watch.* It was named that by mistake. By the end of the 18th century, the varnish on its surface darkened so that the painting looked like a night scene. It was only after the varnish was removed during a restoration in 1946 did anyone realize the truth. Even though the background is dark, you can see that the figures in the foreground are lit by the daylight sun. But the name *The Night Watch* stuck, and we still call it that today."

Letitia raised her hand and remarked, "It seems like much more than just a group portrait, almost as if it were telling a story."

"Yes, it does, doesn't it?" Helga agreed with a smile. "Nobody really knows exactly what that story was. All we know is that the scene is full of dramatic activity."

Pointing to more details, Helga said, "For example, a little boy is running away with a gunpowder horn. A guardsman seems to be loading his musket. Another guardsman has just fired his musket, apparently by accident, narrowly missing the lieutenant's head! A dog is barking at a drummer, who pounds away furiously on his drum. And if you look carefully behind the main characters, you'll see Rembrandt himself looking out over the scene! What is going on here, exactly?"

Helga shrugged and continued, "There have been lots of rumors and legends—including that Rembrandt brought about his own financial ruin by revealing a murder plot in this painting. I personally doubt that. I suppose the painting will never give away all of its mysteries."

London's eye was drawn to an image that she remembered strongly from her childhood visit here. The brightest figure in the whole painting was a girl dressed in gold, who seemed almost eerily out of place among the military men.

"Who is that girl?" she asked.

"That's a good question," Helga said. "She was probably modeled on Rembrandt's wife, Saskia. She seems to be some kind of a symbolic figure, a mascot for the company."

Honey asked, "Is that a dead chicken tied to her waist?"

"It certainly is," Helga said with a laugh.

"That's kind of weird, isn't it?" Honey said with a snap of her chewing gum. "I mean, is it supposed to mean something?"

"Oh, yes," Helga replied. "A chicken's claws were part of the coat-of-arms for this company of *Kloveniers*. And the chicken might also be a visual pun on the name of the captain—Banning Cocq. There he is standing in front of the others …"

Cyrus Bannister interrupted with a question, "What can you tell us about the restoration?"

Helga shrugged and tilted her head.

"Well, not as much as somebody on the team. Let's see if we can get their attention."

She rapped gently on the glass, and the one of the restorers turned toward them. He was the male member of the group—a bald man with tight-looking features that seemed too small for the rest of his face. He was more formally dressed than the other workers, including a yellow cravat.

Helga waved for the man to come outside.

He hesitated briefly, then stepped down off the platform and came on out of the glass enclosure.

"Well?" he said to Helga a bit gruffly in Dutch. "Is there some sort of a problem?"

"Oh, no problem at all," she replied in Dutch. "I just have a group of visitors who are curious about the restoration process."

The man shook his head.

"They can find out all they want to know online," he said.

"Oh, don't be like that!" Helga said, poking him playfully in the shoulder. Then she spoke to him in English. "Let me introduce you to a group of American tourists and their social director, London Rose. Ladies and gentlemen, I'd like you to meet Pier Dekker, one of our restorers."

Poking him again, Helga said teasingly, "Meneer Dekker is the oldest person on the restoration team." She added with a hearty chuckle, "And as you can see, he is the only man working on this shift."

The man frowned sharply at her remark.

"More is the pity," he said in English.

London was a bit startled by this exchange. Pointing out the man's age seemed kind of rude on Helga's part. And the man sounded a bit defensive about the gender issue. It seemed clear that Helga and Dekker didn't especially like each other.

Helga said to Dekker, "What would you like to tell them about the restoration?"

Dekker crossed his arms and said, "Well, for one thing, I wish we were the first team to undertake this task. The painting has been cleaned and restored more times than anybody really knows about. And those efforts have done at least as much harm as good."

He gazed at the painting with a sorrowful expression.

"This masterwork had suffered a great deal at human hands," he said.

"It has even been vandalized, hasn't it?" Cyrus remarked.

"Oh, yes—three different times, and for utterly insane reasons. In 1911, a shoemaker slashed it with his knife, apparently on account of finding himself unemployed. In 1975, another man slashed it—at God's orders, he said. In 1990, an escaped psychiatric patient splashed sulfuric acid on it—an act of pure madness, apparently."

With a bitter sigh, he added, "It's amazing this masterpiece has survived—and not just from the attacks, but from the ignorant efforts to repair the damage they'd caused. No one is to blame, I suppose. It is only now that we have the means to treat this painting with the care it truly deserves."

London was struck by the note of sympathy in Dekker's voice, as if the painting were truly alive.

And in a way, maybe it is, she thought.

Dekker continued, "We are now able to use technology that earlier generations of conservators couldn't even dream of. We are using x-radiography, spectroscopy, infrared imaging—the same technology NASA has used to study the chemical makeup of objects on Mars."

Pointing to the scanning machine, he added, "By the time we're through, we'll have taken 8400 photographs of every square inch of the work in ultra-high resolution—five thousandth of a millimeter, to be exact. We can examine pigment particles right down to the molecular level."

"It sounds like you're doing a great deal more than cleaning and restoring it," Cyrus said.

London heard a note of displeasure in his voice.

"Oh, yes," Dekker said. "We are learning things about *The Night Watch* that no one ever hoped to know."

Pointing to a figure wearing a helmet, he said, "For example, our digital technology reveals something about this character that even the x-ray techniques used in the past could not show us. Originally, there was a feather in this gentleman's helmet. Rembrandt changed his mind and painted it over."

"I suppose you could offer evidence that Rembrandt made that change himself," Cyrus remarked sharply.

Meneer Dekker frowned at him.

"I can assure you that we are positive that Rembrandt made that very change. And yes, I could offer you evidence of it, if you doubt my word."

"I don't doubt it for a moment," Cyrus said, crossing his arms.

Dekker's frown deepened, and his small eyebrows drew together.

"Do I detect a note of disapproval, Mr. …?"

"Bannister. Cyrus Bannister."

"What is your area of expertise, Meneer Bannister?"

"I am merely a humble art lover," Cyrus said.

London grew more worried. As far as she was concerned, Cyrus never sounded "humble" under any circumstances.

Dekker audibly scoffed.

"Well, as one humble art lover to another, I'd be glad to show you a digital image of the feather that has been concealed by layers of paint and varnish for almost 400 years. I can show you dozens of other long-hidden details that practically document every stage of Rembrandt's three-year process as he painted this masterwork."

Looking worried, Helga began, "Meneer Dekker, please—"

Dekker snapped at her in a snidely condescending tone, "This is not your affair, my dear. Kindly let me handle it."

London and Bryce glanced at each other apprehensively.

It was Cyrus's turn to scoff.

"I don't think it's any of my business to look at a feather that Rembrandt himself chose for me not to see, let alone any other details that he deliberately hid away. Frankly, I don't think it's anyone's business—and certainly not yours."

Dekker's face reddened with anger.

London realized that she'd better intervene. She touched the argumentative passenger on the arm.

"Cyrus, we are guests in Amsterdam," she said.

Trying to be helpful, Bryce added, "Maybe we could have this conversation among ourselves after we leave."

A few passengers murmured in anxious agreement. But Dekker made it clear that it was too late to avoid a quarrel. He stepped toward the taller man and peered angrily up at his face.

"Oh, but I *do* insist on having this conversation, right here and now," he said. "Do you object to the work we are doing here, Meneer Bannister?"

"Not at all," Cyrus said, looking down at the conservator. "Restoring and preserving a masterpiece is a noble endeavor, requiring skill. However, it involves no creative effort or insight, merely advanced knowledge of the latest high-tech gadgetry and trickery. It is not fitting for a technician to go poking and prodding into the workings of a great creative mind. And that, I fear, is what you're doing by exposing Rembrandt's secrets."

Dekker let out a low-pitched growl.

"A technician, am I?" he said.

"Surely you don't claim to be an actual artist." Cyrus snapped back.

The conservator stepped forward with a dark scowl on his face.

Cyrus stood his ground with a superior expression on his.

London knew she needed to defuse this situation somehow.

CHAPTER THIRTEEN

Before London could intervene, the argument heated up even more.

"You have no right to assume otherwise," Dekker snarled.

London spoke before Cyrus could reply to that.

"Cyrus, that's enough."

"Don't make this any worse," Bryce added.

Cyrus hesitated, obviously about to fire back. Then he shook his head and turned away silently.

London figured she'd better make amends.

She said to Dekker, "Sir, on behalf of my group—"

"Yes, yes, you apologize," the conservator said, interrupting again. "And with very good reason. This unfortunate incident would never have happened if you were the least bit good at your job."

London felt suddenly baffled.

"Sir, I'm not sure I know what you expected—"

"No, I don't suppose you do. The requirements of your work are quite beyond your female comprehension. It's an all-too-common problem in these dreary times of so-called equality."

London's mouth dropped open.

My "female comprehension!" she almost exclaimed aloud.

"'So-called equality'?"

Bryce opened his mouth to protest, but London silenced him with a poke of her arm. She didn't want to get this confrontation started up again.

But then Dekker spoke to London again.

"And now, I must insist that you and your people leave our museum."

Helga let out a gasp of alarm.

Speaking Dutch now, she said, "Meneer Dekker, you know perfectly well that you don't have the authority to expel patrons from this museum."

Dekker replied to her in Dutch, "No? Then perhaps *you* do. If so, you should exercise that authority at once. But you lack the necessary fortitude. Like I said, it's an all-too-common problem these days."

Helga looked genuinely angry herself now.

London gave Bryce another nudge to keep him quiet. She knew she had to extricate herself and her group from the situation as quickly and painlessly as possible.

She spoke in Dutch to both Helga and Dekker.

"Really, there's no need for this situation to get any worse. Helga, I told you earlier that this would be the last stop on our museum visit. We were about to leave anyway. Thank you for a very informative tour."

"Very well, then," Helga said, still glaring at Dekker. "Meanwhile, sir, I'd like a word with you in private."

London's group seemed more than ready to leave as she began to escort them out of the Night Watch Gallery. She glanced back and saw that Helga and Dekker had already exited separately. She also saw that some of the museum patrons were staring at her and her group.

We really made quite a scene, London realized. *What an unpleasant experience.*

And she had an uneasy feeling that wouldn't be the end of it.

She could feel her face burning as she led the group back through the Gallery of Honor on their way out of the Rijksmuseum. That had an unfortunate ending to what ought to have been a happy, enriching experience for everyone involved. Why had it degenerated into an ugly scene?

Confrontations with local guides and other experts were rare in her work on tour boats. She had to admit, she'd had the occasional disagreement with locals—police captains, for example.

But this one seemed different.

Of course, the museum conservator was a highly trained professional who had reason to be annoyed with Cyrus Bannister's high-handed comments.

"Surely you don't claim to be an actual artist," Cyrus had said. Even if Cyrus was right about that, calling the man a mere technician had been an unnecessary insult.

But why had Pier Dekker become so angry when she had attempted to apologize? The conservator had even insulted her personally. London wasn't sure whether she felt more embarrassed or angry.

As the group continued on their way into the tunnel that led outdoors, London was aware of Bryce walking along beside her.

What must he think? she wondered. He'd had little opportunity to see her working at her job, and this certainly hadn't been her best day.

"That man really ought to apologize," Bryce muttered. "Maybe we should both go back and—"

London interrupted, "Oh, Bryce, please, let's don't. It would only make things worse."

Even so, she felt herself relax a bit at his words. At least Bryce didn't hold her responsible for the way the tour had ended. But the passengers walking along behind them were being uncharacteristically quiet. She wasn't sure what any of them might be thinking.

When they reached the open plaza in front of the museum, at least one of the passengers answered that question.

Stepping out into the sunlight, Honey Jarrett commented loudly, "Wow, does that restorer guy have a problem with women or *what?*"

Several other passengers laughed or nodded their heads in agreement.

"He practically admitted it," Honey continued. "I mean, look at the way he treated you. It was Cyrus he was arguing with, but he didn't take out his anger on him. He took it out on you, just because you're a woman. He argues with men, but he bullies women."

Of course, London realized.

Honey had just answered her unasked question—why had the man lashed out at her like that?

London cringed as she remembered what Dekker had said to her.

"The requirements of your work are quite beyond your female comprehension."

Honey shook her head and added, "I've known men like that all my life. Maybe their mothers didn't treat them right. But that's no excuse. Men can be such a pain in the neck."

"You don't mean me, I hope," Honey's husband said.

Honey gave Gus an affectionate tweak of his cheek.

"Oh, no, not you, sweetie—at least not most of the time. You've got to admit, you're not always perfect."

Then she added to Bryce, "And I don't mean you, either, handsome—not *ever*. You're always a darling in every way."

Honey gave London a knowing wink as she and Gus strolled away across the plaza. Obviously, Honey had some idea of what was going on between London and Bryce.

So does just about everybody, probably, London thought.

Since there didn't seem to be much point in hiding it, London took

Bryce by the hand, and he gently squeezed her hand in return. The show of mutual affection felt nice after what had just happened.

London realized that at least she'd ended the tour right on schedule, and everybody in the group was now free to spend the rest of their stay in Amsterdam doing whatever they liked. Most of them were already chatting about what to do next.

She saw that Cyrus Bannister and Audrey Bolton had stepped off to one side, where they seemed to be carrying on an animated conversation.

She told Bryce, "I'm not as upset with Dekker as I am with Cyrus. I have some responsibility for the behavior of our passengers, especially on our organized tours. And anyway, Cyrus started the whole thing."

"Maybe we should have a word with him," Bryce said.

"Leave the talking to me," London said. "Taking care of these kinds of issues is part of my job."

Reluctantly, she let go of Bryce's hand. He nodded, and the two of them hurried over to Cyrus and Audrey.

"Cyrus, we need to talk," London said.

Cyrus replied, "I take it you disagree with what I said to that—that technician."

"Whether I agree or disagree is beside the point."

"Then what is the point?"

London took a deep breath to control her rising frustration.

"It's not normally my practice to criticize our passengers. But your behavior back there was not acceptable. Outbursts like that reflect badly on us all. It's the kind of behavior that gives American tourists a bad name."

Audrey abruptly took hold of Cyrus's arm and said to London, "What do you expect him to do, apologize to that man?"

"Yes, I think that's what she expects me to do," Cyrus said.

"I'm not telling you what to do," London said, surprised at the apparent solidarity between two of her oddest passengers. "I'm just letting you know that I think your behavior was way out of line. And I hope it won't happen again."

Audrey snapped back at London, "Aren't *you* out of line, criticizing him for speaking his mind? I think he showed lots of integrity. I wish more people could be so honest—especially men."

Audrey snuggled up against her companion's arm as the two of them turned and walked away.

London stared after them. Where had Audrey's sudden attraction to Cyrus Bannister come from? In fact, she'd never heard Audrey and Cyrus say a single word to each other. But now …

"What's going on between those two?" Bryce asked.

"I think she's just developed a crush on him," London said.

"I wonder whether the feeling is mutual," Bryce said.

London had no idea. There were 100 passengers on the *Nachtmusik,* and she didn't even try to keep track of their personal relationships. Anyway, she was sure that Cyrus would enjoy Audrey's admiration.

Meanwhile, others in the group had made their decisions and were heading off to explore Amsterdam on their own. Some hadn't yet been to the Anne Frank House and headed that way. Others decided to visit the Royal Palace. Others chose to see the Rembrandt House, where the great painter had lived and worked during his happiest and most productive years. Others headed out for shopping sprees in the boutiques, galleries, and perfumeries of the Kalverstraat. Still others, their appetite for art whetted by the visit to the Rijksmuseum, headed for the Van Gogh Museum.

London was glad everybody seemed to have their own destinations in mind. Again, she found herself thinking about that mysterious address …

65 Poppenhuisstraat, Amsterdam

Pretty much since she'd disembarked, she hadn't had a spare minute to think about her slim hope of finding Mom right here in Amsterdam. But now that all the passengers had headed off on their own, maybe she finally had a chance to track down that location. Of course, it was a long shot. She knew that finding Mom at all was unlikely after all these years. But for some reason, she had a strong urge to try—at least to check out any lead that she came across. Maybe this was her best chance.

Better yet, Bryce was right here at her side and could join her on her quest.

So far, she hadn't even found an opportunity to tell him about the situation.

"Bryce, I wonder if you could help me with something."

"Sure, just name it."

"Well, it will take a bit of explaining …"

London struggled for a moment, wondering how to begin. But before she could even start telling Bryce the story of her missing mother, one of the passengers came scurrying up beside them.

It was the large and energetic Letitia Hartzer.

She had a spring in her step and a lilt in her voice.

"London, you simply *must* join me for lunch!"

London stifled a groan of despair.

"We need to celebrate right now!" Letitia declared.

CHAPTER FOURTEEN

Shot down again, London thought.

She was beginning to feel a bit grumpy about the repeated barriers to checking out that address. But she could think of no way to say "no" to this particular request. She knew that Letitia needed approval and support right now.

"What are you celebrating?" Bryce asked Letitia.

"Well, let's just call it a little moral victory," Letitia replied with a satisfied chuckle. Giving London a confidential nudge, she added. "London knows what I mean."

Of course, London did know what she meant. Letitia felt rightfully proud of herself for conquering her urge to shoplift the pretty pen back in the Rijksmuseum gift shop. And of course, Letitia deserved her wholehearted support for her little feat of self-control.

"What do you have in mind?" London asked.

"I saw a lovely little outdoor cafe on my way here. It's very close by. Let's have lunch there. And let's … well, let's do whatever the Dutch do when want to celebrate something special. Won't you join London and me, Bryce?"

Bryce shook his head and said, "I wish I could join you, but I can't. I've got to get back to my own kitchen, make sure everything's going smoothly there, and my assistants haven't mutinied or something in my absence."

Oh well, London thought, holding back an audible sigh. Even if she could get away right now, Bryce wouldn't be able to go with her. Maybe lunch would be brief, and she could slip away on her own afterwards. The ship wouldn't be leaving Amsterdam until after midnight.

Meanwhile, Letitia was calling out to Gus and Honey, who were still wandering about the plaza.

"Yoo-hoo! Do you two want to join London and me for lunch?"

The Jarretts eagerly agreed.

"It's a party," Letitia cooed with delight.

Bryce walked along with the group until they got to the cafe—the

Hongerig Kanaal, it was called. It was, indeed, a charming little place with striped awnings and outdoor tables overlooking the canal.

Before Bryce continued on his way, he checked out a whiteboard on an easel.

Then he told London, "I see that the special of the day is a dish called *stamppot.* I need for you to do something for me."

"And what's that?" London asked.

"Order the *stamppot* and savor it very carefully. Give me a detailed report of your eating experience the next time we see each other."

With a sly wink he added, "It's a matter of professional curiosity, you understand."

"Of course," she agreed.

She knew that he was just encouraging her to especially enjoy what he expected to be a perfectly delicious dish.

A hostess escorted London, Letitia, and the Jarretts to a table for four. As soon as they were seated with their menus, Honey dug a little Dutch-English phrasebook out of her purse.

"What are you going to do with that?" Gus asked with surprise.

"What do you *think* I'm going to do?" Honey said with a snap of her gum. "I'm going to talk to the waiter in Dutch. It's about time one of us tried talking with locals in their own language."

As soon as a white-shirted waiter came to her table, Honey started reading clumsily but earnestly from her phrase book.

"Mign naam is, eh, Honey. Wat is jouw naam?"

London smiled at Honey's surprisingly successful attempt to tell the man her name and ask him to tell his.

"Mign naam is Evert," he said with a smile. *"Het is me een genoegen je te ontmoeten."*

Poor Honey stared at the man with perplexity. London could tell that she couldn't understand a word he'd said after he'd told her his name.

Then Evert said to the whole group, *"Ik geef je even de de tijd om naar je menu's te kijken."*

Then with a cheerful and courteous nod, he walked away.

Gus nudged Honey and asked, "So what did he say?"

"Uh … that his name is Evert … I think."

Gus let out a chuckle at Honey's expense.

"Huh! It sounded like he said a lot more than that!"

Honey started nervously and hopelessly thumbing through her

phrasebook. London smiled sympathetically. She'd experienced the same problem herself. It was easy enough to figure out how to greet someone or ask a simple question in an unfamiliar language. But the flood of words in reply was often beyond comprehension.

"Don't bother, Honey," London said. "Phrase books aren't much good when it comes to making actual conversation. He told you he was pleased to meet you. Then he told us he'd give us a moment to look at our menus."

"Oh," Honey said, looking rather deflated.

London added, "Don't feel bad. I could tell he was pleased that you at least tried to speak to him in Dutch. It's always a courteous thing to do in a foreign country, even if you don't know the language. For future reference, just being able to say "hello" and "please" and "thank you" can go a long way. But don't worry. My guess is Evert speaks at least some English. If he doesn't, I'll do my best to translate for everybody."

London and her three companions looked over their menus, which were written in both Dutch and English. London happened to glance up in time to notice a familiar face among the nearby pedestrians.

Helga van den Heugel was walking along at a brisk pace. London caught her eye and waved to her. But instead of waving back, Helga looked oddly startled and kept right on walking. Then she disappeared into the Meyer Fijne Kunst gallery.

I guess she has some business there, London figured.

When Evert came back to the table, the group ordered their meals. As London had correctly guessed, Evert spoke perfectly good English. Then the waiter stepped back inside the restaurant and returned with a platter.

He put it on the table and announced, "Amsterdam is rightly famous for cheeses, this one in particular."

On the platter little yellow cubes were scattered around a small bowl of dark yellow dip.

Evert said, "This type has been traded in the markets of our town called Gouda since the Middle Ages. However, there are many types, and they all have their special flavors. A lot of gouda is manufactured now, but these are authentic farmhouse goudas, made in the traditional fashion."

Gesturing at one side of the platter he said, "These are young gouda, made just four weeks ago. You'll find it very mild."

"A canal boat I took this morning was named *Young Gouda,"* London said.

"How appropriate," Evert commented.

London picked up a cube of cheese and popped it into her mouth. The taste was a familiar slightly sweet nutty flavor, but better than gouda she'd eaten in other parts of the world.

"And these on the other side are more mature gouda," Evert pointed out.

When she tried one of those cubes, London realized that it was quite different—crunchier for starters.

"It's almost fruity-tasting," Letitia observed.

"Sweet," Honey commented as she munched. "I like it."

"Good stuff," Gus agreed.

Evert looked pleased. "Some especially like to use the mustard dip with the older goudas. Or they pair their cheese with beer or wine. So can I bring you something to drink while you await your meals?"

Before anybody else could speak, Letitia asked, "What do Dutch people drink when they want to toast something really special?"

Evert replied, "That would be a straight shot of *jenever,* a Dutch spirit distilled from juniper berries. For a chaser, we'd have some good Dutch beer—a pale lager would be my recommendation."

"Excellent!" Letitia said. "Please bring us four shots of *jenever* and four glasses of pale lager."

As Evert left the table again Gus asked Letitia with surprise, "What are we toasting, anyway?"

Letitia glanced at London with a slight giggle, then said to Gus, "Oh, I don't know. How about a toast to life?"

Gus chuckled heartily.

"I'll *always* drink to that!" he said.

"Me too!" Honey said.

Presently the waiter returned with shot glasses of the clear spirits and served them with glasses of pale beer. While the beer glasses were damp with the usual condensation, London noticed that the shot glasses were actually frosty to the touch. She guessed that the glasses had been freshly taken out of a freezer, and that maybe the *jenever* had been refrigerated.

Letitia raised her glass and spoke to her companions.

"Here's to … well, whatever anybody wants to drink to!"

London and the Jarretts raised their glasses, and everybody clinked their glasses together. As London lifted the *jenever* to her lips, she paused to notice its faint but pleasant aroma.

A bit like gin, she thought.

Which was hardly surprising, since the waiter mentioned that *jenever* was also distilled from juniper berries.

Before London took a taste, she heard Gus call out, "Down the hatch!"

Gus swallowed the contents of his glass at one gulp.

London took a sip from her glass as well. Like all spirits, *jenever* was very strong to the taste. At the same time, it was surprisingly mellow, with an aftertaste that reminded her of wine. The liquid went down smoothly and didn't burn her throat. Even so, she followed it with a sip of the full-bodied beer, which complemented the taste of *jenever* quite nicely.

Honey and Letitia also looked pleased as they tried the *jenever.* Meanwhile, Gus was waving to the waiter and calling out to him.

"I'm ready for another!"

"Take it easy with that stuff, Gus," Honey said as the waiter brought him a second frosted shot glass.

"Hey, don't worry," Gus said. "One or two more won't hurt me. They wouldn't hurt the rest of you, either. Come on, drink up! I'll pay for drinks."

Everybody, including Honey, politely declined. London was glad of that. The last time Honey had over-imbibed, she'd wound up tearfully—and publicly—singing "Home on the Range" to the accompaniment of a German *oompah* band. Letitia had tipsily sung "Lili Marlene" and "We'll Meet Again," accompanied by an accordion player. London was glad the two women were exercising some restraint. She only hoped Gus wouldn't overdo it.

Soon the waiter returned with their food orders. Letitia had ordered a salad followed by skewered lamb, while Honey and Gus had ordered a Dutch rice dish for two.

London herself ordered the *stamppot,* just as Bryce had suggested. As soon as the dish was placed in front of her, she could see—and smell—that it was an excellent choice. Consisting of a length of sausage nestled in potatoes mashed together with other ingredients, it was obviously classic comfort food, Dutch style.

As London got ready to take her first bite, she reminded herself of Bryce's instruction.

"Savor it carefully."

He'd said he expected a "detailed report" of her "eating experience."

London smiled, feeling more than glad to oblige.

She remembered reading on the menu that the sausage was called *rookworst,* which meant smoked sausage. As she took a taste, she guessed that it was a delicious mix of ground pork, veal, and bacon.

Mixed among the mashed potatoes, London detected kale and green onions, all lusciously seasoned with salt, pepper, and garlic and sprinkled with chopped scallions. London made mental notes with every bite, so she could properly report her impressions to Bryce.

Meanwhile, everyone at the table shared bites of each other's meals. Letitia's mouth-wateringly tender skewered lamb came with grilled vegetables, couscous, and a coriander-lime sauce. Honey and Gus's Dutch rice ditch was a rich potpourri which combined stewed beef with onions, boiled potatoes, red cabbage, sausage, and gravy.

After dinner, all four of the diners agreed to a simple but traditional Dutch dessert called *appleflap,* pieces of pastry dough stuffed with apples, raisins, sugar, and cinnamon.

All during dinner, London monitored Gus's enthusiastic intake of *jenever* and beer. He had seemed to be holding up pretty well, but when it came time to leave, he wobbled as he stood up, then sat quickly back down again.

"I warned you," Honey said, wagging her finger at him.

"I'll be fine," Gus said, still speaking quite clearly.

"You will be, once I get you back to the *Nachtmusik,*" Honey said, coaxing him out of his chair and supporting him by the arm.

Meanwhile, the waiter had observed the situation.

"Would you like me to call for a boat?" he asked Honey.

"You mean like a cab?" Honey asked.

"That's right."

"Oh, that would be a great help, thanks!"

The waiter made a cellphone call, and within moments a motorboat pulled up in the canal. Gus didn't seem at all steady on his feet as Honey led him across the street to the canal bank.

Letitia laughed and said to Honey, "Maybe I should come along and make sure he doesn't fall into the water."

"Yeah, that might be a good idea," Honey said.

London breathed a sigh of relief as Honey and Letitia loaded Gus aboard, and the boat pulled away and headed toward where the *Nachtmusik* was docked.

At last! she thought.

For the first time today, she had time to go looking for that address. But before she could bring up a map of Amsterdam on her cellphone, something caught her eye among the nearby pedestrians.

It was a forlorn, lost-looking face, and it seemed to demand her attention.

CHAPTER FIFTEEN

The passenger who had caught London's attention was wandering in her general direction, although he didn't seem to be aware of her presence. Actually, the short, stooped, elderly man didn't seem to be aware of much of anything. After the brief puzzled glance around when she had spotted his face, he had tucked his head down and seemed to be completely absorbed by a hamburger he was eating.

London felt a flash of worry. She was sure that the aspiring mystery writer wasn't accustomed to making his way through strange cities alone. The only place he'd even come ashore had been back in Bamberg, Germany, and he'd always been with his new boon companion, Bob Turner.

But now Bob was sick, or at least he was said to be. And here was Stanley Tedrow, wandering the streets of a foreign city looking more than a little lost, as if he were walking—and eating—in his sleep.

As London made her way toward him, he almost walked by without noticing her.

"Hi, Mr. Tedrow," she said.

He stopped in his tracks and stared at her, chewing on a bite of his hamburger.

"Oh, I know you," he said. "You're the ship's *maître d',* or major domo, or superintendent, or …"

"I'm the social director," she said.

"Yeah, right. London somebody. Your last name's a flower. London Lilac, London Clover, London Marigold … ?"

"London Rose," London said.

"Of course, that's it, London Rose."

Then he scratched his head with his free hand and chuckled.

"I guess I almost didn't recognize you without your dog."

London certainly didn't feel hurt to hear him say that. After all, when she and Sir Reggie had sat down with Mr. Tedrow in the Amadeus Lounge last night, he'd been markedly more interested in talking to the dog than to her.

He took another bite of his hamburger and stood there looking down at the sidewalk.

"How are you today?" London asked, wondering if maybe she could strike up a conversation with him just this once.

"OK, I guess," he replied.

Then, looking around, he added, "This is a strange sort of city, though. There's water everywhere."

"We're in Amsterdam," London said.

"Ohhh, yeah," Mr. Tedrow said with a nod. "It's on our itinerary, isn't it? I should have figured. Nice town. Lots of water, though. Too much of it, if you ask me."

London wasn't really surprised that Mr. Tedrow didn't know what city they were in. He'd shown the same sort of absent-mindedness in the past. But she still found it odd to find him out here all by himself.

"How is your book going?" she asked.

"The book? Oh, it's going OK, I guess. But I'd rather not talk about it. I don't want to spoil it for you."

London remembered him saying almost exactly the same thing in the bar last night.

Mr. Tedrow continued, "But I've realized that my brain gets kind of cramped up if I stay cooped up in that room too long at a crack. Ideas get all clunked together. That's why I came out for a walk—to get the creative juices flowing."

London couldn't help smiling at the irony of that remark. She wondered if it ever occurred to Mr. Tedrow that one good way to get the creative juices flowing might be to pay some attention to what was going on around him, especially when he was in a fascinating city like Amsterdam. But she wasn't going to start giving him that sort of advice.

"You must have been walking for quite a while," London observed.

"You think so? Why?"

"Well, we're pretty far from the *Nachtmusik.*"

"I guess we are," Mr. Tedrow said, glancing around. "Actually, it seems like I just left there a short while ago. Soon as I came ashore, a guy in a motorboat pulled up alongside me and waved to me and offered me a ride. I figured a boat ride would be fun, and he seemed friendly, so I got aboard."

Mr. Tedrow shrugged and took another bite of his burger, which was almost gone now.

"He kept asking me where I wanted to go, and I kept saying I didn't really care, wherever he felt like going. Pretty soon he started getting kind of impatient. Finally, he pulled up the bank and told me to get off. That was fine with me, he wasn't such great company after all. Then he said I owed him some money, I didn't know what for, and anyway I didn't have any of the local currency on me. When he pulled away, he was waving his fist and jabbering pretty heatedly—in Dutch, I guess."

"Um, Mr. Tedrow," London said, "the boat was kind of a water taxi, and he expected to be paid for giving you a ride."

Mr. Tedrow's narrow eyes widened a bit.

"Is that right?" he said. "Well, I guess that explains it. I wish he'd just told me. Maybe we could have worked something out. I'd go looking for him if I had any idea how to find him. Anyway, he dropped me off right near a McDonald's about a block away from here, and I was getting kind of hungry by then, so I bought a hamburger. Used my credit card."

Mr. Tedrow finished his burger and tossed the wrapper in a nearby wastebasket.

"Say, where is that dog of yours, anyway?" he said. "Not sick or anything bad, I hope."

"No, Sir Reggie is fine," London said. She didn't especially want to get into explaining why she'd left the dog aboard the ship.

"Glad to hear it," Mr. Tedrow said. "There's some kind of bug going around, you know. Did I mention that Bob Turner's got whatever it is? He's locked up in his room—self-quarantining, he says. I'd sure hate to have Sir Reggie come down with it."

Mr. Tedrow wiped his hands with a napkin, which he also threw into the wastebasket.

"Well, it was nice running into you, Miss, uh …"

"Rose."

"That's right, Rose. I guess we'll be seeing each other around."

London spoke to him as he started to wander away.

"Mr. Tedrow, wait. Where are you headed next?"

Mr. Tedrow looked surprised at the question.

"Well, back to my room. To get back to work. I'm beginning to feel those ideas flow again and need to write them down."

London hesitated, then asked, "Do you, uh, know your way back to the boat?"

Mr. Tedrow tilted his head curiously.

"Now that you mention it, I don't guess I do," he said.

London held back a discouraged sigh. Now was obviously no time for her to go searching for that mysterious address. Her own quest would have to be put off for a while again.

"Let's go back together," she said.

London flagged down a water taxi and asked the pilot to take them to where the *Nachtmusik* was moored near the *Westerdok.* During the ride, the mystery writer seemed to have again withdrawn into the story he was trying to tell. He had nothing at all to say.

The water taxi followed the same route London had taken into Amsterdam. Although the sights were familiar, the face of the city was changing now. It was late afternoon, and the sky was darker, and the surrounding buildings looked more shadowy. At the same time, the reflection of sunlight on the water shimmered brightly.

London had a sinking feeling that hours and minutes were passing by, more and more quickly. The *Nachtmusik* would leave Amsterdam soon after midnight. And between then and now, whatever time she had left to go looking for that address was getting shorter. She hoped she could leave the ship again quickly once she had Mr. Tedrow safely aboard.

When they got back to the ship and entered the reception area, Mr. Tedrow still seemed completely lost in thought. He headed obliviously to the elevator.

Although London followed after him, she was stopped in her tracks by a noisy crash from not very far away. She stood back as Mr. Tedrow got into the elevator and the doors closed in front of her.

That crashing noise had come from the nearby Amadeus Lounge. London figured she'd better go and find out what was going on in there.

London headed past the library and into the lounge. The large room was unusually busy even for late afternoon. That was because of the special discounts, of course.

The source of the sound was immediately visible. Amy was here to help out again, but apparently she had just dropped an entire tray full of drinks. Several customers had been drenched, and broken glasses littered the floor.

Amy stood there looking stunned and helpless while Elsie's assistants scurried around trying to clean up with the mess and make peace with the wet customers. Meanwhile, Elsie had caught sight of London from behind the bar and was waving to her in a frantic appeal for help.

I guess I've got to pitch in, London thought with a sigh.

*

It was night by the time London was able to get away from the ship. She'd expected the lounge rush to last only a couple of hours, but it had continued in wave after wave as more and more passengers returned from their excursions into Amsterdam. London simply hadn't been able to extricate herself from her work until much later than she'd hoped.

Finally, things quieted down a bit, and other crew members were recruited to help out in the bar. At long last, London hoped to be able to coax Bryce to join her on her errand. But when she went down to the *Adagio* deck, she saw that the Habsburg Restaurant was still far too busy for Bryce to get away.

She was on her own. But this was her last chance to check out that Amsterdam address. She stopped by her stateroom and scooped up her delighted little dog to go along with her.

As she descended the gangway with Sir Reggie on his leash, her spirits began to rise. As they set foot on the dock, she took out her cellphone and brought up a map to find that address:

65 Poppenhuisstraat

"Good news!" she said to Sir Reggie. "It's just a short walk from here. We won't even need to take a water taxi. Who knows? Maybe we'll find Mom shortly!"

Sir Reggie let out a cautionary growl.

"I know, I'd better not get my hopes up," London said to him. "It's a long shot at best. Still, I can't help thinking maybe I've got luck on my side this time. And if not—well, a little sightseeing won't hurt us. According to the map, this address is right near the *Oude Kerk*—the 'Old Church.' It's the oldest building in Amsterdam, and it's supposed to be quite beautiful. We can stop by and pay it a visit if our search for Mom doesn't pan out."

As they continued across a low bridge over a canal, London observed that Amsterdam was even more charming by night, and still bustling with foot and bicycle traffic. Here and there the narrow streets with their neatly laid stones and bricks widened out into small plazas.

Still open and busy were a range of businesses that included bars, cafes, pancake houses, restaurants, karaoke bars in full swing, and parlors for tattoos and body-piercing.

Friendly, smiling pedestrians kept waving to London and saying *goedenavond*—"good evening"—as they passed by, and she waved and said *goedenavond* in return.

Others stopped to tell her, *"Je hebt een aardige hond"*—"You have a nice dog"—and even asked permission to pet Sir Reggie, who was, of course, perfectly delighted by all the attention.

"I wonder whether Mom likes dogs," London said to Sir Reggie as they continued through the winding streets. "I hope so. I guess we'll have a lot to learn about each other."

Again, Sir Reggie let out that skeptical growl.

"I know, we might not find her," London said, "but even so …"

London's words trailed off as they rounded a corner. There was a marked change in their surroundings. Instead of streetlamps, candlelit outdoor cafe tables, and lighted storefronts, there seemed to be a sudden explosion of garish neon everywhere.

"Oh, dear," London murmured to Sir Reggie. "I hadn't expected to wind up *here."*

CHAPTER SIXTEEN

As London stopped in her tracks and took a look around, she noticed a peculiar smell hanging in the air.

Marijuana, probably, she realized.

Which confirmed what she'd already suspected. She had accidentally stumbled into De Wallen, Amsterdam's *Rosse Buurt*—its red-light district, where both cannabis and prostitution were legal and regulated.

Sure enough, as she approached the nearest building facade, she saw a row of vertical plate glass windows. Behind each window was a scantily clad woman.

One of those women smiled and waved at London and mouthed the word *goedenavond.*

"Uh, *goedenavond* to you too," London mouthed back to her with a shy wave of her own.

As London looked around, she noticed that, in some ways, her surroundings hadn't really changed. The area was neat and tidy, and the glare of neon was augmented by same ordinary streetlights she'd seen before she got here. The pedestrians looked as respectable as they did elsewhere in Amsterdam, although a larger percentage of them here were male.

There were no prostitutes on the streets at all. They were all doing their advertising from indoors, behind those large windows, where they struck sexy poses for prospective clients. Some of the women were bathed in red light, while others wore body paint that glowed under black light.

"Well, this is a surprise," London said to Sir Reggie.

Sir Reggie let out a whine of agreement and sniffed the drug-scented air with curiosity. London hoped the small animal wouldn't get high off the smell alone. She'd read quite a bit about the *Rosse Buurt.* But since she hadn't planned to come here herself, she hadn't bothered to look for the district on a map. When she'd found the address on her cellphone map, she hadn't noticed that she would be passing through this neighborhood of legitimized vice.

"I should have been better prepared," she said to the dog.

But what did this mean for the address she was looking for? She reminded herself that *65 Poppenhuisstraat* was located right near the *Oude Kerk*—the "Old Church," which she assumed wasn't part of the *Rosse Buurt*.

"The address must be beyond this area," she said to Sir Reggie. "Come on, let's keep going."

As she and the dog kept right on walking among the sex shops, sex theaters, peep shows, and brothels, London couldn't help but feel self-conscious and embarrassed to have wound up here.

"At least I don't see anybody else from the *Nachtmusik,*" she said to the dog. "And that's probably a good thing, because …"

But before she finished her sentence, Sir Reggie gave his leash a telltale tug, as if he wanted her to see something.

She looked, and sure enough, she *did* see a couple of familiar faces.

They were about the last people she would have expected to find here—Walter and Agnes Shick, the elderly couple she'd last seen riding away from the Rijksmuseum on a tandem bike.

Walter was simultaneously reading something on his cellphone and eyeing the women in the windows.

"Come on, Walter," Agnes said, tugging him by the arm. "I'm sure we've seen enough."

"Not yet, Agnes," Walter said. "This is really quite educational."

For a moment, London hesitated to make her presence known. She didn't want to explain what she and Sir Reggie were doing here. But on the other hand …

What are Walter and Agnes doing here?

Agnes turned around and caught London's eye. Even in the red light from the nearest window, London could see that she was blushing.

"London!" she said. "Oh, dear!"

Walter turned and looked embarrassed as well.

"Uh … I can explain," he said. "This isn't how it looks. We were just out for an evening stroll, and we stumbled into this area."

London had no doubt that he was telling the truth.

"Something like that happened to me," London said.

Agnes scoffed and added, "I haven't been able to get Walter to leave. He's been looking up all kinds of information about this area online—and taking in the sights, as it were."

"Like I said—it's educational," Walter said, skimming over

something on his cellphone as he kept glancing into the windows.

"That's no excuse for all this window shopping," Agnes said.

"It's not window shopping," Walter said defensively. "It's merely observing. And learning all kinds of interesting stuff."

Pointing to some text on his cellphone, he added, "For example, did you know the tradition of regulated prostitution in this area dates all the way back to the Middle Ages? The Dutch have never been prudish, that's for sure."

"Oh, for heaven's sake," Agnes said to her husband. "Come on, it really is time we got back to the ship."

But at that moment, something caught Agnes's eye.

"Oh … my… goodness!" she exclaimed.

London looked where Agnes was looking. Standing in a row of windows were several other people advertising their wares—although these people were men. They were even more scantily clad than the women, and they flexed their muscles when they caught sight of London and Agnes.

Agnes clucked her tongue and tilted her head.

"Well … this *is* rather … educational."

London tried not to laugh at Agnes's sudden change of attitude. Her husband, too, was singing a rather different tune now.

"Now, Agnes, dear, there's no need to ogle," he said, wagging his finger at her.

"It's not ogling," Agnes said. "It's merely observing—remember? Walter, check something out online for us. Find out what percentage of the workers in this district are, well, male."

"I'll do no such thing," Walter said.

"Oh, for goodness sake, *give* me that thing," she said, grabbing the cellphone away from him.

As Agnes started running her own search, Walter said to London, "Maybe you can talk some sense to her."

London couldn't help but chuckle.

"I can understand her curiosity," she said.

Meanwhile, Agnes had found some information on the cellphone.

"I see here that only five percent of the workers in this area are male."

Walter let out a huff as he crossed his arms.

"Hardly enough to make for any serious sightseeing," he said.

"To the contrary, my dear," Agnes said. "The scarcity of male specimens simply makes the search more … well, sporting. Besides, I see this district has its very own sex museum. I wonder if it's open at this hour. If so, I'll bet it's fascinating. Let's go look for it."

"But darling—" Walter began.

"Let's get moving, Walter. The game's afoot!"

As Agnes trotted on ahead, Walter turned toward London with a shrug of resignation.

"We'll be seeing you back at the boat, I guess," he said, and hurried to catch up with his wife.

"Don't be too late," London called after them. "Remember the ship will be leaving tonight."

For a second or two, London wondered whether she and Sir Reggie ought to follow along after the elderly couple, just to make sure they wouldn't get into danger. But as she took another look around, she wondered …

What danger?

Aside from the smell of pot in the air—perfectly legal here in Amsterdam—and the human merchandise in the windows, this neighborhood looked …

Well, almost wholesome.

The pedestrians looked as respectable here as they did anywhere else in Amsterdam. London certainly didn't get any sense of any actual criminal activity. In fact, she saw a couple of friendly policemen idly walking their beats and saying hello to passersby. Considering how well-regulated De Wallen was, the Shicks were probably just as safe here as they would be anywhere else in Amsterdam—maybe even safer.

"Come on," London said to Sir Reggie. "Let's be on our way."

London kept following the map on her cellphone. The route took her and Sir Reggie past the nearest canal, where she happened to notice a plastic cup floating nearby. To her surprise, the piece of trash was actually moving, as if being carried by a current.

A current? London wondered. *In these canals?*

But the phenomenon didn't seem worth wondering about, and she and Sir Reggie continued on their way.

Soon the stately Gothic spire of the *Oude Kerk* came into view. As the broad facade of the church came more into view, something startling occurred to London. The church wasn't outside the *Rosse Buurt,* or even on its outskirts.

It's right in the middle of the red-light district, she realized. And the address she was looking for was nearby. This is where her search for Mom had led her.

What could that possibly mean?

When she and Reggie continued on their way across the broad paved square surrounding the church, she saw a bronze statue up ahead that she assumed to be of some religious saint. But when she and the dog drew closer, London saw that it was of a full-busted, scantily clad young woman standing at the top of some steps in what appeared to be a doorframe.

London looked at the plaque at the base of the statue and saw that the woman had a name—"Belle."

There was also an inscription on the granite base of the statue:

Respecteer sekswerkers over de hele wereld.

London mentally translated the inscription, which meant, "Respect sex workers all over the world." The statue was dated 2017.

It was a striking sight to find directly in front of the oldest building in Amsterdam, let alone a church.

"I guess this tells us a lot about Holland, doesn't it?" London said to Sir Reggie. "Here, prostitution is regarded as just another way to make a living. There's nothing shameful about it at all."

Still following the map, London walked a little faster. On the other side of the church was street she was looking for—*Poppenhuisstraat.* The neighborhood's character didn't change, and London felt a sinking doubt that they would find anything the least bit like what she'd hoped to find.

Sure enough, when she and Sir Reggie got to street number 65, she found herself facing another facade full of windows. Each woman on display here was standing in front of a flag of some European country. What little clothing they wore was suggestive of the traditional dress of those various countries—a *dirndl* bodice for Germany, a red velvet bonnet for Italy, a lace veil for Spain, an embroidered vest for Poland, a flowered apron for France, and so forth.

And a sign across the building displayed the exact same message London had found on the mysterious website:

Reis Lust

elke Europese taal

The first two words literally meant "wander lust," and the line below it translated as "any European language."

London heaved a long sigh of disappointment.

"I should have known," she said to Sir Reggie. She felt dizzy with the overwhelming disappointment and her stomach churned with the bitter taste of failure.

Then she reminded herself sharply that this had been an unlikely lead anyhow. When she'd found the webpage, she had jumped to the conclusion that *Reis Lust* might be a name Mom was currently using, since she'd harbored a similar suspicion of a German tutor who had put out an advertisement under the name *Fern Weh.*

Both phrases meant "wander lust" in English. But in this case, the words weren't the name of a person, but a name of the establishment itself.

"I guess the word *'lust'* ought to have tipped me off," London said aloud.

The webpage hadn't been for a tutoring service at all, but for an altogether different sort of service. This particular brothel was staffed with workers of all European nationalities, who could cater to clients in any European language.

And it certainly had nothing to do with Mom.

And that's just as well, London told herself, *considering the circumstances.*

She'd been foolish to get her hopes up over such a fragile clue.

Now she was just sure of one thing—she should never do this again.

Her search had come to an end. Maybe she could have had more fun here in Amsterdam if she hadn't spent the whole day wondering about this address.

There seemed to be nothing to do now but head back to the *Nachtmusik.* London looked at her watch and saw that she had a couple of hours before she needed to be back aboard. There was no need to catch a water taxi right this minute. Instead, she and Sir Reggie walked along the nearest canal for a few moments until they found a bench overlooking the water.

She picked up Sir Reggie and set him in her lap.

She said to the dog, "OK, this is the part where you tell me how foolish I've been about this whole thing, and you warn me never to let my imagination and good sense run away with me ever again, and you tell me there's no point in looking for Mom anymore, because she definitely doesn't want to be found. Go ahead and scold me. I've got it coming."

Instead of growling in a critical matter, Sir Reggie gave her an affectionate lick on the nose.

London laughed and said, "Aw, you're too much of a pal to give me a hard time about it, aren't you? I'm not so sure Bryce would have been so sympathetic if he'd come with me. I guess I'm lucky you're here and he's not. Even if he'd been nice about it, I'd be a lot more embarrassed than I am already."

But Sir Reggie suddenly seemed to have something else on his mind. He turned his head toward the canal and sniffed the air and let out a worried whimper.

"What is it, boy?" London asked.

Without so much as a whine in reply, Sir Reggie hopped out of London's lap. Before she could catch the end of his leash, he headed straight to the canal bank. The little dog stood at space in the railing, staring down into the water.

Puzzled, London got up and walked over beside him and looked down herself.

At the base of a short ladder was a narrow, floating wooden dock that ran parallel to the bank. Moored to the dock was a line of small rowboats, padlocked by bicycle chains to avoid theft.

"I don't see anything odd," she said to Sir Reggie.

But Sir Reggie clearly disagreed. He jumped off the bank and landed straight on the dock. Although London called his name, he dashed along the dock and then stopped at one of the boats.

"What is it boy?" London asked.

Staring into the boat, Sir Reggie let out a yap of alarm.

London felt a sharp tingle of worry.

I've got a bad feeling about this, she realized.

She climbed down the ladder and walked over to the boat that had caught Reggie's attention.

A man was sprawled there in the bottom of the boat, and London could tell at a glance that he wasn't taking a nap.

He's dead, she realized with a gasp.

She also recognized his face.

CHAPTER SEVENTEEN

London gulped hard as she looked down at the body lying in the bottom of the boat.

This can't be possible, she thought.

How could another person she had recently met have come to such a fate?

But maybe I'm wrong. Maybe it isn't who I think it is.

And for a moment, she thought maybe it wasn't. Not a lot of light reached down to the boat from the street. Maybe her eyes were playing tricks on her.

As Sir Reggie whined worriedly beside her, London stooped down for a closer look.

Then she let out a groan of despair.

There was no mistaking those tight features, the peculiar eyes, nose, and lips that looked too small for the man's bald head.

The dead man in that boat was definitely Pier Dekker, the quarrelsome conservator she had seen back at the Rijksmuseum. He was wearing the same clothes he had been then, except that his collar was open and he didn't have on that yellow cravat.

Even his expression looked much the same—more cross and irritable than frightened or in pain. His throat looked a bit red.

London jumped to her feet and called out in Dutch as loudly as she could.

"Helpen! Politie!"

In what seemed like a split second, a young blonde woman appeared at the railing above her. She was wearing the yellow-striped black jacket of a *surveillant,* a Dutch patrol officer.

"What is the matter?" the *surveillant* called down to her.

For a moment, all the breath seemed to have fled London's lungs. All she could do was point into the boat.

The *surveillant's* eyes widened and her mouth opened into a gasp. Then she scurried down the ladder and over to where London and Sir Reggie were standing.

"Oh, no!" she said. "It's Meneer Schat!"

London was startled at the sound of the name. For a second, she wondered—had she made a mistake? Was the murdered man not Pier Dekker after all? But as she looked at those frozen features again, she was sure of it.

The *surveillant* touched London on the shoulder with concern. London saw from her nameplate that her name was Kaat Dijkstra.

"Are you alright?" *Surveillant* Dijkstra asked London in Dutch. "Do you need to sit down for a moment?"

London shook her head and replied in Dutch, "No, I'm fine. But I'd like to get back onto the shore."

London picked up Sir Reggie and walked over to the ladder and reached up to set him at the top.

As she started to climb after him, *Surveillant* Dijkstra asked, "Are you American?"

London wasn't surprised that the woman had noticed her accent.

"Yes, I'm American," she said. "I do speak a little Dutch, but my vocabulary …"

London had been going to say she wasn't sure that her Dutch vocabulary was large enough to discuss a situation like this. But she was struck by the realization that she'd had to talk about similar situations in Hungarian, Austrian, and German—and that this was a truly terrible way to develop her language skills.

The policewoman replied in English, "Don't worry, I speak pretty good English."

When London was back on solid ground again, she carried Sir Reggie straight over to the bench where they'd been sitting just a few moments ago. As she sat back down with the dog in her lap, *Surveillant* Dijkstra stepped a short distance away and spoke into her shoulder mic, apparently calling for assistance.

Reggie was shivering with alarm now. The discovery had obviously come as a shock to him as well as to London. She hugged and petted him to soothe his nerves.

Soon *Surveillant* Dijkstra came over to the bench and sat down beside London. She didn't say anything for a moment. She didn't even look at London. Her mouth hung open, and she looked pale, as if she were in shock. For a moment this struck London as odd. As a policewoman, hadn't Dijkstra ever been involved in a murder case?

Of course not, London quickly realized. *Her beat is the* Rosse Buurt*—the red-light district.*

After all, De Wallen might be a den of vice, but it was legalized vice, and London had already noticed lots of police patrolling the area. There probably wasn't much violence here in the *Rosse Buurt,* and certainly very little actual homicide. For all London knew, this might be the safest district in Amsterdam. Maybe Dijkstra had never seen a murder victim before.

I wish the same was true for me, London thought gloomily as she struggled to control the trembling that threatened to take over her whole body. Although she'd discovered other murder victims while on this trip, she couldn't imagine ever getting used to it.

Then she heard the noise of approaching sirens.

Dijkstra shook off her shock and said, "Don't worry, help is on the way. Do you have any idea how it happened?"

London shook her head no, then asked, "What name did you call him by just now?"

"Meneer Schat."

London squinted curiously at the policewoman.

"Um, doesn't that mean 'Mr. Sweetie'?" she asked.

"That's right," Dijkstra said. "It wasn't his real name, of course. But that's what the sex workers around here always called him. So did I, actually. Whenever I saw him, I'd always say, 'How are you doing tonight, Meneer Schat?' He'd always grumble that he was fine. I don't think he liked being called that. But since I didn't know his real name, what else was I supposed to call him?"

"His name was Pier Dekker," London said.

The policewoman's eyes widened.

"How do you know his name?" she asked.

Before London could answer, Dijkstra added hastily, "No, you'd better not try to explain it to me. Wait until *Hoofdinspecteur* Braam gets here. It won't be long. The Burgwallen police station is just a few blocks away."

London recognized the word for "chief inspector."

Dijkstra pointed and said, "Here he comes right now."

To London's surprise, Dijkstra was pointing to a uniformed man riding a bicycle across the nearest canal bridge. But London quickly realized that a bicycle was probably the fastest mode of transportation among these canals and narrow streets, at least when it came to short distances.

Meanwhile, she could still hear sirens, and could see boats with flashing lights approaching along the canal. *Surveillants* like Dijkstra were also gathering on foot, keeping gaping onlookers away and trying to set up some sort of perimeter with police tape.

Hoofdinspecteur Braam cut an almost comical figure as he approached on his bike. He was a tall, lanky man, and the bicycle appeared to be too small for him. He stopped in front of the bench, flipped down the kickstand, and got off the bike.

"What is the matter, *Surveillant* Dijkstra?" he asked the policewoman in Dutch.

"I will show you," Dijkstra said.

She and Braam left London and Reggie sitting on the bench as they went to the ladder and down onto the dock. London could see their heads bobbing as they stood talking on the floating platform while they looked at the body.

London sighed as she said to Sir Reggie, "Why do you have to be so observant? This didn't have to be our problem, you know."

Sir Reggie let out a defensive-sounding whine.

"I know, I know. You were just doing your civic duty. You really are a very conscientious little animal. I would have done the same thing, of course."

Three small police cars arrived, and two large motorboats with police insignias pulled up to the bank. The area was starting to burst into activity.

Dijkstra and the *Hoofdinspecteur* climbed back up the ladder. Braam took out a pad and pencil and strode purposefully toward London. She could see him more clearly now. He had a thin face with chiseled features. Although he was far from bad-looking, there was a kind of reptilian skepticism in his expression.

"Your name, please," he said a bit curtly to London in English, preparing to write the name in his notebook. Apparently, Dijkstra had already told him that London was American.

"My name is London Rose," she said. "And I'm the social director aboard—"

Hoofdinspecteur Braam interrupted, lifting his eyes from his notebook.

"Would you repeat your name, please?"

"Uh, London Rose."

"And you work aboard a tour boat belonging to Epoch World Cruise Lines called the *Nachtmusik?"*

"That's right."

"And is the *Nachtmusik* currently docked here in Amsterdam?

"Yes."

Braam arched one eyebrow, and his lips twisted into a hint of a smirk.

"Well, well, well, Mevrouw Rose," he said. "Your reputation precedes you."

CHAPTER EIGHTEEN

London felt a chill of alarm.

My reputation precedes me—how? she wondered, startled by the police chief's sinister declaration.

"Uh, what do you mean?" she asked.

Braam shrugged and chuckled a bit darkly.

"Well, until just this minute, I wasn't quite sure you were real. I thought you might be … how is it said in English? A sort of 'urban legend.' You see, you are quite the talk of law enforcement people all over Europe. After all, you are the woman who has discovered some three dead bodies in three different countries just during the last couple of weeks. And now you've discovered a fourth, right here in Holland. I am quite intrigued, naturally."

London held back a moan of despair. She knew she shouldn't be surprised that she'd developed something of a reputation.

And apparently not a good one, she thought.

Choosing her words carefully, she said, "*Hoofdinspecteur* Braam, I don't know exactly what people have been saying about me. But I never murdered anybody. In fact, I was the one who actually solved all three of those crimes and brought the killers to justice."

With some help from Sir Reggie, she almost added.

But somehow, she suspected now was not the time to praise the crime-fighting prowess of her Yorkshire Terrier.

"Yes, quite the detective, aren't you?" Braam stated. "Or so it is said."

He sounds like he doesn't believe it, London thought.

And in a way, she could understand why he wouldn't believe it. She still didn't quite believe it herself.

Braam lowered his notepad and looked intently into her eyes.

"And now … it appears that events are repeating themselves. What is more, *Surveillant* Dijkstra says you happen to know the victim's name. How can that be?"

"I took a tour group to the Rijksmuseum earlier today," London said. "You see, Meneer Dekker was on the restoration team that's currently working on Rembrandt's *The Night Watch.*"

"You sound like you knew him quite well," Braam said.

"Oh, no, I didn't know him at all," London protested. "The docent who gave my group the tour through the Rijksmuseum asked him to talk to us about the restoration process. He did tell us about it, and what he said was very interesting, but I'm afraid things got … rather unpleasant …"

Her voice trailed off as she realized that her account wasn't sounding good to the *Hoofdinspecteur.* He was glaring at her suspiciously. Even *Surveillant* Dijkstra had a frown on her face.

"Indeed?" Braam asked.

"Yes, one of my passengers made some impolite comments about the work Meneer Dekker was doing. The restorer got rather angry—not just with that passenger, but with the whole group."

London hesitated, then added, "And with me, I'm afraid. I'm not sure why …"

She paused again, wondering if she was being less than honest.

Of course, she was pretty sure she *did* know why Dekker had gotten angry with her. As Honey had pointed out earlier, Dekker seemed to have a serious problem with women, especially ones with any kind of authority.

Should I tell Braam that? she asked herself.

She quickly decided not to. It didn't seem appropriate of her to try to account for Dekker's state of mind.

Braam said, "Of course I must know the name of the passenger who quarreled with the victim."

London queasily told him Cyrus Bannister's name.

This is going to get worse and worse, she thought, picturing the arrogant passenger at odds with this skeptical policeman.

Braam peered at London silently, as if he were deciding whether or not to arrest her.

Then he turned to *Surveillant* Dijkstra and said in Dutch, "You said you recognized the victim."

"That's right," Dijkstra replied in Dutch. "Although everyone around here called him Meneer Schat."

"So he came around for the … usual reasons?" Braam asked her.

"Yes, he was pretty well known among the local workers. I don't think they liked him very much. But they never complained that he was violent or abusive, just … well, sullen and grouchy. I think Meneer

Schat was kind of a sarcastic nickname."

"Can you give me a list of some of the women he … frequented?" Braam asked, still speaking in Dutch.

"Certainly," Dijkstra said, taking out her own notebook and jotting some names.

London was starting to feel uncomfortable that the *hoofdinspecteur* now was insistently speaking to the policewoman in Dutch. London guessed that Braam probably thought she couldn't understand what they were saying—which of course wasn't true.

Should I tell him? she wondered.

Fortunately, the policewoman seemed to be worried about the same thing.

"The witness understands Dutch," she said to Braam.

"Oh, I see," Braam replied English, looking at London with a scoff. "Well, so much for trying to exclude you from the conversation. There's no point in not being perfectly transparent. Tell me, Mevrouw Rose, would you rather continue this discussion in English or Dutch?"

"I … it's … whichever you prefer."

"Dutch it is, then," Braam said. Then he asked Dijkstra, "What else can you tell me about the victim?"

"Well, he was sort of a furtive type. Most of the men who come around here don't care whether they're recognized. But some care a lot. They're embarrassed, I guess. They won't tell the workers their real names, and that's why they wind up with nicknames. They also try to sneak in and out of the *Rosse Buurt* without being noticed. Some wait until after dark and come here by rowboat from various parts of the city."

Pointing to the dock, she continued, "The boats down there belong to men like that. I think the boat we found the body in was the victim's own."

"And it is chained to the dock right now …" Braam mused.

Braam scratched his chin for a moment in silent thought. London could imagine some of the questions he was asking himself. For example, had Pier Dekker been murdered right here in his boat, or had he been killed elsewhere and then moved here?

But most of all, she was sure Braam wondered …

Did I have anything to do with it?

Her heart sank at the thought of having to prove her innocence all over again.

Then Braam said to London, "How long is the *Nachtmusik* scheduled to stay in Amsterdam?"

"We're supposed to set sail for Copenhagen tonight," London said.

Of course, London knew what the *hoofdinspecteur* was going to say next.

"I'm afraid that's not going to be possible. Tell me how I may contact your captain right away."

London gulped anxiously as she told him Captain Hays's phone number. She wished she could call ahead and break the news before Braam did. But she felt sure that the *hoofdinspecteur* would rather be the first to call.

I'll be hearing from the captain soon enough, she thought.

Meanwhile, London could see that a several policemen were loading the covered body into a boat marked *Lijkschouwer,* which London knew meant "coroner."

Hoofdinspecteur Braam pointed to one of the nearby police boats and said, "I'll have one of our pilots take you back to the *Nachtmusik.* I hope I needn't tell you not to leave Amsterdam until we've resolved this matter."

"I won't," London said, picking up Sir Reggie. As she followed Braam toward the boat, a new worry nagged at her mind. She thought maybe she knew the cause of the victim's death.

But should I tell him? she wondered.

Wouldn't that just make him more suspicious than he was already?

Maybe so, she thought. *But I'd better be as upfront with him as possible.*

"There's something I should tell you," she said nervously. "I think the victim might have been strangled."

"Is that right?" Braam said, sounding a bit surprised. "And why would you think that?"

"It's just a guess," she said. "But he was wearing a cravat earlier, back at the museum. He wasn't wearing a cravat when I found him, and his collar was unbuttoned. His throat looked a bit red to me, maybe even bruised. I think the killer may have subdued him and strangled him with his own cravat."

Braam's eyebrow tilted suspiciously, and his smile twisted into more than a hint of a smirk.

"I can see why you've got something of a reputation as a detective," he said. "Of course, I can think of one reason you might *know* the cause of the victim's death for absolute certain."

London felt a flash of resentment. Of course he was insinuating that she, herself, might be the murder.

She replied in a tight voice, "Yes, I know what you're thinking. But then, if I were really guilty, would I be telling you how I did it?"

Braam didn't reply for a moment. He seemed to be mulling over London's question.

Then he said, "I don't suppose we'd find that cravat if we searched your person."

London cringed at the idea of a body search but knew she better than to push back against it.

"You can have *Surveillant* Dijkstra search me if you like," she said.

Braam chuckled darkly.

"I'm sure there wouldn't be any point," he said. "If you *are* a killer, I'm sure you're a very clever one. You won't give yourself away that easily."

He turned toward the policewoman and said, "Dijkstra, I'd like you to accompany Mevrouw Rose back to her ship."

Surveillant Dijkstra offered London a hand to help her and Sir Reggie into the police boat, then climbed in after them. The engine roared as the pilot pulled away from the bank and turned around for the short trip back to the *Nachtmusik*.

London sat down facing Dijkstra with Sir Reggie in her lap. She and the policewoman didn't speak to each other for a few awkward moments.

Finally, *Surveillant* Dijkstra tried to break the ice.

"You have a nice dog," she said over the sound of the engine.

"Thank you," London said. "His name is Sir Reggie."

"What kind of dog is he?"

"A Yorkshire Terrier," London said.

Dijkstra simply nodded, and the two of them said nothing. There didn't seem to be much point in trying to make conversation.

I guess she suspects me too, London thought.

It was a weird feeling to be suspected of murder all over again.

An "urban legend," Braam called me, she thought.

Which made her wonder—what kinds of wild stories might he have heard about her recent adventures? He didn't seem the least bit satisfied to believe that she had actually solved those murder cases herself. But how could he believe otherwise? She'd been officially cleared of suspicion of all three murders. Surely the *Hoofdinspecteur* knew that perfectly well.

Or does he?

London's imagination was churning with speculations about an international rumor mill. She envisioned messages and conversations in various languages, in which she was cast in the role of some kind of criminal mastermind with a peculiar genius for framing other people for her own dastardly deeds. Her spirits sank even further as she realized it might be harder than usual to clear her name this time.

Her phone buzzed.

London stifled an unsurprised sigh as she saw that the call was from Captain Hays.

CHAPTER NINETEEN

The phone shook in London's hand as she took the call.

"Well, well, well, London Rose," the captain said in his dry English manner. "I just got an interesting call from a gentleman claiming to be the *Hoofdinspecteur* for Amsterdam's Burgwallen district. I hope you can assure me it was some sort of prank call, albeit a rather tasteless one."

"I'm afraid it wasn't a prank, sir," London said.

"Another murder, eh?"

"Apparently so."

"But none of our own passengers was the victim?"

"No."

"And not the killer either?"

"No."

Captain Hays let out a grunt of annoyance.

"I suppose I should be relieved. But this particular cloud seems to come furnished with an unusually small silver lining. And I get the impression that the *Hoofdinspecteur* has doubts that the murderer isn't ... well ... you."

London began to stutter a reply.

"Sir ... I don't know how to explain ..."

"Of course," captain went on, "I'll make a general announcement that our departure will be delayed. Where are you right now?"

"On a police boat on my way back to the *Nachtmusik.*"

"What is your current condition? Not drenched in beer again, I hope."

London cringed a little at the memory of how she'd found a murder victim drowned in a vat of lager back in Bamberg. She and Bryce had both plunged into the vat to try to pull him out, only to find that he was already dead. She'd thought she'd never get the smell of beer out of her pores.

"No, I'm perfectly dry this time," she said.

I didn't even get dunked in a canal, she thought.

"That means you can come to my quarters as soon as you're back aboard," the captain said. "I expect to see you momentarily."

He ended the call without another word.

By then the patrol boat was approaching the *Westerdok,* and the *Nachtmusik* was in view. A few moments later the boat pulled up to the pier where the ship was moored. London climbed out of the boat and set Sir Reggie down, and they both walked up the gangway. They found that the reception room was bustling with people and conversation. Sir Reggie leaped back into London's arms to escape being stepped on.

Letitia was the first person to catch sight of her.

"Oh, London, is it true?" she said, rushing over to her. "The captain just announced that we won't set sail for Copenhagen tonight."

"I'm afraid not," London said.

"But what on earth has happened?" Letitia asked.

With a nudge and a wink, she whispered, "Not another murder, surely."

Of course, Letitia was joking—or at least *thought* she was joking. But London couldn't bring herself to reply.

Letitia's eyes widened.

"Oh, dear," she whispered. "There *was* another murder!"

London took Letitia by the arm and whispered to her urgently.

"Please, please, don't tell anybody. At least not yet."

"I won't," Letitia replied with a nod. "I promise."

Still holding onto Sir Reggie, London pushed through the crowded reception room toward the elevator. Of course she was bombarded by questions.

"How long will we be staying in Amsterdam?"

"What's going on, anyway?"

"Does this mean more great deals and discounts?"

London kept her head down and muttered over and over again, "I can't say anything about it right now."

Finally, she made her way into the elevator, still carrying her little dog. When they exited on the *Allegro* deck, she put Sir Reggie down.

"I'll bet you're tired, boy," she said. "You don't have to come with me to see the captain. You can just go back to our stateroom and in through your doggie door."

But Sir Reggie let out a loyal-sounding yap, as though he had no intention of abandoning her in her time of need. London felt grateful for his company as he trotted alongside her. The captain's call had been rather abrupt, and she wasn't at all sure what his attitude was going to be over her discovery of yet another murder victim.

"Thanks for the support," she whispered to Sir Reggie.

Captain Hays answered the door at London's knock.

"First things first," he said as she and Sir Reggie came into the room. "I want you to look me straight in the eye and tell me you didn't kill anybody."

London looked into his eyes and said firmly, "I didn't kill anybody, I promise."

The captain nodded and said, "That's all I needed to hear. I'm more than willing to take you at your word. After all, you haven't killed anybody else since the tour started. You've got a pretty clean record as far as homicide is concerned. You didn't *kill* any of the corpses you found, after all. You've just had jolly bad luck. Have a seat, let's talk."

London sat down with Sir Reggie in her lap while the captain took a seat behind his desk.

The captain steepled his fingers together and said, "You seem to have had a rather eventful day, my dear. I first got word of your adventures earlier this afternoon."

London's eyes widened with surprise.

"Sir?" she said.

"Yes, I was meaning to tell you whenever I saw you. A docent at the Rijksmuseum—Helga, I believe her name was."

"Helga van den Heuvel?" London said.

"Yes, that was it. She called me about how a certain museum staff member had been rude toward you and your tour group earlier today. She said the man's behavior was most inappropriate, and she wished to apologize wholeheartedly on behalf of the Rijksmuseum."

That was kind of her, London thought.

She remembered catching sight of Helga heading for the Meyer art gallery, but Helga hadn't seen her. If she had, maybe she'd have apologized in person.

The captain continued, "Of course I'm sure the earlier incident was in no way connected with what happened more recently."

London couldn't help groaning aloud.

"I wish that were true, sir," she said. "The man who spoke to us rudely at the Rijksmuseum was the murder victim."

"Really!" the captain said, his bushy eyebrows rising with surprise. "That does rather complicate matters, doesn't it? I suppose it has something to do with why the *Hoofdinspecteur* told me he'll come aboard tomorrow to interview Mr. Cyrus Bannister."

"Yes, sir. It was really Cyrus who started the argument."

"Whatever were they arguing over?"

"I think it was about whether or not restoring paintings was an art."

"Hmm. It sounds like a rather thin reason to suspect anybody of murder. But I suppose the *Hoofdinspecteur* has to cover all leads."

The captain stared at London curiously for a moment, as if he had a rather sensitive question to ask.

"You found a body in the red-light district, eh?"

"That's right," London said.

"Hmm. Well, I won't ask what you happened to be doing there. You're a grown-up adult, and lots of interesting vices are perfectly legal here in Amsterdam. It's really none of my business."

London felt herself blush deeply. She wished she could explain that she'd wound up in the *Rosse Buurt* by mistake in a futile effort to look for her mother. But now wasn't the time or place to get into all that.

London said, "I gather you made an announcement over the PA about our delay."

"I did."

"But you haven't told anybody the reason for the delay—not yet, anyway?"

The captain tilted his head.

"That's not quite the case," he said. "No sooner had I made the announcement than Amy Blassingame came right here to my quarters demanding to know more about what had happened. Well, I couldn't very well keep the truth from a staff member. So I told her what little I knew at the time. I did ask her to be discreet about it for the time being."

London fought down another groan of despair.

The idea of Amy being discreet about anything struck her as highly unlikely.

Captain Hays added, "I also had to tell Mr. Bannister to expect a visit from the *Hoofdinspecteur* tomorrow, although I didn't go into any details about why. I can't say he was very pleased. However, the *Hoofdinspecteur* isn't demanding that anyone else stay aboard the *Nachtmusik*. As for yourself, he expects you to stay in Amsterdam and be available for questioning at a moment's notice."

"I'll certainly do that, sir. As long as the *Nachtmusik* stays."

Captain Hays leaned back in his chair and shook his head.

"Meanwhile, I have to figure out how to break the news to our CEO. I tried to call Mr. Lapham before you arrived, but he wasn't available. I left a message that I needed to talk to him about something urgent. I imagine he'll be calling back shortly. It's five hours earlier where he is in New York, so I'm sure he's wide awake. Don't be surprised if he wants to talk to you in the near future."

"I understand, sir," London said.

Her heart sank at the thought of how Jeremy Lapham was going to take the news. She'd spoken to the mysterious CEO of Epoch World Cruise Lines on several occasions, including about the previous three murders. He'd struck her as an eccentric man, but also as kind-hearted and nothing if not patient.

She hated the thought of how he might take this awful news. She hoped he wouldn't make any drastic decisions, like canceling the rest of the cruise. That would surely be ruinous to Epoch World Cruise Lines, which she understood to be in precarious financial straits already.

Captain Hays stood up and walked around toward London.

"Well, I don't suppose there's anything more we can do about the situation tonight," he said. "You must feel exhausted after this dreadful ordeal. I suggest you get a good night's sleep. Tomorrow is liable to be a long and difficult day."

"I agree, sir," London said, standing up with Sir Reggie in her arms.

Captain Hays scratched Sir Reggie on the head.

"I hadn't meant to ignore you, my fine fellow," he said. "In circumstances such as these, it's always reassuring to know we've got such a dedicated and valiant animal on board. You get a good night's sleep tonight as well. You may have your work cut out for you as a crime fighter tomorrow."

Sir Reggie nodded as if in agreement. London and Sir Reggie left the captain's quarters and headed back to their stateroom.

So much had happened today, she really needed a chance to think things over—to try to make some kind of sense out of this awful situation.

*

A short time later, London lay in bed with Sir Reggie snuggled at her side, her head buzzing with worry and confusion. It truly was a bizarre coincidence that she and her group had had an altercation with the murder victim at the Rijksmuseum …

Or is it?

Were that quarrel and the murder connected somehow? As she replayed the ugly scene in her mind, she remembered how it had begun. Pier Dekker had boasted about how the restoration team had discovered a feather on a helmet that Rembrandt had painted over. Cyrus Bannister had taken offense about that.

"I don't think it's any of my business to look at a feather that Rembrandt himself chose for me not to see," Cyrus had told him, *"let alone any other details that he deliberately hid away."*

It had struck London as a petty complaint at the time. But had it been more than a mere complaint? Had Cyrus been angry enough with Dekker to … ?

To do what?

Murder him?

Although she found that hard to imagine, she remembered how Cyrus had been behaving oddly even before that moment. When the group had been looking at the museum's Van Gogh collection, Cyrus had stared with keen interest at a painting of tulips, with his nose almost up against the canvas.

When London had asked him about his behavior, he'd denied that he'd noticed anything interesting about the painting …

"Except, of course, that it's a masterpiece."

She'd suspected at the time that Cyrus wasn't telling her the whole truth. And now she couldn't help but wonder—were all of today's unfortunate events somehow connected She tried to think of some link between the Van Gogh painting and Rembrandt's *The Night Watch* and the argument between Cyrus and Dekker and …

Soon London's brain overloaded completely, and she felt a deep and welcome wave of exhaustion. As she lay drifting off to sleep, her head was full of images of those Van Gogh tulips. Then the tulips parted, and she saw Pier Dekker's tight, mean face peering out from among the blossoms, staring straight and London.

You'd better find my killer, he seemed to be saying silently.

CHAPTER TWENTY

Staring into her bathroom mirror the next morning, London remembered dreaming about the murdered man's face peering at her. She couldn't recall any more of the nightmare, so she forced herself to focus on the immediate problem—her own hair.

As she tugged a brush through the auburn tangles, she thought she heard a sound and stopped to listen.

It came again, louder this time.

Someone was knocking on her stateroom door.

London felt chills run over her body.

Is it the police?

She hadn't expected to hear from *Hoofdinspecteur* Braam or anybody on his team so early in this morning. Since there were no immediate demands on her time this morning, she'd hoped to be able to get out and check out a few things on her own before she had to talk to the police.

She hastily gave her hair one more pat with the brush and left the bathroom.

"Well, at least I'm dressed," she said to Sir Reggie. The little dog was busily eating his breakfast, apparently unconcerned about whoever was knocking. London figured the visitor must not be a total stranger.

There was yet another knock, and London called out.

"Who's there?"

"Room service," came the reply.

Room service? London thought with surprise.

She certainly wasn't expecting room service. In fact, she was just getting ready to head up to the Habsburg Restaurant for breakfast.

She opened the door to see Bryce Yeaton standing there, handsomely clad in his white chef's jacket and floppy white hat. He held a silver tray raised up on one hand.

"Oh, my!" London said, feeling butterflies in her stomach at the sight. "I wasn't expecting this!"

"I'm full of surprises," Bryce replied with a grin.

London ran her hand through her hair, hoping it wasn't still too wild looking.

Delicious smells followed, as he swept on inside and set the tray on the little table near the windows.

He said, "I thought maybe you could use some special attention today. I've heard you had kind of a tough evening."

"Word gets around fast, I guess," London said.

"Yeah, I'm afraid the rumor mill has been hard at work, as usual."

I'll bet it has, she thought.

Bryce lifted the cover off a plate to reveal exactly the meal London would have expected—her favorite breakfast of Eggs Benedict with coffee, fresh-squeezed orange juice, and a fruit plate.

Bryce sat across the table and poured himself a cup of coffee as London started eating.

"I'm sorry about my hair," London said.

"What's wrong with it?" Bryce said. "You look great to me."

London decided not to debate the matter with him, even if he was just being polite. She hadn't slept well last night, and she was sure she didn't look her best.

"Do you want to talk about what happened last night?" Bryce asked with concern.

Yes, I do, London thought, feeling grateful for Bryce's unexpected company, and especially his show of concern. It occurred to her that this was the first moment the two of them had really been alone since their kiss a few nights ago up on the *Rondo* deck.

But this hardly seemed an opportunity for another romantic moment, even though the memory made her feel warm all over.

Then she realized that the lack of romance was just fine.

What I really need right now is a friend.

And she definitely had a friend in Bryce.

She took a sip of the delicious, fresh-brewed coffee.

"I guess you heard that there's been another murder," she said. "And that I happened to discover the body."

"Yes, I did hear that. I'm awfully sorry."

"What else did you hear?" London asked.

"Well, that you found the body in a boat in …"

Bryce's voice faded and he shrugged awkwardly.

"Oh, dear," London said. "You heard I found the victim in the red-light district, didn't you?"

"Tongues will wag," he replied.

"Bryce, I can explain what I was doing there. In fact, it's something I've been meaning to talk to you about for some time. And now … well it's a long story, and there's so much going on, and I …"

"I understand," Bryce said with a smile. "You can tell me all about it in your own good time. Believe me, I assumed you had your own good reasons for being there."

"Thanks for understanding," London said, feeling grateful that he was such a wonderfully patient and understanding man. Then, as she was savoring a bite of fresh pineapple from the fruit plate, she reflected on his earlier words.

Tongues will wag?

Obviously she was a topic of shipboard gossip.

London asked hesitantly, "But how could anybody aboard the ship have known … ?"

Then her voice trailed off as she remembered something the captain had said to her last night.

"Amy Blassingame came right here to my quarters demanding to know more about what had happened."

"It was Amy, wasn't it?" London said to Bryce. "She's been going around saying I was in the red-light district when I discovered the body, hasn't she?"

"She told me so directly just a little while ago," Bryce said with a nod. "And she's been telling anybody else who will listen. A lot of people have heard about that by now. One of the reasons I came here was to warn you—passengers are liable to be treating you a little oddly."

"I imagine so," London thought.

"I hope this news doesn't put you off your Eggs Benedict," Bryce said.

"Oh, anything but," London said, relishing a rich, buttery mouthful. "In fact, it's just what I need right now—perfect breakfast comfort food. But I need to tell you one thing you probably don't know. The victim was the restorer in the museum."

Bryce's eyes widened.

"You mean the bad-tempered fellow?"

"Yes, Pier Dekker."

"That's very strange. But a coincidence, surely."

"Well, the police aren't so sure," London said. "And the fact that Dekker said some angry words to me means that I'm at least a person of interest myself, and potentially an actual suspect. I'm afraid it's up to me to clear my own name—as usual."

"How can I help?"

London thought for a moment.

"I don't know yet. I'm planning to go ashore and look for clues. But I'm sure you're very busy this morning, and you're taking too much time away from your job as it is. Maybe I'll need your help later."

Bryce finished his coffee and got up from the table.

"Well, you know how to reach me," he said. "I'll do anything I can."

"I appreciate that," London said.

Bryce leaned toward London, and they shared a quick but welcome kiss. As he turned to head out the door, Sir Reggie stepped in front of him and sat up on his haunches, growling in obvious discontent.

Bryce laughed as he reached into his pocket and produced a bag of treats.

"I hadn't forgotten you, boy. Far from it. Here are some of my latest doggie treats, fresh baked from my kitchen. It's even a new recipe. I hope you like liver."

Sir Reggie yapped with approval and caught the treat as Bryce tossed it to him. Bryce handed London the bag and gave her another quick kiss on his way out of the stateroom.

As London finished the last bites of her breakfast, she could feel it energizing her for what was bound to be a demanding day.

Sir Reggie climbed up onto the chair Bryce had just vacated and waited expectantly.

"It's about time we got going," she finally said to the dog. "I assume you want to come along."

Sir Reggie let out a yap of enthusiasm.

"I'm glad to hear it," London said, getting up from the table and scratching his head. "I love the companionship, and I'm liable to need your help before the day is through."

London went back to the bathroom and finished brushing her hair, then put Sir Reggie on his leash. They left the stateroom and waited for the elevator to take them up to the *Menuetto* deck where the gangway was attached.

When the elevator door opened, London met with an angry face glaring at her. For a moment she flashed back to the peering face in her nightmare, but this was a different man, taller, darker, and much more enigmatic.

"Just the person I came down here to see," Cyrus Bannister declared as he stepped out of the elevator. "I'd like a few words with you, London Rose."

CHAPTER TWENTY ONE

London stifled a discouraged sigh as Audrey Bolton stepped out of the elevator behind Cyrus Bannister. They both looked furious, and she didn't relish dealing with this alliance right now.

But there they stood, blocking her way.

Audrey pointed her finger at London and snapped, "You ought to be ashamed of yourself."

"Why?" London asked Audrey. "Ashamed of what?"

"Of telling the police that Cyrus was a murderer."

"I didn't tell them anything of the kind," London replied, shocked by the accusation.

Cyrus scoffed, "Then I'd like to know why the captain told me I can't leave the boat today until the police come aboard and question me about a certain dead body."

"A dead body that *you* happened to find," Audrey said to London, crossing her arms.

"I didn't tell the police anything but the truth, Cyrus" London replied. "You had an argument with the murder victim at the Rijksmuseum. It was hardly any secret. And I'm pretty sure withholding information from the police is illegal here in Holland, just like it is pretty much everywhere else in the world."

"By telling them that, you've as much as made me a suspect," Cyrus grumbled.

Join the club, London thought.

"Excuse me," she said, stepping around the pair. As she and Sir Reggie got into the elevator, she added, "I have work to do."

As the doors closed behind them, Cyrus called after her with a final wag of his finger "This isn't over."

I guess those two really are an item, London thought, relieved that they hadn't followed her onto the elevator. She had actually gotten to like Audrey, despite the woman's initial prickliness. The tall, awkward woman had a lot of spunk and had actually helped catch a killer at their last stop. But Cyrus was a more disconcerting character.

She'd been puzzled by his behavior at the museum yesterday. How sure could she be that he wasn't the killer?

When she and Sir Reggie got out of the elevator on the *Menuetto* deck, London noticed that everyone in the crowded reception area was staring in the same direction—directly at her.

Oh, no, she thought.

The rumors Amy had started had apparently been effective. Now it seemed that even some of the *Nachtmusik's* passengers suspected her of murder.

"Come on, boy," she said to Sir Reggie as they continued out onto the gangway. "It looks like we've really got our work cut out for us this time."

London shivered as she and Reggie walked across the gangway and away from the *Nachtmusik.*

There wasn't a chill in the air.

Actually, it promised to be a warm, sunny morning. Even so, London felt a cold dread deep inside. She knew it was because she and Sir Reggie were following the same route they had walked along last night when they had discovered the dead body.

And judging from how Sir Reggie was hugging close to her ankles and making little whining sounds, he was anxious too.

"Don't worry, Sir Reggie," she told the little dog. "There's nothing to be afraid of."

Then she muttered to herself, "Of course there isn't."

There was no feeling of any threat. The winding streets, bridges, and canals of Amsterdam were quaint and cheerful by day. Shop owners were opening their doors and cranking open their awnings, and streets were starting to bustle with morning pedestrians, bicycles, and little cars. Everybody London saw looked happy and cheerful.

Amsterdam seemed like the last place on earth where any kind of violence could happen.

But something violent did happen here last night, she reminded herself.

They didn't have to walk very far before they passed into the De Wallen district. Last night London had been taken aback by the sudden change of surroundings as they entered the red-light district. But in the daylight, those red and neon lights didn't glare in the same way.

Even so, business was already getting underway here, just as it was elsewhere in Amsterdam. Although some windows were vacant, many of them were occupied by preening, posing, dancing young women wearing as few clothes as possible. Some appeared to be just setting up for the workday, sitting in the windows wearing bathrobes and putting on makeup or even eating breakfast.

Prospective clients were also up and around, starting to cluster and browse around the windows. But today London realized something she hadn't quite noticed last night. At least half of the gawkers didn't appear to be clients at all, but merely tourists not unlike Agnes and Walter Shick, whose interest in the red-light district was purely that of curiosity. London could hear a fair number of them speaking English.

She could again smell the aroma of marijuana in the air, and she noticed small groups of people standing around having a morning chat while enjoying a smoke together.

As she and Reggie followed the familiar route toward the crime scene, they came to the large square surrounding the stately and dignified *Oude Kerk*—the church that was the oldest building in Amsterdam, and that happened to be planted square in the middle of the red-light district.

And there was the statue that London had noticed before, the buxom sex worker who stood in a doorframe like some kind of guardian saint.

She paused in front of Belle and took a closer look. The bronze figure had a mysteriously knowing expression, as if few things ever happened here in the *Rosse Buurt* that she wasn't fully aware of.

London wished that was true, and that Belle could explain this murder to her.

In wry voice, London said in Dutch, "Good morning, Mevrouw. I wonder if you could help me with something."

She and Sir Reggie both jumped to hear a woman's voice reply in Dutch.

"I'd be glad to. What can I do to help?"

The sloshing of water drew London's attention to a short, stout woman wearing a gray maintenance uniform. She had just poured out a bucket of soapy water onto the brick pavement on the far side of the statue. Now she glanced up with a grin, then focused on scrubbing those wet bricks with her mop.

London stepped around the statue of Belle to get a better look at the woman who had answered her question. After viewing rows of shapely and available young women, the perfectly ordinary cleaning woman struck London as a jarring sight. But she quickly sensed that the woman didn't feel the least bit out of place here in the *Rosse Buurt*, mopping around a statue dedicated to Amsterdam's sex workers.

Just one more person going about her job, London thought.

When she felt a tug on the leash, she looked back and saw Sir Reggie had come to a halt and was staring at the spreading water. Her Yorkie obviously didn't want to get his feet wet, so she scooped him up and carried him.

London approached the woman shyly and spoke to her in Dutch.

"Um … I wonder if you happened to hear about a murder that took place near here last night."

"Oh, yes," the woman said, clucking her tongue with dismay. "Such an awful thing. I was at home at the time, but I've heard a lot of talk about it this morning."

"Did you happen to know the victim?"

The woman tilted her head as she resumed mopping.

"Meneer Schat, you mean? Only enough to say hi to him. He was a grouchy fellow, never said hi back. Still, it was a terrible thing to happen to anybody."

"Have you heard anybody say anything about … ?"

"Who might have killed him?" the woman said, completing London's thought. "Oh, nothing like that."

The woman paused mopping and looked at London curiously.

"You must be English—or maybe American."

"American," London said, aware that the woman had picked up on her accent.

"Why are you asking about it? Are you a journalist or a writer or …"

"I'm … just an interested foreigner," London said, hoping not to have to explain how she'd found the body.

"Well, if anybody around here knows anything about what happened, it's probably Evert Cornellison."

Pointing, she added, "He owns the Zacht Coffeeshop just a few doors down that way."

"Thanks for the help," London said.

"Anytime," the woman said. "You have a nice dog. May I say hello?"

London gladly introduced the woman to Sir Reggie, who was happy to have her scratch him on the head. Then London picked him up and carried him as she continued down the block toward the establishment the woman had mentioned.

It was impossible to miss—there was a sign that read Zacht Coffeeshop jutting out from the storefront. When she and Sir Reggie stepped inside, she saw several patrons seated at small tables and a few more with their elbows propped on a long counter. Some were snacking on treats that looked rather like banana cake and specials of the day were written in colorful chalks on a large blackboard.

The place looked perfectly ordinary, but in at least one way this was distinctly different from any other coffeeshop she had ever visited.

It was the aroma.

She'd gotten more or less used to this particular smell on the streets in this area, but it was much thicker here indoors and she couldn't help coughing.

London rubbed her eyes, cleared her throat, and walked over to the front counter where a burly, smiling man stood by a cash register.

"Welcome to the Zacht Coffeeshop," he said in Dutch. Then he added with an amiable chuckle, "You look a bit confused. I'll bet you're a foreigner."

"Uh-huh," London said, trying not to start coughing again. Sir Reggie himself sputtered a little bit.

"Are you here to buy some coffee?" the man said with a broad, mischievous smile.

"Uh, a cup of coffee might be nice," London said.

"That's too bad!" the man said, letting out a peal of good-natured, teasing laughter. "Because we don't sell any!"

Several nearby customers joined him in his laughter.

Most of them were smoking—and it was certainly no mystery to London *what* they were smoking.

The man leaned on his elbows toward London.

"Foreigners often make this mistake," he said. "They think a *coffeeshop* is place where you buy coffee. But that's not true here in Amsterdam. If you want coffee, you have to go to a *cafe.*"

In a few moments, London's eyes stopped stinging and she could see more clearly. The menu posted across the bar was divided into four lists—*Joints, Weed, Hash,* and *Edibles.* Under the last category were listed a variety of so-called "space cakes."

Suddenly the name of the place—Zacht Coffeeshop—made a lot more sense.

After all, the word *zacht* meant "mellow" in Dutch.

Although London already knew that hashish and marijuana were perfectly legal here, it hadn't occurred to her that there were cafe-like establishments where those drugs could be purchased and enjoyed.

London felt a bit dazed from the smoky atmosphere. For a moment she could barely remember why she'd come in here.

"Would you like to sample some of our wares?" the man asked.

"I—I don't think so," London stammered. "I was wondering if I could speak to the owner. His name is Evert Cornellison."

"You're speaking to him," the man said with a hospitable smile and a nod. "How can I help you?"

"I was wondering what you could tell me … about a certain Meneer Schat."

The man's jolly expression suddenly darkened. He looked positively angry now.

"Who is asking?" he growled at London. "And why?"

CHAPTER TWENTY TWO

For a moment London wondered whether she and Sir Reggie should just hurry away without further ado. As jovial as Evert Cornellison had seemed just a moment before, he certainly wasn't the least bit *zacht*—mellow—now.

And all the other faces in the coffeeshop were turned toward her with expressions ranging from curious to hostile.

But then she reminded herself that this was the only lead she had at the moment.

Trying to keep her voice steady, she asked in Dutch, "Did you know that Meneer Schat was found dead last night?"

"Oh, I heard, all right," the man said sharply. "The police were here about an hour ago. *Hoofdinspecteur* Braam asked all kinds of questions, caused me all kinds of inconvenience. He seems to suspect *me,* of all people. I half-expected him to arrest me. Worst of all, he upset my clientele. You'd think that Schat fellow was somebody important."

Cornellison took out a rag and started wiping down the counter.

"Anyway, I've answered all the questions I'm going to answer about him. Who are you, anyway? What makes you think you've got any business giving me any more trouble?"

London spoke slowly and carefully.

"My name is London Rose, and I'm an American, and I work as the social director of a tour boat that is currently visiting Amsterdam, and …"

She paused for a moment.

"And the police have got some idea I might have killed Meneer Schat."

Cornellison stopped wiping the counter. His eyes widened, and London saw a flicker of that grin of his reappear.

"So Braam suspects you too, eh?" he said. "Well, that makes things much more interesting. We've got something in common, eh? He has definitely cast a wide net for suspects. Why would he suspect a foreigner like you?"

“Well, for one thing, I was the one who happened to …”

Still in her arms, Sir Reggie let out a little “ahem”-like yap to correct her.

“My *dog* and I were the ones who found the body.”

“Sounds like a bit of bad luck,” Cornellison, no longer seeming angry.

Oh, you’ve got no idea, London thought.

“Bad luck is right,” London continued. “You see Meneer Schat’s real name was Pier Dekker, and he was a conservator working on ‘Operation Night Watch,’ the restoration of the Rembrandt painting, over at the Rijksmuseum. I happened to lead a tour group there yesterday afternoon, and he … well, he got rather unpleasant toward us.”

Cornellison’s interest seemed to be rising.

“And Braam suspects you on account of *that?”* he said. “That sounds pretty farfetched.”

Of course, London knew that the *Hooftinspecteur* had more reason to suspect her than just the altercation at the museum. There was also the matter of the three other bodies London had discovered all over Europe during the last couple of weeks. But she decided not to go into that.

Cornellison reached across the counter and scratched Sir Reggie on the head.

“What about this formidable little fellow?” he said with a chuckle. “Do the police suspect him too?”

Reggie let out a soft growl, as if to warn the man to take him more seriously. Cornellison drew his hand back with mild surprise.

“If you don’t mind my asking,” London said. “Why does Braam suspect you?”

“He suspects me because … what was the man’s real name again?”

“Pier Dekker.”

“Right, Dekker. He’d run up an outrageously big tab here in the shop. Once I realized he had no intention of paying up, I kicked him out. That was a couple of days ago. He made a big scene about it, calling me all kinds of names and overturning furniture and upsetting everybody. I had to forcibly throw him out.”

London glanced around and tried to imagine the incident. Dekker had been a small guy, and Cornellison was large and muscular. She guessed Cornellison must have made short work of Dekker.

Cornellison continued, "But did I kill him? That would be ridiculous. Now that he's dead, there is not a chance in the world of my collecting the money he owed me. Not that I'm sad that he's gone. He was no fun to have around here, believe me."

One of the customers nodded and said, "I won't miss him."

Another added, "I never knew anybody else to get so grouchy around this place."

There was a general murmur of agreement from the others in the store.

"Anyway, I told the police I had an alibi," he said. "I was at home watching television with my wife when the body was found. There is no way I could have been the killer."

"Do you happen to know anybody else who might have meant him harm?" London asked Cornellison.

The coffeehouse owner shrugged.

"Anybody who knew him, I suppose," he said. "I don't imagine he had many friends—or any at all, for that matter. I can't say we had any acquaintances in common."

A male customer who was seated nearby spoke up.

"I can think of somebody who knew him. Kaneel Lied is her name—or at least the name she goes by here in the *Rosse Buurt.* I've seen Schat stop by her window where she works and go on inside several times. He was a regular client of hers, I guess."

London realized that the name *Kaneel Lied* meant "cinnamon song."

A sex worker, London thought.

"I don't envy that girl," muttered one of the female customers.

"I can't imagine why she'd deal with a pig like that," said another.

London's curiosity was piqued.

"Can you tell me where I can find her, uh, window?" she asked.

The male customer pointed.

"Just take a left up at that corner. She works on Klaverstaat in window 14A."

London guessed that the customer had a good reason to remember the address. He probably had more than a passing familiarity with Kaneel Lied herself.

"Thanks, you've both been very helpful," London said to Cornellison and the male customer. She carried Sir Reggie out the door, then set him down to walk on his leash. As they continued on their way, London found herself thinking about the rather volatile coffeeshop owner.

"So what did you think of Meneer Cornellison, Sir Reggie?" she asked.

Sir Reggie let out a noncommittal growl.

"I don't know either," London said. "I guess the police will check out his alibi. But it doesn't sound exactly airtight. His wife wouldn't be the first woman to lie to protect her husband. Still, if Dekker owed Cornellison money, why would he want him dead?"

She sighed and added, "There are lots of possible reasons, I guess. I wouldn't want to get Cornellison mad at me, that's for sure. And I definitely got the impression Dekker wasn't popular with any of the customers there."

London sighed. It seemed likely that the *Rosse Buurt* was just full of possible suspects.

She and Sir Reggie turned onto Klaverstaat, where the street was lined with windows for sex workers. As she'd observed walking by earlier, some of the windows were vacant, while others were already occupied and open for business. In her travels as an adult, she'd seen sex workers soliciting customers before, but never quite so openly. As she thought about it, she realized that a prostitute was probably safer behind a glass window than she would be on most city streets.

When she arrived at window 14A, she saw a pair of shapely legs wearing ultra-high heels, but she couldn't see much else of the woman. She was holding a newspaper open in front of her.

London rang a buzzer to get the woman's attention. The woman peeked overtop of her newspaper, revealing a pretty face topped with short hair that was dyed in a rainbow of colors.

The woman touched a button and spoke to London over an intercom.

"Go away," she said.

The woman's face disappeared behind the newspaper again.

London was a bit startled by that gruff response. It was true that she hadn't usually talked with women who lived this particular lifestyle. But now she really needed information about the murder victim.

She pushed the buzzer again and spoke into the microphone.

"Do you happen to be Kaneel Lied?"

The woman looked over her newspaper again, this time with surprise and interest.

"No, I'm Honingraat Hemel," she said. "Why do you ask?"

London mentally translated the name, which meant "honeycomb sky."

She said, "I'm looking for anyone who might have known Pier Dekker—although probably not by that name. He seems to have called himself Meneer Schat whenever he was in the *Rosse Buurt.*"

The woman who called herself Honingraat Hemel set her newspaper down.

"I'll buzz you in," she said.

The glass door opened at the sound of a buzz.

London hesitated for a moment, glancing around and wondering if anyone from the ship might be watching. Then she cleared her suddenly dry throat and stepped through the opening. She followed the scantily clad young woman through a curtain into a plain but tidy little room furnished only with a couple of chairs, a small bed, and a table with a coffeemaker and a couple of mugs.

Glad to be out of sight anyone gazing into that big window, London felt herself relax a bit.

The woman slipped into a bathrobe.

"You're American, I take it?" she said in Dutch, obviously recognizing London's accent.

"That's right, er, Mevrouw Hemel," London said, also in Dutch.

The woman chuckled and began to speak in fluent English.

"You can call me Anouk. That's my real name."

"My name is London Rose."

"Well, London, I take it this isn't a professional visit."

"Oh—no, nothing like that," she replied, hoping that her slight blush wasn't visible.

"I'm sorry if I seemed rude just now. I took you to be a tourist. I can't stand tourists—the people who come around only to gawk and stare, I mean. I especially hate the picture takers. They've gotten to be a real nuisance in this district. They crowd out the real business. Would you like some coffee?"

"No, I—I won't be long," London stammered awkwardly.

Anouk poured herself a mug of coffee and invited London to sit down.

"Kaneel Lied is my business partner, so to speak," she said. "That is, we pay the rent for this window together and work here in shifts. I work days, although there's hardly any business at this hour, so I take things pretty easy during the early morning, as you can see."

With a wink, she added, "I don't always just sit there reading a newspaper, if you know what I mean. Kaneel works nights. That's when things get really busy."

"I don't assume Kaneel—'cinnamon'—is her real name," London said.

"No, it's actually Ingrid. Our hours are so different that I don't see much of her, but I have heard her mention Meneer Schat. And a little while ago some cops came around asking me questions about him—and about her. Is it true that he got murdered?"

"I'm afraid so," London said.

"That's awful. I suppose Ingrid has gotten a visit from the cops herself by now."

"How much did she tell you about, er, Meneer Schat?"

"Oh, hardly anything at all. He's just one of the few clients I've ever heard her mention by name. He is—or I guess he *was*—pretty regular, I guess. A shame what happened to him. You have a nice dog, by the way."

"Thanks," London said.

Anouk leaned toward her and asked, "But why is an American like you interested in what happened to Meneer Schat?"

London stifled a sigh.

"It's kind of a long story, but the police suspect me of the murder."

Anouk's eyes widened with surprise.

"Really?" she said. "Why?"

"It's because I … my *dog* and I … were the first to discover the body."

Anouk laughed as she took another sip of coffee.

"Is that the only reason the police suspect you? Neither one of you strikes me as especially homicidal."

"I assure you, we're not," London said. "But I need to clear my name as soon as possible. You see, I work aboard a tour boat that was scheduled to leave Amsterdam yesterday. As long as I'm under suspicion, the boat can't go anywhere. We're going to wind up way behind schedule."

More behind schedule than we already are, London almost added.

"How can I help out?" Anouk asked.

"Could you tell me where I can find your, er, business partner? Ingrid, I mean?"

Anouk stroked her chin thoughtfully.

"Well, normally I am a stickler for confidentiality, but …"

She paused for a moment, then said, "But you seem like a nice person, and you've a got a real problem, and you need all the help you can get. As it happens, Ingrid and I also happen to be roommates."

She opened a table drawer and took out a note pad and jotted something down.

"I'll give you our address. It's only a short walk away from here. I'll also call her and let you know you're on your way."

Anouk handed London the address and gave directions on how to get there.

"Thanks, Anouk," London said, getting up to leave. "You've been a great help."

"I hope so," Anouk said, leading London back to the front window. "I can't imagine what it's like to be in trouble with the police. Everybody who works around here gets along with them just fine."

London's head buzzed as she and Sir Reggie continued on toward the address. The visit to the sex worker had definitely taken her by surprise. Apart from her scanty clothing and her rainbow-colored hair, Anouk had seemed like a perfectly normal young woman. And something Anouk had said kept rattling through London's head.

"I can't imagine what it's like to be in trouble with the police."

It seemed more than ironic that London kept getting in trouble with the law and this local woman never did.

"We're definitely in whole different world, Sir Reggie," London said to her dog.

Their route took them along the bank of the nearest canal. When they arrived at the address, London's mouth dropped open with surprise. She had to check the paper to make sure she hadn't made a mistake.

"This isn't what I expected, Sir Reggie," she said.

CHAPTER TWENTY THREE

How in the world do two sex workers afford that? London wondered.

She couldn't imagine that Anouk and Ingrid made much money in that plain little room with the large window facing the street. She had been expecting to find themselves living someplace more …

Well, squalid, maybe, she admitted to herself.

She was staring at a small but perfectly charming houseboat afloat in a nearby canal. It was one in a row of cheerful little floating homes. Like most of the others, this one had flowers blooming in pots on a small deck that could be accessed by a set of steps leading down from the waterfront walkway.

Just yesterday *Kapitein* Claes, the pilot of the *Jonge Gouda* canal boat, had talked about these "house arks" —*woonarks*, he'd said they were called. He'd emphasized that the berths alone could be extremely expensive.

London stood wavering on the bank, not sure whether to head down those steps onto the foredeck and knock on the door—not sure, in fact, whether she actually had the right address.

Then the front door opened, and a young woman came out dressed in a gleaming white nurse's uniform.

"We've definitely got the wrong place," she murmured to Sir Reggie. "Come on, let's go."

But as she turned to walk away, the nurse called out in Dutch.

"Are you Mevrouw Rose?"

Surprised, London turned back again.

"Um, yes," she said, picking up Sir Reggie and stepping down onto the deck.

"It's good to meet you," the nurse said with a pleasant smile. "My name is Esmée, and I'm just now leaving for work, but please go on inside. Ingrid is expecting you."

Esmée? London wondered as the nurse went up the steps and hurried away.

Anouk hadn't mentioned anybody named Esmée. But that door was standing open, so London walked on inside. She found herself in an attractive living room with a whole wall of windows looking out over the canal. A small, shiny kitchen was nestled into the other side of the open area.

London was admiring the neat décor when a large woman appeared through a doorway. At almost six feet tall, full-figured and muscular, wearing a blue shirt with a black tie, shoulder insignias, and a badge, she was rather daunting.

Although the woman's expression was markedly less cheerful than Esmée's, she spoke cordially enough, "Oh, you must be the visitor Anouk called about. Come with me."

London followed the woman into a tidy little bedroom with windows overlooking the water. It was furnished with a desk and twin beds. Sitting at the desk was another woman wearing a housecoat and poring over a computer screen through reading glasses. Sheaves of notes and textbooks were stacked up all around her.

"Ingrid, your guest is here," the tall woman said in Dutch.

The studious woman looked around and smiled at London, her eyes sparkling over her reading glasses.

"Oh, yes," she said, shaking London's hand. "Anouk called about you a few minutes ago. Your first name is … the same as a city I think."

"London. London Rose."

"Yes, that's right. What an interesting name. I'm Ingrid, and this is my sister, Femke."

Ingrid patted the bed and added, "Please have a seat, London."

London sat down on the bed with Sir Reggie in her lap, and Femke sat on the other bed facing her. Ingrid stayed seated between them at her desk. Although Ingrid wasn't nearly as formidable as her sister, London could see a family resemblance in their faces.

Meanwhile, Femke's stern expression softened just a little as she looked at Sir Reggie.

"What an adorable little dog," she said, reaching a hand toward him.

"Thanks," London said. "His name is Sir Reggie."

Instead of welcoming the attention, the little Yorkie stayed huddled in her lap. He seemed to be rather intimidated by the uniformed woman, who withdrew her hand and sat staring at London.

Ingrid looked at London with concern.

"This has something to do with Meneer Schat, doesn't it?" she said.

"I'm afraid so," London said. "You see he—"

"Yes, I know," Ingrid said, gently interrupting. "I didn't even know his real name until the police told me. They said it was Pier something …"

"Pier Dekker," London said.

"Yes, and he worked at the Rijksmuseum, didn't he? I had no idea. It was such a terrible thing that happened to him.

Femke scoffed as if she didn't think it was such a terrible thing at all.

"Don't you have to go to work?" Ingrid asked her sister.

"I've still got a few minutes," Femke said to Ingrid, crossing her arms. "The truth is, I don't like the idea of leaving you alone just now."

"Oh, don't be silly," Ingrid said to Femke with a musical laugh. "I'm not in any danger."

Turning toward London, Ingrid said, "The police were here earlier. They wanted to talk to me about Meneer Schat. I guess pretty much the whole *Rosse Buurt* district knows he's one of my regulars."

London couldn't help feeling jarred by those words.

"My regulars."

London could tell by Ingrid's impish smile that she'd noticed London's moment of awkwardness.

"You're American, aren't you?" Ingrid asked London in English.

London nodded.

Ingrid added, "And I guess many things here seem kind of … well, unusual to you."

London nodded again.

"Well, don't be shy about asking questions," she said. "It's really all right, I won't be offended."

London glanced around and stammered, "I—I'm just not sure … I understand this whole …"

"Living arrangement?" Ingrid said.

London nodded yet another time.

"Five of us live here," Ingrid explained. "We've known each other all our lives. My sister Femke is a security guard at the Botanical Garden. Esmée is a nurse at a hospital near here. You might have met her when you arrived. Dora is a hairstylist. She's at work right now. Anouk and I …"

Ingrid's grin widened, and London just nodded, aware that the woman was amused at her discomfort.

"I'm also a psychology student at Vrije Universiteit," Ingrid explained, indicating the books and notes. "And Anouk is a singer-songwriter who plays with a band at night. What we do the rest of the time pays the bills. With five of us, we can afford the rent on this place. It gets a little crowded from time to time, but not very often because we work such different hours. There's another bedroom like this. Anouk and I take turns sharing one bed because we work separate shifts, so we're almost never here at the same time."

London listened with growing fascination.

It really is a good arrangement, she thought.

In fact, she'd known other groups of young people who'd set up housekeeping in much the same way. In her own earlier years working on large ocean-going ships, she'd shared much less comfortable quarters with several other women. The only difference had been that none of them had been sex workers. But of course, here in Amsterdam, that was considered just another job.

Ingrid's forehead crinkled with concern.

She said to London, "Anouk told me something about why you wanted to talk to me, but I wasn't sure I heard it right. Is it true you found Meneer Schat's body?"

"That's right," London said. "My dog and I, anyway."

"And the police suspect *you* of murder?" Ingrid said.

"That's right. And I work aboard a visiting cruise ship, and I've got to clear this up so our departure won't be delayed any more than it has been already. I was wondering if maybe you could help."

"I'll do whatever I can," Ingrid said with a shrug. "I want whoever killed Meneer Schat to be brought to justice. I feel awfully sorry about what happened to him."

Femke scoffed again.

"I can't imagine why," she said, also in English.

"What can you tell me about him?" London asked Ingrid.

"Well, he wasn't very pleasant," Ingrid said. "He was almost always in a bad mood whenever he came around. He said cruel and insulting things from time to time. I think he actually hated women generally. But he was never physically abusive. I was never frightened of him. Or at least I wasn't until ..."

Ingrid paused for a moment.

"A few days ago, when he came around, he told me he wanted to marry me. I was special to him, he said, and I was different from all the women he'd ever known, and he wanted us both to start life all over again together. He talked about how he'd support me, and I'd never have to work at any kind job again or even leave the house, and we'd raise lots of children, and …"

Ingrid paused again and shook her head.

Her sister shuddered and said, "It gives me the creeps just to think about it."

London couldn't help but shudder as well as she imagined the mean, beady-eyed, and apparently disturbed little man offering Ingrid the sort of life London herself had done her best to escape.

"It really was weird," Ingrid said. "I hadn't realized until that moment how obsessed he'd gotten about me, and how delusional. I mean, he didn't even know my name, and I didn't know his. I told him he had to go away and not come back, that I didn't want to see him again. He got very angry, and he said I was just like other women after all, and he stormed away. But he kept prowling around my window, watching me. I must admit, I got very uncomfortable with him then."

"Of course you did," Femke said. "Like you said, he hated women. His obsession with you was just another way of showing it. You weren't a human being to him, just a fantasy. Men like that are dangerous."

"You're being awfully harsh," Ingrid said. "I don't think he was dangerous, just sad and pathetic."

"Hah!" Femke snorted.

"You didn't even know him," Ingrid protested.

"I knew him better than you think," Femke said.

Femke quickly raised her hand to her mouth, as if she'd blurted something she hadn't meant to say. Ingrid looked at her sister with sudden curiosity.

"What do you mean by that?" Ingrid asked Femke.

"Never mind," Femke said defensively.

"You never even met him."

"Never mind, I said."

"No, tell me what you meant."

London tensed up at the awkward silence that fell between the two sisters. Femke crossed her arms and tapped her feet and frowned.

"I *did* meet him, actually," she finally admitted. "He came here to the houseboat once."

"What!" Ingrid said with a gasp.

"It must have been the day after you told him you wouldn't see him anymore. I was the only one here at the time. You were at school."

"Why didn't you tell me?" Ingrid said.

"I didn't want to worry you," Femke said.

"How did he even find out where I lived?" Ingrid asked.

"Maybe he followed you some morning. Or maybe from one of your neighboring workers. Anyway, he turned up here. He didn't know I was your sister, just figured I was a friend. He told me how much he wanted to marry you, but also that he'd said some things to you that he shouldn't have, and you were angry with him, and he wanted me to help patch things up between the two of you."

"What did you say to him?" Ingrid asked.

"Let's not talk about this right now," Femke said, indicating London's presence.

"No, I think we'd better. After all, London came here looking for answers."

Femke let out a growl-like sound and London heard Sir Reggie grumble in response.

"Let me put it this way," she said. "Even if he hadn't gotten killed, he wouldn't have come around bothering you anymore."

"Did you threaten him?" Ingrid asked.

"That's all I'm going to say."

"Why didn't you tell the police about this when they came around this morning?"

Femke let out a sarcastic laugh.

"Why do you *think* I didn't tell them?" she said.

Another silence fell.

London felt awkward, as though she was intruding on a very private matter. She sensed by the tension in Sir Reggie's little body that he felt the same way.

She couldn't help but wonder what Femke had said to the man, but she told herself it was really none of her business.

She actually felt a surge of relief when her cellphone rang.

"Excuse me, I've got to take this," she said to the sisters, who were still glaring at each other.

She stepped out into the hallway and took the call, which was from Elsie.

"London, where are you?" Elsie asked, sounding anxious.

"I'm in town, not far from the boat," London said.

"Can you get back here pretty quickly?" Elsie asked.

"Is it an emergency?"

Elsie let out a sigh of despair.

"It's something I don't know how to handle, anyway. Please come to the lounge right away."

CHAPTER TWENTY FOUR

When London and Sir Reggie reached the Amadeus Lounge, all she could see was the backs of people who were huddled around the bar. She was out of breath from running all the way to the ship from the houseboat and had to wait a moment before she could even ask whether someone was ill or hurt.

"What's going on?" she finally croaked out.

All the faces turned toward her.

Several of them gasped and others just glared.

They're not happy to see me, London realized, flashing back to the stern looks she'd gotten in the reception area that morning. She'd suspected then that ugly rumors were flying about her. Apparently, she was right.

"Nothing is going on," one of the passengers said to her.

"Nothing at all," another said.

Then the group gathered more tightly together as if they were trying to hide something.

Now London knew that something definitely *was* going on here.

And I'd better find out what it is.

She picked up Sir Reggie and pushed her way among the passengers, who moved aside grudgingly.

At the bar she found herself face to face with Amy, whose big dark eyes stared up at her defiantly. And just below Amy's face, another pair of big dark eyes was looking up at London too.

The concierge was clutching something small, furry, and white against her chest.

"You're going to tell me I can't keep her, aren't you?" Amy said in a voice shaking with emotion.

"Who do you mean by 'her'?" London asked. "What is that, anyhow?"

Amy turned away and set a strange looking little white kitten down on the bar. The little creature immediately started lapping milk out of a bowl that had already been set out for it.

The group of people gathered there resumed what they'd apparently been doing before—oohing and ahhing about how adorable the creature was.

From her place behind the bar, Elsie gazed at London imploringly.

"Please help!" Elsie mouthed silently.

London looked back at Amy, who began to explain anxiously.

"I went out for a walk. Now, don't scold me for going AWOL, London. It's not fair that I'm always stuck here working. I was walking through a park when I saw a pair of the loveliest eyes looking up at me through the branches of a bush. I couldn't just leave poor thing there."

As if in agreement, the animal opened its mouth and made a little noise. It was an odd, startling sound—more like a high-pitched series of chattering staccato "yips" than a typical kitten's "mew."

Sir Reggie let out a bark of alarm at the noise. The dog struggled in London's arms until she unfastened his leash and let him scamper away.

London wondered—why was her normally fearless Sir Reggie frightened at the sight of a small kitten?

Maybe this is no ordinary kitten, she thought.

It certainly didn't look ordinary, with its enormous eyes and its large, rounded ears.

"What are you going to do with him?" London asked Amy.

"It's not a *him,* it's a *her,"* Amy grumbled. "You can tell by her beautiful face."

"And you want to keep … her?" London asked.

"I've already given her a name," Amy said, petting the creature. "Dewdrop. don't you think that's a pretty name?"

London shook her head slowly.

"Amy, there are a lot of problems …" she began.

Amy appealed to the people around her. "Didn't I tell you this was going to happen?" she said in a protesting whine. "Didn't I tell you she'd try to make me get rid of my adorable Dewdrop?"

The crowd murmured angrily.

"How could you, London?"

"Can't you see they've bonded already?"

"Can't you see how much Dewdrop already loves Amy?"

The hostility was palpable. London had found it bad enough to realize that some passengers actually suspected her of murder. This almost seemed worse.

"Besides" Amy added, almost in tears now. "You got to keep your dog, didn't you?"

London stifled a discouraged sigh. "Amy, the amount of paperwork involved in taking an animal out of one country into another is just staggering. Surely you know that."

"Well, you managed to skip all that," Amy said in a pathetic voice.

"No, I didn't," London replied. "Sir Reggie came aboard with Mrs. Klimowski, remember? And she had all the paperwork she needed to bring him from the United States. When she was killed, it only made sense for someone aboard the ship to adopt him. But this …"

"It isn't fair," Amy murmured, picking up the animal again and holding it close.

Again, Amy's complaint was echoed by others in the group.

London added, "Besides, this kitten probably already belongs to someone who is worried sick about it."

A male voice spoke up from nearby.

"I'm pretty sure that is *not* a kitten."

London turned and saw Cyrus Bannister standing there, with Audrey clinging to one arm. They had pushed through the crowd and were staring at the creature.

Cyrus disentangled himself from Audrey and held out a hand toward Amy.

"Let me have a look."

"Not a kitten?" Amy was visibly stunned.

She handed the animal to Cyrus. It was small enough to fit in his right hand.

"It's just as I thought," Cyrus said, examining the animal carefully. "What you've got here isn't a kitten at all, or even a close relative. It's not even native to Europe. These creatures normally live in the Sahara Desert and semi-arid regions in the Sinai. I'd be willing to bet that this one is missing from a zoo."

"What is it?" Amy asked weakly.

"This is a baby fennec fox," Cyrus told her. "I've heard of fennec foxes being kept as exotic house pets, but it's a practice I personally frown upon. Full-grown fennec foxes feed on small rodents, lizards, insects, and birds and their eggs—not a diet anybody here is in a position to supply. And this is hardly a hospitable environment for such an animal. Besides, this one is too small to be away from its mother."

A murmur of surprise passed through the group.

"The poor little thing," Audrey added. "And think about how

worried its mother must be."

Looking a bit relieved at this news, Elsie said, "I'll get on the phone and see if I can find out anything about a missing zoo animal."

"You should do that," Cyrus said with a nod. He handed the little creature back to Amy, then turned and gave London a bitter stare. With that, he stalked out of the lounge with Audrey at his side.

They're still mad at me for mentioning his name to the police, London realized.

In a way, she couldn't blame them, but she did wish she could ask Cyrus some questions. For example, how had his interview with the police gone this morning? And why had he been so fascinated by the Van Gogh painting of tulips in the Rijksmuseum? And what was he refusing to tell her about it?

Meanwhile, she had a more immediate matter to deal with.

Amy was just standing there holding the little animal close, with a tear running down her cheek.

"Come on, Amy," London said, taking her colleague gently by the arm. "Let's sit down and talk."

Amy nodded with a stifled sob and followed London to a table where they could talk more privately. When they sat down, she put the little fox on the table and pulled out her cell phone.

"Amy, I'm awfully sorry about this," London said. "I know how much I'd hate to have to give up Sir Reggie. But if Cyrus is right and this really is a lost zoo animal …"

"He's right," Amy said with a sigh. She held up the cell phone, showing a photo of a fennec fox and her kits. The young ones looked just like the animal on the table. The adult had a long fox face and huge ears.

"I really can't keep her," Amy said, wiping away another tear. Then she looked up at London and added, "Sometimes I really hate working on this ship. You're the one who gets to have all the fun and adventures."

London couldn't help but chuckle a little. She knew that Amy harbored a grudge because London had gotten the position of social director that Amy had wanted. But her new career had certainly not been all fun and adventures.

"Amy, right now I'm a murder suspect," London said. "I have to clear my own name. And not even for the first time."

"I hadn't thought of it that way," Amy said.

"It hasn't helped that you've been going around telling everybody that I found the dead body in the red-light district. And now half the ship suspects me of murder and God only knows what else."

Amy just stared at the baby fennec fox, which had gone to sleep on the table.

"Do you really think I killed anybody?" London asked.

Amy shrugged slightly.

"Probably not."

"Amy!" London said with roll of her eyes.

"OK, definitely not."

At that moment Elsie came over to them.

"I made some calls and found out that Cyrus was right," Elsie said. "A keeper at the Artis Zoo accidentally left an enclosure open, and a mother fennec fox and her two babies got loose. The mother and one baby have already been found, but everybody has been worried sick about this one. They've been afraid it might have gotten run over or fallen into a canal or …"

"Or gotten snatched up to be a house pet," Amy said, finishing Elsie's thought. "I understand."

"A couple of zoo employees are coming right over to pick the animal up," Elsie said.

As Elsie walked away, Amy petted the little animal.

She said, "Well, Dewdrop, I guess we'll be saying goodbye pretty soon. I hope you're happy in the zoo. At least you'll be back with your mama."

London looked at her watch. She still needed to get off the ship, to get to the bottom of the mystery of the murdered art restorer. But she felt that her conversation with Amy wasn't finished.

"Amy, what's been going on with you lately?" she asked. "You've been acting oddly, darting around, even hiding. What's going on?"

Again, the concierge just stared at the fox in silence for a moment.

"OK, if you must know," she finally said. "I've been doing everything I can to stay away from Emil."

"I thought so," London said. "But why?"

"Well, Emil and I were just starting to have a little *thing* together …"

"Yes, I know," London said, queasily remembering how she'd caught them making out in the library.

"It was fun at first," Amy continued. "Part of the fun was trying to keep it secret. But I realized pretty quickly that it wasn't going to work out. I mean, we're just so different, Emil and me. He's so stuffy and intellectual and uptight, and I'm … well, so cheerful and spontaneous, such a free spirit."

London managed not to sputter with laughter.

Amy, a free spirit?

"So I broke it off," Amy said. "Or at least I tried to. London, Emil is positively obsessed with me. He just won't leave me alone."

London struggled to make sense of what she was hearing.

"Are you sure about that, Amy?"

"Oh, I'm absolutely sure. And do you know what he did yesterday? He went out and bought some very expensive blue-and-white antique plaque thing that he set up in the library and showed off to everybody. Now, why do you think he did that?"

But before London could reply, Amy continued, "He bought it for *me,* of course."

London's eyes widened with disbelief.

"Did he tell you that?" she asked.

"No, not yet. But why else would a man buy a piece of china?"

Without pausing for an answer to her question, Amy chattered on, "It's obviously a gift for a woman he has a crush on. Which would definitely be yours truly. Haven't you noticed how he's been acting? The man is lovesick. London, what am I going to do? I can't keep avoiding him forever, but I don't want to hurt his feelings. How can I let him down easy? And how can I tell him I don't *want* that plaque? I don't even like it very much."

London's mouth had dropped open. Whatever else might be going on between Amy and Emil, London knew almost for certain that Amy was wrong about the plaque—and probably about a whole lot else.

For starters, that "piece of china" was considered a valuable work of art, and she was certain that Emil had bought it for himself.

He had told her, *"I have wanted an authentic* Delfts Blauw *ever since I was a little boy."*

"Amy, listen to me—" London began.

But before she could continue, she heard a man's voice behind her.

"Mevrouw Rose, I need to have a word with you."

London turned and saw *Hoofdinspecteur* Braam standing there with crossed arms and a stern expression on his face.

CHAPTER TWENTY FIVE

Feeling apprehensive, London stood up from the table. She found the sudden arrival of *Hoofdinspecteur* Braam a bit unnerving. It didn't help that Amy cried out, "London, have the police come to get you?"

She saw other faces in the lounge turning toward her to see what was happening.

"No, I think they're just here for a little chat," London replied, wondering what kind of rumors everybody would be spreading now. She left Amy sitting there with the little fox on the table in front of her and followed Braam across the lounge to a table near a window.

Although she wasn't surprised that Braam wanted to talk with her again, she felt a pit of worry in her stomach. Her discomfort grew when they sat down together, and he just sat silently gazing out the window.

Finally, he spoke to her in English.

"Such a lovely view of my city. I don't often get to see it from this perspective. Amsterdam looks so peaceful from here, doesn't it? It is hard to imagine how something so ugly as murder ever taking place here."

London could hear a note of irony in his voice.

As if he's toying with me, she thought.

"Of course," he continued, "the *Nachtmusik* seems to bring murder with it wherever it goes. I wonder why that is. Do you think you could explain that to me, Mevrouw Rose?"

"I'm afraid I can't," London said. "All I know is that you still seem to suspect me of a murder I didn't commit. And I don't know what to say to convince you otherwise."

Braam leaned back and tilted his head.

"It might help if you explained your activities this morning. I happen to know that you went ashore in order to … well, *snoop* I believe is the word for it in English. I stopped by the Zacht Coffeeshop a little while ago to have another word with the owner, Meneer Cornellison. He told me you had come by to ask him some questions."

London stifled a surge of alarm that the *hoofdinspecteur* had been checking up on her activities. Had he really come here to arrest her?

"That's true," she replied as evenly as she could.

"Now why would you do a thing like that?"

"To help you solve the case."

Braam scoffed.

"I don't remember asking for your help," he said.

London took a deep breath to settle her nerves. She realized that she'd better be upfront with the *hoofdinspecteur*. More than that, she figured it was probably a good idea to stop acting afraid of him.

Anyway, I'm not in the mood for games, she thought, as irritation overcame her anxiety.

"You didn't ask for my help," London said. "But if you persist in wasting time and energy investigating me when I didn't do anything, you can't blame me for pitching in to put you straight. I want to find Meneer Dekker's killer as much as you do. Maybe even more so, since so much is at stake for me."

Braam peered at her silently for a moment. London sensed that gears were turning in his head as he tried to figure out what to make of her. And in a way, London could understand his mystification. From what he'd told her yesterday, European law enforcement was abuzz with rumors about her.

London decided to keep right on being bold and direct.

"Tell me, *Hoofdinspecteur* Braam—what sorts of stories have you heard about me? If rumor has it that I'm some sort of international serial killer, why do I keep investigating the murders I've committed? And what about the culprits I've been catching? Are they really innocent, and I've been framing them? Have I been doing it so brilliantly that I've fooled the police in Gyor, Salzburg, and Regensburg? Is that what you've been hearing?"

Braam's brow knitted thoughtfully. Although he wasn't saying so, she suspected that the rumors he'd been hearing had been just about that crazy.

I'm an "urban legend," after all, she thought.

And she knew that one thing urban legends had in common was they got more and outlandish as they circulated.

But she detected a change in Braam's demeanor. Maybe, she thought, she was getting through to him. Maybe, hearing this scenario from her own lips made it seem less plausible.

Finally, Braam said, "So what have you learned so far?"

London stifled a sigh of relief. It seemed good that he was asking for her help. But was it really? Was he still trying to play a game of cat and mouse with her?

She said, “Well, Meneer Dekker didn’t exactly have many friends in De Wallen, and at least a few enemies—Meneer Cornellison himself, for example. Surely you haven’t ruled him out as a suspect.”

Braam let out a grunt of affirmation.

“I am considering many possibilities,” he said. “Who else did you visit during your little investigative outing this morning?”

London hesitated for a moment.

Just how upfront should I be? she wondered.

Maybe too much honesty would get her into trouble. But keeping her mouth shut didn’t seem to be an option.

She said, “I talked to a young sex worker who goes by the name of Kaneel Lied. Her real name is—”

Braam interrupted, “Yes, I know—Ingrid de Kuiper. So, you paid her a visit too, eh? You have had a rather busy day so far. Did she tell you anything of interest?”

London sensed a shift in Braam’s attitude, as if his curiosity about her was starting to outweigh his suspicions.

“She told me that Meneer Dekker was obsessed with her and that he wanted her to marry him.” London said. “She was shocked and probably a little scared and told him she didn’t want to see him anymore. He didn’t take it well. But I’m sure she told you all this as well. Are you thinking of *her* as a suspect?”

Braam shuffled his feet. London wondered whether he was to decide how much to open up to her, now that she seemed to be opening up to him.

Finally, he said, “My instincts tell me that Mevrouw de Kuiper does not have the makings of a killer.”

London was glad to hear this, for Ingrid’s sake. She too couldn’t believe that the intelligent young woman who was putting herself through college by working in Amsterdam’s sex trade had killed anybody.

And yet ...

London shivered as she realized—she *did* know something that Braam didn’t know. It had to do with Ingrid’s older sister, Femke. When Femke had opened up about it, Ingrid had asked her why she hadn’t told her story to the police.

“Why do you think *I didn’t tell them?”* Femke had replied.

London suddenly wavered. She'd liked both of the sisters, and she didn't want to get either of them in trouble. If she told Braam about the conversation, he would certainly put Femke on his suspects list.

But maybe he should, she thought.

After all, London had no way of knowing whether or not Femke might be the killer.

Choosing her words carefully, London said, "When you visited Ingrid, did you also meet her sister Femke?"

Braam nodded.

"Yes, she's security guard at the Botanical Garden. What about her?"

"Well, Femke told me something that I happen to know she didn't tell you," London said.

Braam's eyes widened with interest.

"And what was that?" he asked.

"One day Pier Dekker came around to the houseboat where the sisters live. Ingrid wasn't home, but Dekker talked with Femke. He tried to talk Femke into helping him get back into Ingrid's good graces."

"What did Femke tell him?" Braam asked.

"I don't know, she wouldn't say," London said.

"Do you think she may have threatened him?"

"I really have no idea," London said.

But maybe that isn't true, London thought, remembering what Femke had told Ingrid about Dekker.

"Even if he hadn't gotten killed, he wouldn't have come around bothering you anymore."

It sure sounded as though Femke might have threatened the man.

Braam stroked his chin thoughtfully.

"Interesting," he said. "I appreciate your sharing this information—that is, if it *is* information and not just something you are making up to deflect suspicion from yourself."

London managed not to roll her eyes with exasperation. She still hadn't convinced Braam of her innocence.

Meanwhile, she noticed that across the lounge two uniformed zoo employees had arrived at Amy's table with an animal carrier. As they coaxed the fennec fox kit away from Amy, the concierge wiped her eyes but didn't put up any resistance.

That's one problem solved, London thought.

She also realized that she had a question of her own to ask the *Hoofdinspecteur*.

"Maybe you could tell *me* something," London said to Braam. "I happen to know that you came around the ship this morning to talk to one of our passengers, Cyrus Bannister. What did you find out from him?"

Braam let out a scoff of annoyance.

"He was not especially cooperative," he said. "In fact, I am pretty sure there is something he is not telling me. Do you have any idea what it might be?"

London's brain clicked away as she tried to think of an answer to that question.

Maybe something to do with the Van Gogh painting? she wondered, remembering Cyrus's strange behavior after he'd stood staring at it. But she couldn't imagine what possible connection there could be between that painting and Dekker's murder.

"I don't know," London said. "But I think he might have had an entirely different matter on his mind."

"Can you think of anything else I should know?"

London shook her head no.

Braam stood up from the table and spoke again with a note of irony.

"Well, then, I suppose that brings this charming little visit to an end. You are an interesting woman, London Rose. Perhaps *too* interesting, one might even say. If you are deceiving me in any way, you can be sure I will find you out. You won't get away with anything. Meanwhile, I will thank you to keep your nose out of my investigation from now on."

With a tip of his cap, he strode on out of the lounge.

Is that all he's got to say to me? London wondered as she watched him leave. While she hadn't exactly expected him to take her into custody, she'd thought he'd at least insist that she stay aboard the ship.

As London mulled over Braam's parting words, she noticed that Amy seemed to have recovered from her grief at the loss of her fennec fox and was now giving Elsie a hand with drink orders. As she delivered drinks to a table and chatted with the customers, Amy glanced over her shoulder at London. The customers, too, were giving London skeptical looks.

She's spreading gossip again, London thought with a sigh.

It was bad enough that she hadn't fully succeeded in shaking off

Hoofdinspecteur Braam's suspicions that she might be the killer. There just didn't seem to be any way to get Amy to stop raising doubts aboard the *Nachtmusik.*

Certain that confronting Amy all over again would be a waste of time, London decided to focus on solving the murder case and clearing her name.

Of course, she knew the *hoofdinspecteur* would not approve. She remembered what he had said just now.

"I will thank you to keep your nose out of my investigation from now on."

But she realized …

It wasn't exactly an order.

Surely Braam wasn't naive enough to think she was going to stop looking for the truth in order to earn his "thanks."

In fact, he probably expected her to do exactly what she was determined to do right now—leave the ship and head back into Amsterdam and leave no stone unturned until the real murderer was caught.

Which surely means that he'll be watching me. Or some of his men will.

Regardless, she figured she'd better get going before something else happened to hold her up.

But as London hurried toward the exit from the lounge, she heard a sound that made her stop in her tracks.

I guess I'd better find out about that first, she told herself reluctantly.

CHAPTER TWENTY SIX

For a moment, London stood frozen in place, torn between her desire to get off the ship and her reaction to the sound that had stopped her in her tracks.

It was music. It sounded to her like Bach, and it was coming from behind the closed door to the library.

Emil is in there, she realized.

She hadn't even seen the historian around at all today. Was he hiding in the ship's library? It was, of course, his domain, but it was supposed to be open to the passengers and crew. Not that there were likely to be a lot of patrons today, with most passengers ashore enjoying Amsterdam. But sooner or later someone was going to want information or a novel or a video.

Of course, Emil's behavior had been very strange lately. And so had Amy's.

She remembered Amy's recent words.

"Emil is positively obsessed with me. He just won't leave me alone."

It seemed high time for her to get to the bottom of whatever was going on between the historian and the concierge.

But do I really want to know? she asked herself.

And did she really want to fix the situation right now, when she had so much else to do?

London sighed. As social director, any discord on the ship seemed to always fall within her realm of responsibilities. She decided she needed to tend to this one as promptly as possible—certainly before she ventured ashore again.

Besides, it should only take a few minutes, London thought.

Or so she hoped.

When she rapped on the door, she received a startling reply.

"Go away."

It was Emil's voice, all right. But it was not the sort of greeting she would expect from him.

She tried turning the knob, but the door was locked.

"Emil, it's London," she said.

"Oh," she heard Emil say, speaking less sharply now. "By all means, come on in."

London tapped her foot impatiently.

"The door is locked," she said.

"You have a key, don't you?"

London stood staring at the door for a moment.

What's the matter with that man? she wondered.

Couldn't he be bothered to walk over to the door and open it?

London didn't have any choice except to use her master key to let herself into the library.

Sure enough, Emil was sitting with his feet up on a long table, gazing raptly at the large blue and white plaque, which was perched nearby on an easel. He was humming along to the music.

"Emil, what are you doing?" London asked.

"What do you *think* I'm doing?" Emil said. "I'm savoring this wonderful acquisition, accompanied by a most appropriate choice in music—Bach's complete Brandenburg Concertos."

As he waved his finger as if conducting the music, London stood glaring at him.

"Emil, how long have you been sitting here?"

"Just during the last hour or so, I suppose," he said. "First I made sure that everyone who was interested had a chance to come around and admire this exquisite object. Then I figured I deserved some time alone with it."

"Are you planning to sit here like this for the rest of the day?"

"Would it be so bad if I did?" Emil said.

"Yes, actually, it would be," London said. "The library is supposed to be available to passengers. In fact, *you're* supposed to be available to passengers."

London walked over to the door and opened it.

"What are you doing?" Emil asked with a note of alarm.

"I'm doing what you should do," London said. "I'm opening the library to the public."

"Please don't do that," Emil said. "At least not today."

"Why not?"

Emil was silent for a moment.

"Well, if you must know," he said, "I'm avoiding Amy."

"Really?" London said with a scoff. "Why?"

"I would really rather not get into all that."

London planted herself in the open doorframe.

"I'm not moving from this spot until you do," she replied firmly.

Of course, the truth was that London was anxious to get away from here as quickly as possible. She only hoped that Emil wouldn't call her bluff.

Emil let out a groan of despair.

"All right, I will tell you," Emil said. "But please close the door first."

London closed the door. She crossed her arms and stood staring at Emil.

"Well?" she said.

Emil shook his head miserably.

"London, there is something wrong with that woman—Amy, I mean. Perhaps you were not aware that she and I had a bit of a … well, a workplace romance, I suppose is one way to put it. Very briefly."

Oh, yes, I was aware, London thought ironically.

Like Amy, Emil seemed intent on forgetting how London had caught them together right here in the library.

"Well, it all happened so quickly," Emil said. "It was much too impulsive on my part. I really was not thinking through the consequences. And in my infatuated state, I overlooked the woman's character flaws. I had not realized that she's actually rather a … well, to put it bluntly, a cold fish. And I, of course, am a rather hot-blooded and impetuous male specimen, if I do say so myself."

London choked back the laughter that threatened to break out.

Hot-blooded? Emil?

"Anyway," Emil continued, "I realized very quickly that I had made a dreadful mistake—in fact, that both of us had made a mistake. I told her so, but she did not take it well. She has been following me everywhere—or almost everywhere. As long as people kept coming into the library to look at the *Delfts Blauw,* she at least left me alone in here. But now that the passengers' interest is quenched, so to speak, I just know she will descend upon me at any moment—that is, if I leave that door open."

Emil shrugged slightly.

"That is why I have shut myself in here," he said. "Do not worry, though. Amy is not a very tenacious and determined creature, let alone a passionate one. Her focus is very limited, and her concentration span is just about nil. Soon she will tire of pestering me if I just keep ignoring her. She will turn her attentions toward a different fellow—someone more appropriately bland and unexceptional, one can hope. You do understand my, er, predicament, eh, London?"

Again, London fought back a sputter of laughter.

"Oh, I understand perfectly, Emil," she said. "Thanks for being so open and honest with me."

Without another word, she turned and walked out of the library and shut the door behind her. She walked straight across the Amadeus Lounge, where she found Amy hovering over a table. She didn't seem to be serving drinks. Instead, she was talking to the customers with what seemed to be gleeful animation.

More gossip, London realized.

For once she was glad not to find Amy trying to do anything useful.

London grabbed her colleague by the elbow.

"Come with me," London said.

Amy blushed as London dragged her away from the table.

"Oh, London, I hope you didn't think I was talking about *you* just now. Whatever is going on between you and the law is your own business, and I respect that. Truly I do."

Hah, London thought.

"But where are we going?" Amy asked as London hauled her out of the lounge.

"To the library," London said.

Amy sputtered, "But—but—isn't Emil in there?"

Exactly, London thought.

She unlocked the door and opened it and shoved Amy inside.

The concierge and the historian stared at each other with mouths agape.

London waved her finger at both of them.

"The two of you have got some issues to sort out," she said. "And you're going to do it right now."

"I don't understand," Amy said.

"What do you mean?" Emil asked.

"Amy, tell me something," London said, pointing at Emil. "Does this man strike you as a hot-blooded and impetuous male specimen?"

"Hardly," Amy said, obviously surprised by the question.

"And Emil," London added, pointing at Amy, "does this woman strike you as a cheerful and spontaneous free spirit?"

"Anything but," Emil said.

"And which of you is trying to break off this little workplace romance of yours?" London demanded.

"I am," Emil and Amy said in perfect unison.

Then they stared at each other with surprise.

London put her hands on her hips and glared at them.

"Whatever is going on between you two, it has got to stop. I'm leaving the two of you together—and I don't want to see either of your faces until you've worked this out and are ready to behave like adults and dependable staff members. And if you don't … well, so help me, I'll find some way to lock you up or even handcuff you together until you do. Is that understood?"

Emil and Amy nodded in mute astonishment.

"Good," London said. "Now if you'll excuse me, I've got to clear myself of suspicion of murder."

London left the library and shut the door behind her. She stood outside listening for a moment. Soon she heard voices inside the library—quietly at first, then growing louder. She sensed that a full-scale argument was about to break out.

Good, London thought. *That's just what they need to clear the air.*

And now she finally had a chance to go ashore and start investigating in earnest. She brushed her hands with satisfaction and headed into the reception area. But before she got to the gangplank, her phone rang.

Her heard jumped up in her throat as she saw who had texted her.

It was none other than Jeremy Lapham, the CEO of Epoch World Cruise Lines.

And the text read:

Video chat. Right now.

CHAPTER TWENTY SEVEN

London wasn't surprised to hear from Jeremy Lapham. Just last night Captain Hays had told her to be prepared for this.

"Don't be surprised if he wants to talk to you in the near future."

And Lapham's message said, *"right now."*

The moment of reckoning had come.

She turned back into the Amadeus Lounge and hurried toward an isolated table in a corner of the big room. As she walked, she couldn't help but wonder if this meant the end of the tour … or at least the end of her job.

Anxiously, she opened up her video chat app on her cellphone.

In moments, Mr. Lapham made his usual enigmatic appearance. His webcam was tilted so London couldn't see his eyes or even most of his face—just his neck and his cleft chin and a pair of thin lips. But she had a clear view of his elegantly patterned velvet smoking jacket and an extremely fluffy black and white cat that lay comfortably in the man's lap.

She could actually hear the creature purring contentedly as Mr. Lapham scratched it under its chin.

But Lapham's first words sounded anything but contented.

"London, I want to talk with you about possibly ending the tour."

"Oh, no," London gasped as she collapsed into a chair at the table.

"I'm afraid that I'm getting rather mixed messages from Alex, my new astrologer. I was rather unsettled by his most recent reading, which was shockingly pessimistic. I suppose I'd hoped he was wrong. Alas, judging by the events of yesterday, it sounds like he has proven to be more than correct."

London wasn't completely surprised at the idea of Mr. Lapham consulting an astrologer. As odd as it had seemed to her, he'd done the same thing in the past.

"Are you sure?" she said. "The passengers have been thrilled with your discounts and vouchers. In fact, most of them are out enjoying another day in Amsterdam."

"I'm pleased to hear that," the CEO's voice softened as he

continued. "But what about this latest unpleasant setback? Captain Hays has been updating me regularly. You don't need to tell me the whole story. Just please put my mind at ease about one thing. Tell me you have *not* been killing all these people."

"I haven't killed anyone," London said, oddly relieved to be telling him the truth about that.

"Very good," Mr. Lapham. "I haven't achieved my success in the business world without being an excellent judge of character. And I sense that you've got very good character indeed. I know I can take you at your word."

"Thank you," London said, her throat catching a little with gratitude.

"And you're quite sure that nobody else aboard the *Nachtmusik* is killing people either?"

London swallowed hard. She wished she could simply say "yes" with complete confidence. But Cyrus Bannister's peculiar behavior yesterday at the Rijksmuseum was still worrying her. And judging by what *Hoofdinspecteur* Braam had told her just now, Cyrus was still on his suspects list—along with London herself, of course.

"I don't know," London admitted. "I hope not."

"Well, the truth will come out, I suppose," Mr. Lapham said with a sigh. "I assume that Bob Turner is hot on the trail of the culprit."

London felt momentarily stymied.

It had actually been Mr. Lapham's idea Bob Turner to help with the boat's security. As far as London knew, nobody had ever told Mr. Lapham that Bob Turner was a pretty poor excuse for a detective. Certainly nobody had revealed to him that London had actually solved all of the murders. She had been glad to let Bob claim all the credit for that, so the CEO still believed that his security man was a crack crime fighter.

London tried to choose her words carefully.

"Mr. Lapham, I'm afraid Bob Turner is … well, under the weather."

"Is he now? What has he come down with? Typhoid? Yellow Fever? Smallpox?"

"Um, I think he has a cold," London said.

"A cold!" Mr. Lapham said with a scoff. "Where is he right now?"

"In his stateroom, sir. I … I think he's worried about spreading whatever it is he's got around the boat."

"So he's self-quarantined with the sniffles while a murderer is at large?" Mr. Lapham said. "That's preposterous. I expect you to pay him a visit and tell him under no uncertain terms that he'd better come out of his shell. He needs to get back to work."

"Yes, sir."

"And now ..."

She sensed that Mr. Lapham was hesitating.

"London, I'm sure you're aware that the future of the entire Epoch World Cruise Lines is in rather serious jeopardy. My company was faltering even before the *Nachtmusik* began its cruise. My hope had been that European river tours would prove to be more profitable that ocean cruises. Alas, I hadn't reckoned on a murder happening every several days."

"I'm sure you hadn't sir," London said.

"I'd also hoped I could mollify customer dissatisfaction with extra benefits. But those perks are costing the corporation untold amounts of money, and at this point, I see no end to them. So what I called to ask you is ..."

Mr. Lapham paused again.

"London, I hired you because of a wide range of abilities, including an excellent aptitude in business. And now I'm hoping you'll help me make a difficult business decision. Do you think I should cancel the rest of the *Nachtmusik*'s voyage and give all the passengers a full refund, then start Epoch World Cruise Lines all over again, completely from scratch?"

Why is he asking me *this?* London wondered.

"Uh, sir, I hardly feel qualified ..." she began.

"Oh, my dear, you underestimate yourself," Mr. Lapham said. "You've proven yourself a versatile and talented employee. I have been deeply impressed by your work and your dedication to the company."

As much as London appreciated the compliment, she felt hopelessly overwhelmed by Mr. Lapham's question.

"Have you ... asked Captain Hays for his opinion, sir?" she said.

"I have," Mr. Lapham said. "He didn't give me an answer. Actually, I'm afraid he got rather agitated about it. He ... well, he sputtered and babbled without really saying anything at all."

Small wonder, London thought.

Mr. Lapham added, "I trust your judgment, London. I really do."

London's mind boggled at what her boss was asking of her.

Whatever she said to him right now would affect the future of Epoch World Cruise Lines—and probably the careers of everyone who worked for it as well. Would he really shut down the cruise if she said to? Would she be responsible for putting everyone in the crew out of a job? On the other hand, what if she insisted that he keep the tour going and the company lost more money and had to shut down completely anyhow? And where was that astrologer he was always talking about consulting?

London decided she needed to put her foot down about the matter.

"Mr. Lapham, I'm sorry, but I just can't help you with this," London said. "It's simply not my place to answer a question like that."

Mr. Lapham fell silent for a moment.

"Yes, of course you are right," he finally said. "We mustn't ignore the fact that higher forces are at work here. I really must Alex to update his reading, give me more astrological data to make an informed decision."

London couldn't help feeling a bit relieved that her boss was shifting the responsibility off her own shoulders. Even so, she felt a little queasy at the thought of an astrologer deciding the future of Epoch World Cruise Lines—and her own future as well.

But what do I know? she reminded herself.

Maybe Mr. Lapham was right to investigate the role of "higher forces." After all, the *Nachtmusik* was experiencing a remarkable run of bad luck these days.

Mr. Lapham said, "My dear, you may go get back to work now. I hope it goes without saying that I don't want you to leave the ship until this unfortunate mystery is resolved."

"Sir?" London asked with surprise.

"What I mean to say is, I absolutely do not want you to playing 'Nancy Drew,' like you did back in Hungary. You almost got yourself killed, remember? And it was my fault, because you were following my instructions. Well, I learn from my mistakes. I hired Bob Turner specifically to keep you out of trouble. Make sure he gets out of bed and blows his nose and gets back to work. You will do that, won't you?"

"I will, sir," London said.

"And can I trust you to stay out of trouble?"

London balked for a moment at answering the question. She'd already been delayed in her quest for answers much too long. She needed to go ashore as soon as she possibly could. But she couldn't bring herself to say so to Mr. Lapham. For all his peculiarities, she'd learned that he had a protective streak, especially toward her. She'd come to like him for that.

The truth was that Mr. Lapham had no idea how much danger she'd gotten herself into on those murder cases in Salzburg and Regensburg.

"I'll stay out of trouble, sir," she said.

"I am very glad to hear you say that," Mr. Lapham said with an audible sigh of relief. "Now I will let you get back to your duties."

He ended the call, and London sat at the table staring at the phone, wondering what had just happened? It was as though a bombshell had been dropped and she didn't yet know if it had been a dud or whether a huge explosion was in progress.

Was she going to be out of a job?

Was everyone?

Could she have said something more helpful?

She'd just told him she would stay out of trouble, and she knew that probably wasn't true. In fact, she could leave the ship right this minute and start investigating again.

But London realized she still had one errand to run. She'd told Mr. Lapham that she'd have a talk with Bob Turner, and she needed to keep that promise, at least.

As she got up from her chair, she heard a familiar yap.

Sir Reggie!

It seemed like the perfect moment for her canine companion to appear. As soon as she finished talking with Bob, she and Sir Reggie could leave the ship together.

But when she turned toward the bark, she saw that things weren't going to be that simple.

CHAPTER TWENTY EIGHT

The yap had indeed come from Sir Reggie.

London's Yorkie was perched in a chair at one of the tables. Across from the little dog sat Stanley Tedrow, talking earnestly to Sir Reggie with animated gestures. London was glad to see that the aspiring writer had made it back to the boat safely after wandering ashore yesterday. She wasn't eager to chat with him right now, but she had to pass by that table on her way out of the lounge. And besides, she hoped her little dog would join her.

As she drew near, Mr. Tedrow was saying, "So you can see my problem, can't you, pal? I just don't know what to do."

Sir Reggie tilted his head, looking as though he understood exactly what was being said.

"Hi, Mr. Tedrow," London said.

Mr. Tedrow looked up at her with surprise.

"Oh, hi there, Miss, uh …"

London almost chuckled aloud. She wondered how many times she'd introduced herself to him, only to be forgotten every time.

"London Rose," she said. "You can call me London."

"Oh, yeah, London. Now I remember."

"How are you doing today?" London asked.

"OK, I guess."

London felt tempted to end the conversation and be on her way. The sooner she checked in with Bob, the sooner she could go back ashore and resume investigating. And yet she sensed that Mr. Tedrow was not exactly "OK," and it was her responsibility to find out why not.

"How is the book going?" she asked him.

London expected him to give her his usual answer—that he didn't want to risk spoiling it for her.

Instead, he said, "Well, that's just what Sir Reggie and I were discussing right now. I hate to admit it, but I'm blocked. Completely stymied. Even getting out and around yesterday didn't stir up the old creative juices."

"Could I help?" London asked.

"Naw, I don't think so," Mr. Tedrow said. "Don't take this the wrong way, miss, but I need someone with more expertise. You know, some real hands-on experience in homicide and criminal investigation and such."

London chose not to mention her own recent experience in such matters.

"What about Bob Turner?" she asked.

Mr. Tedrow shrugged and squirmed in his chair. Then he looked at Sir Reggie as if he were talking only to the dog.

"Well, Bob isn't available right now," he said. "He's holed up in his room, under the weather, as you may have heard."

London felt oddly invisible—as if she were a ventriloquist "throwing her voice" to Sir Reggie, who certainly appeared to be fully engaged in the conversation.

Then Mr. Tedrow asked, "Tell me the truth, now. Do you think Bob is really sick?"

London had been half-wondering the same thing herself. Bob's refusal to even see the ship's medic had struck her as odd.

Mr. Tedrow drummed his fingers on the table.

"You know," he said to Sir Reggie, "Bob has been going around bragging that he's solved two murder cases—no, three—since we set sail. But folks around here are saying he never did anything like that at all. They say some woman has been doing the real detective work. She works aboard the ship doing something—a *maître d'*, or major domo, or superintendent, something like that."

Again, London decided not to set him straight by telling him *she* was the woman he'd been hearing about.

But then Mr. Tedrow added, "Some folks are saying it was this woman who really *did* kill someone, right here in Venice or whatever waterlogged city this is."

London felt a bit stung. If she'd had any doubt that some people aboard the *Nachtmusik* thought she might be a murderer, this confirmed it.

Mr. Tedrow looked Sir Reggie in the eye.

"What I'm wondering is—maybe Bob doesn't have a cold at all. Maybe he's just embarrassed. Now that everybody thinks he's no great shakes as a security guy, maybe he's ashamed to show his face around here."

London felt a flash of agreement.

Mr. Tedrow kept talking directly to Sir Reggie.

"The thing is—I don't really care if the guy's a blowhard. He's fun. He tells great stories. And he does come up with good story ideas. I miss him. And I'm worried about him. What if he spends the rest of his life locked up all alone in that room of his?"

London had to stop herself from laughing aloud. Mr. Tedrow himself had spent days alone in his own room, working on his mystery novel and completely ignoring the first several stops on the tour. But, of course, he was right. That wouldn't be comfortable for the gregarious security man. If Bob Turner wasn't coming out of his room, something must be wrong.

Well, the CEO had ordered her to pay Bob a visit, so she had been on her way there anyhow.

She said to the aspiring author, "You know, I was just going to check up on Bob. Do you want to come along?"

Mr. Tedrow nodded to Sir Reggie and said, "Hey, that's a great idea. Let's go."

London felt her mood improve as the man and the dog got up from the table and followed her. Glancing toward the library as they left the Amadeus Lounge, she saw that the door was still closed. There was no sign of what might be going on in there, but she hoped that Amy and Emil were settling things without causing each other any harm.

As they crossed the reception area, she gave a wistful glance at the gangway outside the glass doors. But leaving the ship and solving the murder would have to wait a little longer.

They walked along the passageway toward Bob's stateroom, and she knocked at the door.

"Who is it?" she heard Bob's usual growly, monotonous voice call out from inside.

"It's me, London Rose. I need to talk with you a minute."

"I'm sick," Bob replied. "I don't want to give you whatever I've got."

"Mr. Tedrow is here too," London said through the door. "And Sir Reggie."

A silence fell.

"OK, let yourselves in," Bob said. "But keep a safe distance. I'm stuffed to the gills with germs of some kind. I'm like some living breathing petri dish."

London used her key to unlock and open the door. Stanley hurried on inside ahead of her. As London stepped inside with the little dog following her, she was startled by what she saw.

The comfortable sitting area and the big bedroom were still impressively spacious. But the décor—hints of early 19th-century Vienna—had had vanished under dirty clothes, snack wrappings, and dirty dishes. Bob clearly hadn't let the ship's maids do their usual cleaning and tidying up.

I guess he likes it this way, she thought.

And she couldn't blame him for wanting to make himself feel more at home. It hadn't been his idea to stay in this luxury suite in the first place. He'd wound up here because no other rooms had been available.

Bob himself was in pajamas, sitting up in bed propped up by pillows. He was watching a crime show on the big screen TV with the sound muted. Reflections of the action flickered in the mirrored sunglasses he always wore.

London noticed an empty space on the wall where a portrait had previously hung.

"What happened to Beethoven?" she asked.

"I shut him up in the closet," Bob growled. "Mr. B and I didn't get along. He looked so grouchy all the time, such a bummer to be around."

Then with a chuckle Bob added, "He was also hard to carry on a conversation with. He's kind of hard of hearing, you know. Hey, I hear there's a lot of great art here in Amsterdam. Do you think somebody could find me a nice big painting of Elvis to hang there?"

Before London could say that was pretty unlikely, Mr. Tedrow pulled up a chair next to the bed.

Bob protested, "Hey, Stan, didn't I just tell you to keep your distance?"

"I don't need to," Mr. Tedrow said. "I've never been sick a day in my life. I'm immune to every contagious disease known to man. You couldn't make me sick if you tried."

The two men both looked a bit alarmed as Sir Reggie jumped onto the bed to join them. London remembered Mr. Tedrow telling her about Bob's mystery illness.

"I'd sure hate to have Sir Reggie come down with it."

She said, "Guys, don't worry about Sir Reggie. I'm pretty sure dogs don't catch most human diseases."

London obediently kept her distance from the bed, even though she found herself doubting that Bob was really the least bit sick.

"So, what's up, fellas?" Bob asked Reggie and Mr. Tedrow.

London felt a flicker of worry as Mr. Tedrow cleared his throat, apparently trying to decide what to say. Was he going to confront Bob with his suspicion that the security man was hiding out of embarrassment over his own incompetence?

But Mr. Tedrow's expression softened.

"I'm having trouble with my book," he said. "I thought maybe you could help me."

"You came to the right place, as usual," Bob said. "What's your problem, Stan?"

"Well, it has to do with moving a body. A dead body. After a murder."

"And?" Bob asked.

"Well, I don't know how to do it."

"How to do what?"

"Move the body."

Bob looked puzzled, and London felt the same way.

Bob said, "Well, strictly speaking, Stan, *you* don't have to move anybody's body. I mean, you're just the writer. You're not actually a character in the story."

"Yeah?" Mr. Tedrow said, as if surprised by this insight.

"Yeah. Now I've done lots of research on the subject of moving bodies around, read lots of forensic reports, including FBI stuff that would make your hair stand on end. But if you want my help figuring out how it's done, you're going to have to give me more info to work with. You know, facts, data, details, specifics, particulars."

"Such as?" Mr. Tedrow said.

"Well, for example, do you want the body dumped out in the open, or deliberately concealed? Is the victim dressed, or partly dressed, or stark naked? Has the victim just been plopped there, or was he or she put into some kind of peculiar pose or position? What do your autopsy reports and crime scene photos tell you about who moved the body and how?"

"Um, well," Mr. Tedrow said cautiously, "strictly speaking, *nobody* is supposed to move the body."

"Huh?" Bob said.

"It just … well, moves."

Bob scratched his head. London felt as if she shared his increasing perplexity.

"Uh, Stan, this might be kind of a problem," Bob said. "Corpses don't tend to have a lot of ambulatory function. They're called 'stiffs' for a reason. They stay put if they're left alone."

"They don't move even by accident?"

Bob stared at him for a moment. Then a light seemed to come on in his eyes.

"Maybe it could happen," he said. "Like, maybe because of some natural disaster."

"Like a mudslide?" Stan asked.

"Yeah, or maybe an avalanche."

Mr. Tedrow snapped his fingers excitedly.

"Hey, maybe I could set my book in a ski resort!" he said.

"Now we're talking! It's the perfect locale for a murder! Now let's get down to business …"

Bob's voice faded as he looked at London. Mr. Tedrow looked at her as well.

Bob said, "Hey, London, no offense, but … I'm not sure you should be in on this conversation."

"Bob's right," Mr. Tedrow said. "We don't want to spoil the story for you."

London smiled broadly.

"I understand," she said. "I'll let you guys get right to work."

London was pleased that Sir Reggie jumped off the bed and followed her out of the room. She really did want his company—and perhaps even his help—for the tasks ahead.

She pulled the door shut behind her and stooped down to pet her little dog.

"Well, pal, that went better than we could have hoped for, huh?" she said. "Mr. Tedrow is getting help with his book, and Bob isn't even acting sick anymore."

She thought for a moment, then added, "Of course, I didn't do exactly what Mr. Lapham told me to do. I didn't tell Bob to get to work on the real-life murder case. But …"

Rising to her feet, she said, "I can't help thinking that things are better this way."

But as she started to walk away, London's eye was caught by the name on the door directly across the hall—the Arnold Schoenberg Suite. It was the other grand suite on the ship, and of course London knew who lived there.

She was well aware that the occupant of that suite wouldn't want to talk with her.

But she was eager to get back to solving this murder, and that person could tell her some things she needed to know.

She stepped across the hall and gathered her nerve to knock on the door.

CHAPTER TWENTY NINE

London hesitated before the door to the Schoenberg suite, remembering the scornful glare she'd gotten from its inhabitant just a little while ago. Cyrus Bannister had always been an aloof, superior personality, but his demeanor had been even worse since yesterday's visit to the Rijksmuseum.

Apparently, he hadn't been any more agreeable with *Hoofdinspecteur* Braam. She remembered the inspector's words.

"He was not especially cooperative. In fact, I am pretty sure there is something he is not telling me."

As she stood there, Sir Reggie let out an impatient little yap.

"You're right," London said to her dog. "I've got to be brave."

She knocked on the door and was only mildly surprised when Audrey Bolton opened it. Although at first Audrey and Cyrus had struck London as an unlikely couple, they seemed to be pretty inseparable.

"Oh, London," Audrey said, looking startled to see her. "Uh, how can I help you?"

"I was hoping to talk with Cyrus," London said.

A sort of deer-in-the-headlights look came over Audrey, as if she didn't know what to say. Even her unruly curly hair seemed to leap out in all directions with alarm.

"I—I'll see if he's available," Audrey stammered.

She turned and called across the living area toward a wall of folding doors that had been pulled shut to close off the bedroom area of the suite.

"Cyrus, someone would like a word with you."

"Is it London Rose?" Cyrus called from the other side of the door.

"Yes."

"Tell her to go away."

Audrey looked flustered.

She said to London, "He's still angry about you reporting him to the police."

London stifled a sigh.

"Audrey, I didn't *report* him to anybody. We already talked about this. I simply told the police the truth—that he and the murder victim had an argument. If I hadn't said that much, someone else surely would have. It did happen in a public place, after all."

Audrey stood frozen with indecision. Earlier, she'd seemed to share in Cyrus's indignation, but now she appeared to be thinking everything through again.

Finally, she whispered to London, "Let me talk to him."

Audrey walked over to the folding doors and pushed them partly open. She disappeared into the other area, pulling the doors shut behind her. London could hear Audrey and Cyrus talking. Although she couldn't make out what they were saying, it sounded like Audrey was trying to be persuasive.

As she waited, London also looked around the suite, which she hadn't been in before. Unlike Bob's matching space, everything here was neat and orderly. The décor was strong and simple, with colorful abstract paintings on the walls along with a stern portrait of the composer Arnold Schoenberg.

Sir Reggie let out a discontented little whine, apparently in response to the odd sounds in the suite. The music playing was a dissonant string quartet with no melody that London could pick out.

By Schoenberg, of course, London realized.

"I know how you feel Sir Reggie," London murmured. "It wouldn't be the kind of thing I'd pick out for casual listening. But it seems to suit Cyrus, and maybe Audrey as well."

She wondered about the kind of "thing" Audrey was clearly having with Cyrus. Although Audrey herself had a prickly personality, London had gotten to like her. In fact, they'd wound up working together as a team to solve the murder back in Bamberg.

On one hand, it seemed nice that Audrey had found a little romance in her life.

On the other hand …

What if Cyrus is actually a murderer?

While London was considering that question, Audrey reopened the folding doors.

"Come on in," she said to London.

London and Sir Reggie followed her into the bedroom.

On the far side of a big, neatly made-up bed, Cyrus was sitting in an easy chair with a book in his lap. The book appeared to be a biography of Vincent van Gogh.

"So do you still think I'm a murderer?" Cyrus growled to London.

"It doesn't matter what *I* think," London said. "What matters is what the police think. And right now, they're as suspicious of me as they are of you. Maybe more so."

"That's too bad," Cyrus said unsympathetically. "I don't know what you expect me to do about it."

"Well, maybe you should just tell me the truth," London said.

"About what?"

"About whatever it is you *didn't* tell the *Hoofdinspecteur* this morning."

"I told him everything I know."

"He doesn't think so," London said. "And frankly, neither do I."

Cyrus shrugged and squirmed a little in his chair.

"I didn't like the murder victim," he said. "I had a little spat with him. I'm sure that's not a crime."

"There was more to it than that," London said.

"Like what?"

London thought for a moment, mentally trying to put the pieces of this puzzle together.

Finally, she said, "You were awfully interested in that Van Gogh painting we saw just before we went to the Night Watch Gallery and you got into that argument with Meneer Dekker. The painting of the tulips."

"It's a masterpiece," Cyrus said with another shrug. "Naturally I was interested."

"Not just interested," London said. "Really, really curious. Worried, even. You wouldn't tell me why at the time. I think you should tell me now."

Cyrus grunted and rolled his eyes.

"This is ridiculous," he grumbled.

Audrey was standing nearby watching and listening anxiously.

"I think you should tell her, Cyrus," she said. "Tell her what you told me."

Cyrus grumbled and shuffled his feet on the floor. Then he glanced up at Audrey, who was beginning to look a little impatient with him.

For a long moment, he seemed to be debating silently.

Then, to London's surprise, Cyrus leaned forward in his chair and spoke directly to her.

“Do you remember what that docent, Helga, said about the Van Gogh paintings they had on exhibit in the Rijksmuseum?”

London thought back to Helga’s little lecture.

“Helga admitted that the museum didn’t have many Van Gogh paintings,” London replied. “But she said the ones they did have showed his development as an artist. His early paintings were muted and realistic with subtle brushstrokes. His later paintings were bold and colorful, with thick layers of paint. She said sometimes he even squeezed paint directly of its tube onto the canvas.”

“Exactly,” Cyrus said with a nod. “Now, I happen to know a great deal about Van Gogh’s work. *Tulips* is a very early painting of his. And when you look at it, you can see how consistent it is with his early work. The painting is detailed and subtle, done with restraint and careful brush strokes. Except …”

Cyrus paused and stroked his chin.

“Go on and tell her, Cyrus,” Audrey said.

Cyrus crossed his arms and continued, “There was one petal on one tulip that looked weirdly out of place. It was painted more boldly than the rest, and the paint was very thick. That petal alone looked like something from Van Gogh’s later work. He hadn’t even developed that style of painting when he did the *Tulips.*”

“But how is that possible?” London asked.

“That’s exactly what I wondered,” Cyrus said. “Then the docent took us through the Gallery of Honor and into the Night Watch Gallery, and that’s when we met that awful man.”

“You mean the murder victim,” London said.

“That’s right, Pier Dekker. When he started boasting about cracking Rembrandt’s secrets—the hidden feather on the guardsman’s helmet, for example—I sensed there was something really wrong with the man. He was a mere technician, but he considered himself more than that—a true artist. And right then and there I wondered—had he tampered with the Van Gogh, just for his own pleasure, just so he could gloat about it? If so, how many other of the Rijksmuseum’s masterpieces had he casually toyed with?”

Cyrus shook his head slowly.

“The possibility positively alarmed me. But I didn’t dare confront him about it at the time. I only told him what I felt—that a technician like himself had no business thinking of himself as an artist.”

London’s brain clicked away as she tried to make sense of what she was hearing. She simply couldn't connect all the dots. What could that single peculiar tulip petal on a Van Gogh painting possibly have to do with Pier Dekker's death?

Cyrus took a deep breath and continued.

"I didn't even know the man had been killed until the next morning, when that police chief interrogated me."

London asked, "Did you tell him about the Van Gogh painting?"

"Why should I?" Cyrus said. "I didn't even know what to make of it myself. And I certainly had no reason to think it had anything to do with the man's murder."

Audrey put her hand on Cyrus's shoulder and spoke to London.

She said, "Cyrus didn't tell me about the Van Gogh painting until this morning, after he'd talked to the police chief. I could tell he was really bothered about it. So I told him we should go back to the museum to have another look."

"And that's what we did," Cyrus said. "We went straight to the Van Gogh exhibit and looked again at the *Tulips* and …"

Cyrus's voice trailed off for a moment.

"It looked perfectly normal. The petal that looked peculiar yesterday looked exactly like it ought to look—painted with subtle, careful brushstrokes, nothing bold about it at all."

"What do you think happened?" London asked.

"How should I know?" Cyrus said, his voice rising with exasperation. "For all I know, I only imagined the difference from the very start. Maybe it was a trick of the light. Maybe my eyes were fooling me."

"You don't really think that," Audrey said.

"I don't know what to think," Cyrus said. "All I know is that I want nothing more to do with this whole business. I want to forget it ever happened."

"But if the police still suspect you—" London began.

Audrey interrupted, "Cyrus has an alibi for the time of the murder. He and I were taking a walk through Amsterdam. That's what I told the police."

Cyrus chuckled sardonically and patted Audrey's hand.

"I don't think the police chief took our alibi very seriously, Audrey," he said.

London could understand why they wouldn't. Audrey sounded like someone who would willingly lie for Cyrus's sake. For all London really knew, that was exactly what she was doing.

Cyrus got up from his chair.

"And now if you don't mind, London," he said. "I'm heartily sick of answering everybody's questions. I hope you and your little dog will be so kind as to be on your way."

London could tell that there was no point in pushing the issue. She and Sir Reggie left the stateroom. As they walked down the passageway, London looked at her watch and saw that the hours were slipping by. But at long last, at least she was free from obstacles and interruptions.

"Come on, boy," she said to Sir Reggie. "We can finally go ashore and get to work."

To her relief, no one stopped her for questions or complaints and she and Reggie made their way off the boat and onto the shore. But as they walked alongside the canal nearest the riverboat's dock, London came to a stop.

Sir Reggie looked up at her with an inquisitive "yap," as if to ask, *"What now?"*

"I'm not sure," she replied. "The truth is, I haven't had a moment to think things through ever since I got called back aboard a while ago."

Then something floating in the water caught her eye.

CHAPTER THIRTY

When London stepped to the edge of the walkway to see what was floating in the canal, she was disappointed. The object that had caught her attention was just a paper cup. She couldn't imagine why she had even been drawn to take a closer look. A floating cup didn't seem to offer any clues to a murder investigation.

So she was still left with the unanswered question of where to go now that she was finally off the ship.

Mulling it over, she said to Sir Reggie, "You know, when I went ashore this morning, I had no idea I'd wind up in some smoky *coffeeshop* or meeting with a couple of sex workers. I'd planned to go straight to the crime scene and see if there was anything there the police might have missed. Maybe that's what we should do right now. Come on, it's not a long walk."

Sir Reggie barked with approval.

But then London stopped in her tracks.

As she turned to look back along the water, she glimpsed an odd movement among the pedestrians behind her, as though someone had hastily stepped behind several others. But then no one seemed to be behaving strangely, so the turned her attention back to that floating cup she had just noticed.

It was still there.

It took another moment for London to realize what was bothering her about that cup.

It's not drifting with a current.

The cup she'd observed last night before she'd found the body had been moving along in flowing water.

She asked Sir Reggie, "Do you think some of Amsterdam's canals have currents, and others don't?"

Sir Reggie let out an indecisive grumble.

"That doesn't quite make sense, does it?" London agreed. "These are canals, not creeks or rivers. There's no reason for any of them to flow anywhere."

As London and Sir Reggie continued on their way, London tried to persuade herself that the two floating cups—one drifting, one motionless—couldn't possibly have anything to do with the murder.

And yet …

"I just can't shake off the feeling that it matters somehow," she told Sir Reggie. "Maybe I need to talk to someone who knows a lot more about the canals than I do."

Sir Reggie whined as if asking who such a person might be.

"I know just who we should talk to!" London said, remembering someone who had said he knew these canals *"Like the back of my hand."*

She got out her cellphone and found the number to call for water taxis.

When she got a dispatcher on the line, she asked for a boat to come to her current location.

Then she added, "But I want a certain pilot and a certain boat. The boat is called the *Jonge Gouda* and the pilot's name is …"

London paused as she tried to remember the man's name.

The dispatcher replied in a cheerful voice, "Oh, you mean *Kapitein* Claes Stoepker. He's very popular with tourists, much in demand. And it looks like he's not far from where you are at the moment. I will send him to you."

As she and Sir Reggie stood waiting on the bank, London wondered, *What do I expect him to tell me exactly?*

Soon the charming little boat painted with a bright red hull and a yellow prow to look like a block of gouda cheese appeared. The smiling, red-bearded pilot waved his nautical cap as he pulled the boat against the stone embankment.

"Hello, there!" he said in English. "You are the American woman I met yesterday, eh? And your name is London—like the city."

London smiled.

"That's right," she said. "London Rose."

He chuckled and added, "I never forget a passenger's face or name!"

No wonder he's so popular with tourists, London thought as she picked up Sir Reggie and climbed into the boat with him.

Kapitein Claes peered at Sir Reggie curiously.

"I do not remember this fine fellow from yesterday," he said. "Perhaps you would like to introduce us, Mevrouw Rose."

London laughed and said, "I'd like you to meet Sir Reggie,

Kapitein Claes."

"Welcome aboard," Claes said, scratching Sir Reggie on the head.

Claes took his place at the wheel and London and Sir Reggie sat close to him. As he started up the purring engine and pulled away from the embankment, London again noticed some odd activity among the people nearby. She fancied she saw a figure darting away. She figured if someone actually was following her, she had a pretty good idea who it might be. In any case, he must have been flummoxed by her taking off in a boat.

"So where would you like to go?" the pilot asked.

"I want to stop at a place in De Wallen near the *Oude Kerk.* It's a little dock where rowboats are tied up."

"It is not very far away," Claes said.

Then something seemed to dawn on him.

"Wait a minute. I am familiar with that dock. That is where the body was found last night, wasn't it?"

"That's right," London said with a prickle of anxiety.

"An American woman found the body in a docked rowboat—that was you, was it?"

"Yes, that was me," London said.

She was worried now that the *kapitein* might not want to help her.

"Why do you want to go back there?" Claes asked.

London decided to tell him the truth without mentioning the unpleasant fact that she was a murder suspect.

"I'm trying to help the police find the killer."

"Are you, now?" Claes said with an enthusiastic twinkle in his eye. "Well, consider me to be at your service. It is not very often that an Amsterdam taxi pilot gets a chance to help solve a murder case. How can I help you?"

"I was wondering," London said, "what you could tell me about currents in the Amsterdam canals. Last night, shortly before I found the body, I saw a plastic cup in the canal. It seemed to be floating with a current. But just a few minutes ago, before you picked me up, I saw another plastic cup, and it was motionless."

"How very observant of you," Claes said. "I believe I can explain. Perhaps you have also observed that Amsterdam's canals are remarkably clean—cleaner than they have ever been in the city's history. You won't find much trash in them, anyway. That is because the trash is regularly flushed out, so to speak."

"Flushed out?"

"Yes, clean water is pumped in from the IJsselmeer, the large bay to the east of Amsterdam. This causes currents that sweep dirty canal water all the way through the city to locks on the other side, were garbage is netted and scooped up. This happens three times a week. Last night was one of those times. That was why you saw a cup moving with the current."

London was intrigued by what she was hearing.

"So that's also why there's no current this morning," she said.

"Correct," the *kapitein* said. "Those currents only happen during the scheduled pumping procedures. But what has this got to do with the murder?"

That's a good question, London thought, pausing to think it over.

Her gut was telling her that the current mattered a great deal.

But why?

She suddenly flashed back to the conversation between Bob and Mr. Tedrow about Mr. Tedrow's case of writer's block, and his problem with moving a dead body in his book.

"Strictly speaking, nobody *is supposed to move the body,"* he'd said.

"It just ... well, moves."

Bob had suggested some phenomenon like a mudslide or an avalanche.

London felt as though a major piece of the puzzle was falling into place.

As the boat approached its destination, London saw that the narrow dock with the rowboats was cordoned off with police tape. Claes pulled his boat up near the dock and stopped the engine.

"I guess you will not get a very close look," Claes said.

London had a tingling feeling that she wasn't going to need one.

"Let's just stay right here a minute," she said to Claes.

Claes kept the *Jonge Gouda* motionless in the water. As London gazed at the boat where she and Sir Reggie had found the body, she remembered what *Surveillant* Dijkstra had said about what these boats were for. Clients who didn't like to be recognized in the *Rosse Buurt* would use them to arrive here furtively by night. Pier Dekker was one of those clients, and the boat he'd been found in was apparently his own.

Claes asked London, "Are you getting any ideas?"

"Maybe so," London said. "Last night the *Hoofdinspecteur* wouldn't tell me his own theories. But I think I have a fair idea of what he was thinking. He thought maybe Dekker had been killed right there in his boat. Either that, or someone killed him nearby and put him into his boat. But now I'm considering another possibility …"

"Of course!" Claes exclaimed. "Last night's current might have brought the boat here, body and all!"

London nodded and said, "If so, maybe the victim wasn't killed near here at all. He might have been killed elsewhere in Amsterdam."

She gasped at the realization of what that might mean. If Dekker had been murdered somewhere else, that opened up a lot more possible scenarios and provided a lot more possible suspects. But then she realized she was overlooking something important.

"There's one problem with my theory," she told *Kapitein* Claes. "The boat was chained to the dock when I found the body. It couldn't very well have floated here from somewhere else and chained itself to the dock."

"No, I don't suppose so," Claes said, scratching his head.

Then another object caught her eye—a long pole with a hook on it that was fastened to the embankment wall alongside the dock.

"What is that pole for?" London asked Claes.

"Well, these rowboats have a way of slipping away from you by accident, sometimes when you're trying to climb into them. It often happens. That pole is there to pull back boats when they get away. The canal is very narrow here, and the boats are always pretty easy to reach."

With a chuckle, Claes added, "It is easier than jumping into the canal and swimming to fetch them."

London's mind was buzzing now.

She said, "So if someone *knew* the boat with the dead body was going to float toward this part of the canal, they could have waited here and used the pole to bring it up against the dock and chain it up. That way they could have made it look like the victim had been killed near here, when he had really been killed elsewhere."

"The question is," Claes said, "where did the boat *come* from?"

"And where was the victim killed?" London added.

"Yes, those are big questions," Claes said, gazing along the canal thoughtfully. "You have noticed, surely, that Amsterdam's canals form quite an intricate web."

London pondered over the possibilities for a moment. Then a thought occurred to her.

"What if the victim were killed somewhere near the Rijksmuseum?" she asked.

Claes's eyebrows jumped with interest.

"Yes, if his body was put into a boat last night in the canal nearest the museum, it would certainly have floated here."

London paused to analyze this idea.

She said, "But why wouldn't the killer have just rowed the boat here?"

Claes scoffed.

"And risk being seen rowing the whole way? It would be much safer to just cover up the body and let the boat go. Then if nobody took notice of it, he could intercept it here, pull it in, and chain it up."

"That's right," London said. "So when I found the body, the police naturally assumed the victim had been killed near here.

"It is not a bad theory," *Kapitein* Claes said.

Thoughts rattled noisily through London's head.

Not a bad theory, maybe, she thought.

But that was all it was, a theory. There were still a lot of pieces of the puzzle to fill in. But London had an idea of who else might help her do that.

"Let's go to the Rijksmuseum," London said to *Kapitein* Claes.

He revved up the motor, and the *Jonge Gouda* was on its way again.

CHAPTER THIRTY ONE

As the boat cruised through the narrow canals, Sir Reggie stood up on the prow, obviously enjoying the ride. The gray day hadn't darkened the little dog's spirits at all.

London was, on the other hand, feeling some apprehension. Even if that grand museum held answers to her questions, how could she get to that information? Did she really expect to find out things that the police hadn't even discovered?

She knew she had to keep trying. After thinking hard for a moment, London decided who she wanted to talk to first.

She took out her cellphone and called the Rijksmuseum and asked to speak to one of their docents. "Her name is Helga something … Helga van den Heuvel, I believe."

"I'll see if she's available," the receptionist said.

In a few moments, a woman's voice replied in Dutch.

"This is Helga van den Heuvel. How may I help you?"

London replied in Dutch, "My name is London Rose. We met yesterday. I brought an American tour group to the museum."

There was a brief silence, then Helga said, "Yes, I remember."

"I wondered if we could meet somewhere and talk."

"I suppose we could. I have a break coming up. Would you care to meet me at the museum's cafe?"

"I have my dog with me today," London replied. "Perhaps we could meet at one of the entrances in the passageway that runs beneath the museum."

"May I ask what this is about?"

London heard an understandable note of skepticism in Helga's voice. She figured it was best to be as forthright as possible.

"This is about the death of one of your conservators, the one my group met yesterday. Pier Dekker."

Helga fell silent. For a moment, London wondered whether she might have hung up.

"Yes, that was a terrible thing," Helga finally said. "Such a shock to everybody here. Naturally, the police came to the museum and asked everyone on the staff many questions. I am afraid I had no choice but to mention the little altercation Meneer Dekker had with one member of your group. I'm sorry if that has led to any trouble for you."

"That's not why I'm calling. You see …"

London paused, then gulped hard and continued, "I'm the one who found the victim's body last night in the *Rosse Buurt.*"

Helga fell silent again.

Is she going to refuse to talk to me? London wondered. *Does she think that I might be involved in the murder?*

Instead, Helga asked, "How soon can you be here?"

"In just a few minutes."

"I will wait for you at the entrance."

Helga ended the call without another word.

The boat was now approaching the majestic museum building and *Kapitein* Claes pulled up to a dock alongside the embankment. A variety of small boats were chained up there, ranging from inboard motorboats like the *Jonge Gouda* to rowboats like the one in which she and Sir Reggie had found Pier Dekker's body.

Kapitein Claes commented, "Maybe the murder victim normally kept his rowboat on this very dock."

London nodded in agreement.

"He worked in the museum," she said. "So, this would have been very convenient for him. He could have come straight here after a day's work. He could have rowed from here to De Wallen whenever he wanted to visit the *Rosse Buurt.*"

"Except for last night," Claes said.

"No, last night someone might have killed him—strangled him—right here on this very dock, then sent the boat adrift knowing perfectly well where it would wind up."

As she said the words aloud, London realized that she and the *kapitein* were making a lot of assumptions. Still, that scenario made more sense than anything else she could imagine right now.

Kapitein Claes helped London and Sir Reggie out of the boat and onto the dock.

"Would you like me to wait here for you?" he asked.

London thought for a moment.

"No, I don't know how long I'll be here," she said. "I'm very grateful for the help you've given me already. You've been very kind."

She paid him the taxi fare and added, "Thank you so much."

"I'm very glad to do what I can," Claes said with a tip of his cap. "Good luck with your case. If I can help in any other way, you know how to reach me."

Claes started up the engine and waved as he pulled away from the dock.

London and Sir Reggie climbed a small flight of concrete steps to the embankment walkway and walked straight to the Rijksmuseum. They entered the elaborate tunnel that passed straight through the building, which was bustling as usual with pedestrians and bicyclists.

The docent was waiting for them outside one of the tunnel's entrances to the museum. Dressed in a simple and rather severe pantsuit, the tall, shorthaired woman was an imposing figure.

"I am sorry we have to meet again under such circumstances," Helga said, shaking London's hand.

"I'm sorry too," London said.

"Come, let's walk over to the *Rijksmuseumtuinen,*" Helga said. "We can talk better there."

As they walked out of the bustling tunnel, Helga glanced down at Sir Reggie.

"Your dog is very small," she said, a bit contemptuously.

"His name is Sir Reggie," London said.

Helga nodded without commenting further.

At that moment, Sir Reggie let out a peculiar little growl.

He doesn't like her either.

London, Helga, and Sir Reggie continued walking into the spacious and beautiful *Rijksmuseumtuinen,* the museum gardens with mazes of paths, arches, sculptures, and various flowers in bloom. Even an enormous chessboard with oversized pieces was spread out on the pavement.

Helga led London and Sir Reggie to a circular fountain, where they all sat down on a bench.

"How exactly can I help you?" Helga asked.

London thought for a moment.

Where to begin? she wondered.

There were so many unanswered questions. Would this woman be likely to know anything about the conservator's boat and where it was usually docked?

But something else had been nagging at London—something that seemed irrelevant, but that she sensed was somehow very important.

She blurted out the question.

"Have you noticed anything odd about one of your Van Gogh paintings? The *Tulips,* I mean."

The effect was startling.

Helga sat bolt upright, as if she'd received an electric shock.

"Please explain," Helga snapped.

London hesitated. How much detail did she want to get into? Did she have to mention Cyrus Bannister, or would that just cause him more trouble?

She chose her words carefully—and a bit evasively.

"Yesterday … there seemed to be something odd about that painting. Especially thick strokes on one of the tulips."

Helga was glaring at London now.

"There's nothing unusual about that," she said. "I explained that Van Gogh often used thick brushstrokes and even sometimes squeezed paint straight out of the tube onto the canvas."

London felt a tingle from head to foot.

She remembered something Cyrus had said a little while ago.

"Maybe it was a trick of the light. Maybe my eyes were fooling me."

But now London felt sure that Cyrus's eyes hadn't been fooling him. Judging from Helga's reaction, Cyrus seemed to have observed something very real. But what was it, and what does it mean? Had the conservator done a clumsy restoration job on a priceless masterpiece? Had he failed to fix it properly?

Trying to tread carefully, London said to Helga, "As I understand it … the *Tulips* is a very early Van Gogh work. He was still painting in a realistic style. He wasn't using thick paint or brushstrokes then."

Helga didn't reply, just sat there glaring at London.

"And besides …" London began.

"Well?" Helga said, her eyes narrowing grimly.

London was starting to feel a bit frightened now. Was it her imagination, or had the afternoon sky actually darkened as they sat there talking? She glanced around and realized that there was nobody else nearby. She more than half wanted to scoop up Sir Reggie right now and walk away from here without saying another word.

But I've really got to know.

"Today that tulip didn't look the same," she told the docent. "Not thickly painted, I mean. It looked smooth and realistic, just like the rest of the painting."

Helga's already pale face went white with anger and alarm.

"What are you suggesting?" she demanded.

"I'm not suggesting anything," London said, since she still had no idea why the change might be so important. "I was hoping you could explain it to me."

Helga leaned toward London menacingly.

"Does anybody else know about this?" she hissed.

London gulped hard. Should she mention Cyrus now? Should she tell Helga that he was the one who had noticed the difference?

No, I shouldn't.

London had a terrible gut feeling that she'd told Helga too much already.

"Never mind," she said, rising from the bench and picking up Sir Reggie. "It was nothing. I'm sorry to have troubled you."

But Helga leaped to her feet and grabbed London by the arm.

Towering over her, the conservator said, "You will not leave here. Not until you tell me."

London gasped with horror as she felt Helga's strong fingers dig painfully into her arm.

CHAPTER THIRTY TWO

As London tried to pull away from Helga's grip, she heard the woman cry out in surprise. Sir Reggie was still in London's arms, and he had sunk his teeth into Helga's hand. For a moment London was almost free.

Then the attacking woman swatted the little dog away, and he fell to the ground with a yelp.

"Sir Reggie," London gasped, struggling to see if her precious sidekick was all right. But her assailant grabbed each of her arms with strong hands and shook her.

"Who have you talked to?" Helga demanded in Dutch.

London was relieved to hear Sir Reggie barking fiercely as he darted around the docent's feet. But then Helga began to kick at the dog to keep him from biting her ankles and London was as frightened for Sir Reggie as she was for herself. She didn't doubt that the woman would gladly crush the tiny animal underfoot.

But she couldn't get free of Helga's grip.

Suddenly there was a swarm of movement and the hands on her arms let go.

Two men seemed to appear out of nowhere and pulled Helga away from London.

"Who are you?" Helga yelled. "Let go of me! I'll call the police."

But at that moment, *Hoofdinspecteur* Braam himself came riding toward them on his bicycle. The policeman seemed to be all elbows and knees as he peddled to her rescue, but he was a most welcome sight to London.

He shouted at the woman, "Helga van den Heuvel, you are under arrest.

London realized that the men holding Helga were plainclothes policemen. With a sigh of relief, she collapsed back onto the bench where they'd been sitting. Sir Reggie jumped up into her lap and bared his teeth at everybody else in sight.

"Whatever for?" Helga shouted back at Braam as the two policemen began to put her into handcuffs.

"To begin with, for blackmail," Braam said. "And I believe also for murder."

"I have no idea what you're talking about," Helga said.

"Oh, I am sure you do," Braam scoffed.

London felt dazed now, but not totally surprised by the policemen's arrival. After all, she'd been aware of being watched ever since she'd left the *Nachtmusik*. And now she was glad she'd been followed. She didn't know what Helga might have done to her—and to Sir Reggie—if the policemen hadn't shown up.

"You can't prove any of this," Helga hissed at Braam, her hands now cuffed behind her back.

"Your bank statements offer most of the proof we need," Braam said. "Or are you going to deny that you received some highly suspicious payments directly from the murder victim?"

Helga's eyes bulged with fury and confusion.

"But I didn't kill anybody!" she shrieked as the policemen hauled her away.

Braam smiled ironically at London.

"Well, well, well, Mevrouw Rose," he said in English as he sat down beside her. "Perhaps you'd control your guard dog so we can talk this over."

London wasn't all that comfortable with the *hoofdinspecteur* sitting next to her and asking questions. But there were things she wanted to know from him, so she hushed Sir Reggie, reminding him that *Hoofdinspecteur* Braam was a legal authority. The little dog quieted down and sat in her lap watching the policeman suspiciously.

"It seems like only minutes since our last chat," Braam said to her. "And if I remember correctly, I humbly requested that you keep your nose out of my investigation."

He chuckled and added, "Of course, I knew better than to expect you to do any such thing. That is why I had you followed—for your own safety mostly, but also to find out what you might get yourself up to. As it happens, some of my men were also just getting ready to arrest Helga van den Heuvel. We've had her in our sights all afternoon. Her behavior toward you just now confirms her guilt."

He leaned toward London and Sir Reggie let out a warning grumble. She stroked the dog's head and Braam continued.

"Meanwhile, I assume you have been living up to your reputation as a brilliant amateur detective. May I ask what your own investigative efforts have turned up?"

London didn't speak for a moment. She was waiting for a feeling of relief to kick in, now that it seemed as though the killer had been caught, and the case was closed. But the truth is, London felt nothing but confusion. She really had no idea exactly what had just happened.

Nevertheless, she figured she'd better at least tell the *Hoofdinspecteur* whatever she could.

"All I've got is a theory," she said to Braam. "It's probably nothing you haven't already considered."

"Enlighten me," Braam said with a sly grin.

"I think Meneer Dekker wasn't killed in De Wallen. I think the murder happened very close to here—perhaps at a nearby dock."

"Indeed?" Braam said with interest. "Then why did we find the body in a boat in De Wallen?"

"I think the killer set the boat adrift with the body when the canals were flushed out last night. If so, the boat would have floated to De Wallen in the current. When it did, the killer pulled it to the dock and chained it up to make it look as though the murder happened right there."

Braam gazed at London intently. She guessed that her theory was *not* something he had yet considered. He also seemed to be impressed with her for thinking of it.

"An intriguing scenario," he said. "It fits very well with what I've already deduced. Perhaps you should consider a career change, London Rose. Criminal investigation seems to suit you."

London didn't feel exactly flattered.

"Now maybe you can answer a few of *my* questions," London said.

"Such as?"

London took a deep breath.

"Such as, what does Van Gogh's painting of tulips have to do with all this?"

Braam squinted at her and tilted his head.

"Why do you think it does?" Braam asked her.

"I'm told by … um, an expert on many topics … that the painting somehow changed in appearance, and then changed back again. I'd like an explanation for that."

Braam stared at her, and his lips twisted enigmatically. London could barely keep herself from chuckling.

"You don't have any idea what I'm talking about, do you?" she said.

"I hope you'll be so kind as to tell me," Braam said with a flicker of a smile.

Of course, London knew that he wasn't making a polite request. It was more of an order, and she had no choice but to comply.

London said, "I'm talking about a Van Gogh painting in the museum called *Tulips*. Yesterday one of the petals on one of the tulips looked all wrong and out of place. Today it looked exactly as it ought to look."

"And you think this has to do with the murder somehow?"

"Well, the docent *did* physically attack me when I mentioned it. So yes, I think it does."

Braam put his hands in his pockets and stared off into space.

Finally, he said, "I'm sure Mevrouw van den Heuvel will tell us everything in short order. The evidence we have against already her is pretty airtight. And I'm sure we'll find more information when we search her premises. There's not a doubt in my mind that she killed Pier Dekker."

He brushed his hands together with satisfaction, as if putting an end to the whole matter.

"For the time being, Mevrouw Rose," he said, "I hope you enjoy the rest of your visit to our lovely city."

To London's astonishment, he stood up and walked toward his bicycle.

"Wait a minute," London said, getting to her feet and striding after him with Sir Reggie trotting at her side. "Is that all? Aren't you going to tell me anything else?"

Braam turned toward her and shrugged.

"What more is there?"

"A great deal, I think," London said. "For example, is the *Nachtmusik* free to set sail for Copenhagen?"

"I am not ready to say," Braam said. "But I am quite sure that your ship's delay here in Amsterdam is coming to a prompt end. It won't be long now. I'll call your captain when I know more."

London stood with her mouth agape as Braam climbed onto his bicycle and rode away.

London looked down at her dog.

"I don't like that man, Sir Reggie, she said. "I don't like anything about him."

Sir Reggie let out a small growl of agreement.

London continued, "I don't like the way he had me followed without telling me. Don't get me wrong, I appreciate that he was thinking of my safety, but he didn't have to keep it a secret, did he? And now that it's all over, the least he could do is thank me for helping with his investigation. Or better yet, tell me he's sorry he ever treated me like a murder suspect."

Just then London's phone rang. She was pleased to see that the call was from Bryce.

"Hi, London," he said. "I'm about to take a break, and I wondered whether we could meet somewhere. I just keep hearing wilder and wilder rumors, and I've been worried about you."

"I'd love that," London said. "But I'm in town, near the Rijksmuseum."

"I can get away. Where would you like to meet?"

London realized she was hungry. She hadn't eaten since that morning, when Bryce brought her that lovely breakfast. She remembered the name of the restaurant where she and several passengers had been yesterday.

"How about the *Hongerig Kanaal?* I'm close to it right now. Why don't you join me there?"

"I'll do that," Bryce said.

They ended the call, and London and Sir Reggie headed out of the museum grounds. As they continued on their way, London found herself thinking about what Braam had said just now.

"There's not a doubt in my mind that she killed Pier Dekker."

I hope he's right, London thought.

But Braam hadn't told her anything about what evidence he had. He had only referred to bank statements and blackmail. And he obviously knew nothing about the Van Gogh painting—the very mention of which had driven Helga to attack her. Did Braam really have a solid murder case against the docent?

She remembered the dumbfounded expression on Helga's face when the policemen took her away.

"But I didn't kill anybody!" Helga had screamed.

London felt a shiver of doubt. That protest had sounded very real.

Is Braam even on the right track? she wondered.

She really needed to talk this out with someone smart enough to understand her questions and qualms.

CHAPTER THIRTY THREE

"So do you think the whole thing is really over?" Bryce asked after London described her day's adventures. They were sitting at an outdoor table at the *Hongerig Kanaal* café, where she and her tour group had eaten lunch yesterday. London had picked this one out to wait for him, because she figured the table's broad umbrella would keep them dry if it did rain a little. Although the sky was still overcast, London had felt more cheerful as soon as Bryce arrived.

Since she hadn't eaten anything since breakfast, she had ordered a delicious bowl of split pea soup cooked with hearty slabs of bacon. The soup was so thick London could stand her spoon in it—perfect comfort food after her ordeal. London could feel herself calming down with every mouthful. She shared the accompanying slices of smoked sausage with Bryce and Sir Reggie, who was perched in a chair of his own.

"I hope it's over," London told him. "But I've got my doubts. I wish *Hoofdinspecteur* Braam hadn't been so tight-lipped about everything."

London took a bite of freshly baked rye bread and thought for a moment.

"Braam told Helga he was arresting her for *blackmail* as well as murder," she said. "He seemed to have proof of odd payments in the form of bank statements."

"But why?" Bryce asked.

"I have no idea. I can only guess it had something to do with that Van Gogh painting. And maybe with other paintings as well. Judging from his argument with Cyrus, Dekker seems to have had a streak of vanity. He fancied himself to be more than just a restorer. He thought of himself as an artist. Maybe he was going around tampering with some of the masterpieces on display in the Rijksmuseum, just out of sheer egotism. Maybe Helga caught him doing that."

"I guess that makes sense," Bryce said, although he sounded doubtful.

London shook her head with frustration.

"No, it doesn't, Bryce," she said. "Every idea I can think of seems farfetched to me. Blackmail and murder are two different things. Why would Helga kill somebody if she was successfully extorting money from him?"

"Maybe he refused to keep paying her and things got ugly," Bryce suggested.

"Maybe so," London agreed. But somehow that didn't sound exactly right to her.

She and her two companions fell silent as she ate the last delicious spoonsful of her soup. She glanced around the quaint streets of Amsterdam, wishing she'd had more time to enjoy the city while she'd been here. She also observed that some of the nearby pedestrians kept looking upward as if worried about rain.

Then she let out a gasp as a memory came back to her.

"Bryce, yesterday I saw Helga one more time after we left the Rijksmuseum. I was sitting right here at this table. And Helga walked by—she seemed to be coming right from the museum. She looked like she was in a hurry. And she gave me a very odd look as she rushed by."

"Where was she going?" Bryce asked.

London pointed and said, "I saw her go into that art gallery over there, the one we were in yesterday with Emil—Meyer Fijne Kunst. Maybe that gallery has something to do with the mystery."

"Like what?"

"I've got no idea. But let's go over there and see what we can find out."

London and Bryce paid the cafe check, then trotted with Sir Reggie over to the corner storefront gallery.

The door was open as they approached and, standing inside, London saw the same formidable man who had been standing sentinel there yesterday. Again, he was dressed in what appeared to be a butler's uniform, but the microphone on his shoulder and his shaved head suggested that he was more like a security guard.

London stopped in her tracks.

"Oh, my," she said to Bryce and Sir Reggie. "I doubt that dogs are allowed inside. Maybe you two should wait out here while I go inside and investigate."

But at that moment, London was surprised to see the guard's stern-looking face explode into a wide grin. But he wasn't smiling at her.

"Why, what have we here?" he called out in Dutch. "I do believe this is some sort of terrier—a Yorkshire Terrier, unless I'm much mistaken. Come in, come in!"

London and her two companions entered the gallery, and the guard stooped down to make friends with the dog.

"His name is Sir Reggie," London said.

"An aristocrat, no less!" the guard chuckled. "I'm honored to make your acquaintance, Sir Reggie. My name is Jurjen Smit."

Then he asked, "Does this fellow know any tricks?"

"I've taught him a few," Bryce said. "Hold out your leg."

Smit held out one leg and laughed with delight Sir Reggie jumped back and forth over it several times.

"Ahem," a nearby voice grumbled crossly.

The hefty man with wavy, steel-gray hair and a silver watch chain in his vest pocket looked anything but pleased as he stepped toward them. It was Axel Meyer, the gallery owner, and he was clearly unhappy about the dog.

"I assume these people are here to do business," he said to Smit.

Smit didn't seem to be especially perturbed by his boss's displeasure.

"I'm sure they are, Meneer Meyer," he said. Then he added to London, "I think I've got some items in my lunch box that he might enjoy. May I take him into our back room and play with him a bit while you are talking art?"

"Of course," London said, handing him some of the kitchen-made treats she carried with her. "He likes these."

The delighted security guard and Sir Reggie exited through a door in the back of the gallery.

Axel Meyer glared after him with annoyance. Then he turned toward London and Bryce with a stiff, professional smile.

"You two were here yesterday, were you not?" he said in Dutch. "With the German fellow, if I remember right—the one who bought the *Delfts Blauw* piece."

"That's right," London replied.

Axel Meyer looked at them curiously.

"How may I help you?" he asked, gesturing toward some nearby artworks. "Perhaps you'd be interested in this fine landscape by Esaias van de Velde. Or perhaps this one by Van de Velde's pupil, Pieter de Molijn."

"Very nice," Bryce commented, and the gallery owner smiled

widely.

London guessed that Meyer had been very happy with the price Emil had paid for the plaque. For a moment London wondered whether there was any advantage to be gained by bluffing Meyer into thinking she and Bryce were here to do serious business.

But London doubted that she'd get away with it. For one thing, she didn't have Emil's keen knowledge of fine art. She also figured she didn't look like a promising customer, dressed as she was in her company uniform. It seemed best to get right to the point.

"We're wondering what you could tell us about a woman named Helga van den Heuvel," she said.

Meyer squinted warily.

"I don't believe I know anybody by that name," he said.

He's lying, London realized.

"Are you sure?" London said. "I saw her come in here yesterday afternoon."

Meyer didn't reply, but his expression darkened. London got an unmistakable tingling feeling that she'd touched a nerve. If she could just get Meyer to talk, he'd surely be able to tell her and Bryce something important.

"Are you aware that Mevrouw van den Heuvel was arrested a little while ago?" she asked.

The man's face reddened, and he tugged at his collar.

He said in a tight voice, "Even if I did know the woman, I'm not in the habit of discussing my clients with total strangers. And now, if you're not here to make a purchase, I'll thank you not to waste my time."

London felt a flash of panic as he turned to walk away.

I've got to get him to talk to me, she thought.

But before she could think of anything else to say, she heard a series of loud barks coming from the back of the gallery, followed by a human shout of alarm.

In an instant, Sir Reggie came dashing through the door, carrying a rolled-up canvas by the piece of cloth it was tied up with.

Sir Reggie ran toward her with his prize.

As she took it, she recognized the cloth that was tied around the canvas. It was actually a yellow cravat—the same kind of cravat Pier Dekker had been wearing in the museum.

But the murdered man hadn't been wearing a cravat when London and Sir Reggie found his body.

London shivered deep down in her bones.

The murder weapon! she realized.

CHAPTER THIRTY FOUR

As Sir Reggie trotted proudly in circles with his prize in his mouth, the guard dashed out of the back room yelling, "Stop that dog!"

But stopping him wasn't necessary. Sir Reggie skidded to a halt at London's feet and dropped the canvas right in front of her. London stared down at the yellow cravat with horror.

She remembered her own words to *Hoofdinspecteur* Braam shortly after finding the body.

"I think the victim might have been strangled."

She'd thought then the victim might have been strangled by his own cravat—*this* cravat, which the hadn't been wearing when London found him dead. And now it suddenly appeared that she was probably right.

Worse than that—the killer might well be right here at this very moment.

The gallery owner had frozen in place when the dog appeared, but now he went into action.

"Give me that!" Axel Meyer shouted.

But before the bulky gallery owner could stoop down to pick up the object, Sir Reggie gave the yellow bow a tug, untying it. Suddenly the canvas rolled open right there on the floor.

London gasped aloud, and she wasn't the only one. She heard Bryce gasp as well, and both Smit and Meyer let out strangled cries.

There on the floor was Vincent van Gogh's *Tulips*—the very painting that had caught Cyrus's attention back at the Rijksmuseum. A short while ago, Helga van den Heuvel had flown into a desperate rage at the mere mention of this painting.

London stooped down to look at it more closely and immediately saw the detail that had troubled Cyrus—a single petal that appeared to be painted in a thicker, bolder style than the rest of the image.

But what does this mean? London asked herself.

Were there two almost identical Van Gogh paintings of tulips?

But she knew exactly what the yellow cravat must mean.

Sir Reggie had cracked the murder case.

Because her dog had been the first to find the body last night, he must have recognized the victim's scent on the cravat, which he'd run across while playing with the guard. Intrepid detective that he was, Sir Reggie had brought the evidence straight to London.

London stood up, holding the yellow cravat and staring back and forth between the gallery owner and the security guard.

Which one was the killer?

She waved the yellow cravat and said, "One of you killed Pier Dekker. You strangled him with this cravat."

The next few moments revealed which one it was.

"Pier Dekker?" the gallery owner scoffed. "I've never heard of anyone by that name."

The guard, Jurjen Smit, let out an incredulous snort.

"You're lying, Meneer Meyer," he said. "Dekker came here very often. You knew him well."

"So what if I did?" Meyer blurted. "It doesn't prove I killed him."

The guard stepped toward Meyer accusingly.

"You did, I'm sure of it," Smit said. "I've suspected for months that there's something rotten this business, and especially your dealings with Pier Dekker. I've known there was something rotten about *you.*"

Meyer's eyes darted among the faces around him.

"None of you can prove anything!" he yelped in a voice of rising desperation.

"No, but I imagine the police can," Smit said, reaching for his shoulder microphone. "I'll call for them right this minute."

Meyer stood frozen with terror for a moment. Then he rushed out of the store and tore away down the street.

"We've got to catch him!" Smit said.

Bryce waved him back. "No, you stay here, in case he doubles back. You'll need to explain things to the police when they arrive. We'll get him."

London, Bryce, and Sir Reggie dashed out of the store, but they didn't see the fleeing man anywhere.

Then Sir Reggie barked and tugged on his leash.

"He's caught Meyer's scent," London said.

"Let's follow his lead," Bryce said.

Sir Reggie pulled hard on his leash as London and Bryce struggled to keep pace with him. London glanced up and noticed that sky was darker than before. She only hoped it wouldn't start raining before …

Before what? she wondered.

Before they caught up with Axel Meyer?

London wasn't even sure they *could* catch up with him.

And if they did, what were they going to do then?

But somehow, they had to stop the man from escaping.

Sir Reggie led London and Bryce around a corner, where a bridge across one of the canals stretched out before them. If Meyer was up ahead somewhere, London couldn't pick him out among the cars, bicycles, and other pedestrians. She could only hope that Sir Reggie wouldn't lose the scent.

And that Bryce and I can keep up with him, she thought.

The dog was pulling harder and harder on his leash as they ran trailing behind him. It was obvious that the two humans couldn't run as fast as the tough little dog could. London was sure that Sir Reggie wished they'd just let go of his leash and let him give chase on his own. But then he would surely disappear in the distance, and she would have no idea how to find him.

Weaving among puzzled pedestrians, London made a hasty apology as she bumped into a teenage boy, spinning him around. Then she and Bryce sprinted across a bridge following the little dog. Bryce bumped into a large man and fumbled out an apology in English, but neither of them could stop to explain why they were in such a hurry.

At one point, London thought about calling out to a nearby policeman for help. But what could she tell him? That they were in pursuit of a killer? By the time they could explain, Axel Meyer would be long gone.

The little dog took another sharp turn, then another, and yet another bridge over yet another canal stretched out ahead.

"Are you sure Sir Reggie knows where he's going?" Bryce asked breathlessly.

"I hope so," London gasped.

But they were definitely tiring faster than the dog.

After several minutes tearing along busy thoroughfares and crossing several canals, London recognized the changing neighborhood. She and Bryce were now entering the *Rosse Buurt* of De Wallen, with its narrow, twisting streets.

She felt her own heart pounding and her lungs burning. Neither she nor Bryce was by any means in bad physical condition. Even so, London wondered how much longer they could keep on like this.

To make matters worse, it was starting to rain now, and pedestrians were fleeing from the street. Sir Reggie slowed down to a walk and began to sniff around, going one way and then another, apparently unable to follow the scent in the falling rain.

"This isn't good," Bryce said.

"No, but we can't give up," London said. "He must be somewhere just ahead."

"We need to split up," she told Bryce. "We can cover more options that way."

Bryce took a turn to the right, and London and Sir Reggie went off to the left. Instead of running, London and Sir Reggie walked along as she looked carefully on all sides, hoping to catch a glimpse of the fleeing man or to spot him if he was trying to hide somewhere.

The rain was falling in a steady shower now. This street was too narrow for cars, and no pedestrians were in sight. But surrounding were quite familiar, including rows of windowed booths, the bronze statue of "Belle" the sex worker, and the Zacht Coffeeshop.

At one corner, she wavered for a moment trying to decide which way to go.

London didn't hear the man over the sound of the rain. She only caught a glimpse of movement in her peripheral vision before she felt a viselike grip take hold of her wrist.

She turned her head and saw Axel Meyer, his face twisted with anger. To her surprise, the man was immensely strong as well as bulky.

Strong enough to kill a man with a cravat, she thought.

He grinned at her cruelly, ignoring the water that was streaming down his face.

"I'm tired of running, aren't you?" Meyer said in Dutch.

London's breath had fled her lungs. She wanted to scream, but no sound escaped her throat. She heard Sir Reggie growl, but Meyer simply ignored the sound.

He chuckled grimly.

"Yesterday I found out how it feels to kill someone," he said to her. "Do you know how it feels?"

London stared at him mutely, still unable to yell for help.

"It feels good," Meyer said.

She and the killer seemed to be entirely alone there in the falling rain.

Then in a flash, Sir Reggie was barking ferociously and snapping at

Meyer's heels and ankles. Trying to kick at the dog, the man let out a yelp of his own as he slipped and almost fell on the wet pavement.

London seized the moment to twist her wrist loose from his grasp. She had enough presence of mind to sweep Sir Reggie into her arms before she fled.

As she broke into a run, she was dimly aware of a nearby clatter of footsteps, but she didn't dare turn to look.

But when she dashed around the corner of a building, her heart jumped up in her throat at what she saw next. She and Sir Reggie had fled into a tiny cul-de-sac, a short length of alleyway that ended in a brick wall.

There's no way out! she realized. Was her sleuthing going to end in disaster right here in this alley? She closed her eyes and braced herself for whatever was coming next.

But then she thought furiously, *No. Not like this.*

London closed her eyes and opened her mouth and shouted as loudly as she could.

"Help!"

As if in reply, she heard a noisy thud. She opened her eyes and turned around.

Axel Meyer was lying face down on the wet pavement. Three women were standing over him, as if daring him to move.

One of those women was Ingrid, who was wearing regular street clothes and standing above the prone man with her arms akimbo. Another was Anouk, wearing little else but the bathrobe she'd worn when London had met with her earlier. Anouk had removed one of her spiked-heel shoes and was obviously prepared to hammer Meyer in the head with it if he put up a fight.

The third woman was Ingrid's large and formidable sister Femke, dressed in her security guard uniform. Femke sat down Meyer's back and brushed her hands with satisfaction.

"I believe you called for help," Femke said to London with a smile.

CHAPTER THIRTY FIVE

London just stood gaping at the three women who were looking quite pleased with themselves in spite of the falling rain.

Then she finally stammered, "Uh … thank you."

Sir Reggie let out a grateful bark of agreement.

But the pinned-down gallery owner was complaining, even with his cheek mashed against the wet pavement.

"How dare you!" Meyer growled, "Unhand me at once!"

"I don't think so," Ingrid said, nudging him with her foot.

"Not just yet, anyway," Anouk added, tapping him on the head with her shoe.

Femke just shifted her weight as she sat on Meyer's back, making him writhe and groan uncomfortably.

London sputtered, "But how … did you … ?"

"Femke and I were in the neighborhood," Ingrid explained.

"We often stop by to visit Anouk during the day and bring her a snack while she is at work," Femke said.

Anouk added, "We happened to look out my window when you and your dog ran by, all wet and worried looking. We came out just in time to see this big guy grab hold of you and hear him threaten you. We thought maybe you could use some help.

"You were so right," London said, laughing with relief.

Just then Bryce came dashing up with a policewoman at his side. London immediately recognized *Surveillant* Kaat Dijkstra, the patrol officer who had appeared last night when London and Sir Reggie had found the body.

Bryce stared at the scene with surprise.

He said, "It looks like the situation is … under control."

Then he added with a laugh, "Sorry to arrive late."

"Better late than never," London added, chuckling.

Dijkstra gazed upon the situation with amusement.

"Hello, ladies," Dijkstra said with a pleasant wave.

"Hello, Kaat," the women replied in unison.

Obviously the *surveillant* and these women knew each other well.

"It looks like you've been busy," Dijkstra said to them.

"Just a little," Femke said with a chuckle.

"I didn't do anything wrong!" Meyer shouted from his prone position. "I'm innocent, I tell you!"

Anouk said, "An innocent man doesn't threaten to kill anybody."

Meyer looked up at *Surveillant* Dijkstra with a pleading expression.

"Who are you going to believe?" he asked the policewoman. "A respectable gallery owner or a sex worker?"

"Hmm," Dijkstra said in a wry voice, coaxing the women away and helping Meyer to his feet. "Let me think about that."

She immediately started to put Meyer in handcuffs.

"All right, I've decided," she said. "You are under arrest."

The policewoman told the others, "I have a police van parked on the next street. I'm taking this prisoner off to the station." As she marched the subdued gallery owner away, she added, "I will notify *Hoofdinspecteur* Braam."

"Come on, let's all get inside and dry off," Anouk said.

For the first time London realized how soaking wet she was. She saw that Bryce and Sir Reggie were no better off, and the three women who had rescued her were getting pretty wet as well. She was grateful when Anouk escorted them all to the little room where she and Ingrid did business.

Ingrid brought some blankets and towels, and Anouk poured some hot tea for everybody. The women took turns drying Sir Reggie, who was delighted by the attention. The room was crowded, but warm and comforting.

Everybody was a little dryer when there came a knock on the outside window. Anouk looked out and called "No business today" in Dutch. Then she said, "Oh" and disappeared through the door.

In a moment she returned, escorting *Hoofdinspecteur* Braam, who was wearing a wet poncho.

"He just came riding up on his bicycle." Anouk informed the others.

Bryce and Braam shook hands, and then Anouk invited him to sit down with the others and offered him some tea as well.

"Thanks, perhaps some other time," Braam said to her.

Then he looked at London with a quizzical tilt of his head.

"Tell me, Mevrouw Rose," he said. "Do you think you are quite through with this investigation of yours at long, long last?"

"I hope so," London said with a grin.

"I hope so too," Braam said. "But I do suspect we're now getting to the bottom of things. I just had an interesting phone conversation with the security guard at the Meyer Fijne Kunst gallery. He mentioned a certain yellow cravat—and I believe you said that a yellow cravat was missing from Dekker's body when you found him. I'm sure a little forensics work will prove it to be the murder weapon. It is what I believe you Americans call a 'smoking gun.'"

"What else did he the guard tell you?" Bryce asked.

"Oh, just some theories of his own about Meyer's nefarious activities," Braam said. "Meyer's gallery seems to have been a front for his real business, which was fencing priceless stolen paintings for unscrupulous private buyers. He did most of his business with Pier Dekker, who was an expert art forger as well as a restorer."

"But why did Meyer kill Dekker?" London asked. "And what did Helga van den Huevel have to do with this whole scheme?"

Braam let loose a peal of laughter.

"Mevrouw Rose, did anybody ever tell you that you ask far too many questions? Suffice it to say that we've already found plenty of incriminating in Mevrouw van den Huevel's home, and she is telling us everything she knows now that we've got her in custody. Still, we've got a fair number of loose ends to tie up. I'm sure you'll be able to read about everything in the newspapers during the coming days."

London bristled with frustration.

The newspapers? she thought.

After the role she'd played in solving the mystery, she felt as though she deserved a more forthright explanation than that. But she was starting to realize that Braam actually enjoyed teasing her like this.

Bryce asked the *hoofdinspecteur,* "Does this mean the *Nachtmusik* is free to set sail?"

"A funny thing about that," Braam said with a chuckle. "I called your captain just a little while ago to tell him your ship was no longer detained. That was before this little incident—and a bit premature of me, I now realize. But there is certainly no reason to delay your voyage any longer."

Hoofdinspecteur Braam took his leave with a jaunty wave and rode away on his bicycle. It had stopped raining now, so London, Bryce, and Sir Reggie made their farewells to the three women started on their way. Although it wasn't very far to the ship, London and her two companions were sore and exhausted from their chase, so they caught a water taxi to take them back to the *Nachtmusik.*

As they sat together during the short ride back, Reggie sat in London's lap. Bryce put his arm around London's shoulders, and she cuddled against him and put her head on his shoulder.

"London, is this sort of thing going to happen in every port?" Bryce said with a sigh.

"I don't know what you mean," London replied with a laugh.

"Of course you do," Bryce said. "You seem to get into life-and-death situations at every opportunity. Are things always going to be like that?"

"I'll try my best to stay out of trouble," London said. "But then, I do that all the time. I don't go looking for trouble, Bryce. I really don't."

"I know you don't, but …"

Bryce hesitated, then added, "I get scared for you London."

London felt a sudden surge of warm emotion. It felt really lovely to have someone in her life who was really concerned about her like this. She snuggled more closely against Bryce and petted Sir Reggie.

"There's no need to be scared for me," London told Bryce with a slight laugh. "I'll always have Sir Reggie to protect me."

Bryce laughed as well.

"Yes, that *is* reassuring," he said.

London and Bryce didn't say anything for a few moments, just watched the quaint buildings as the boat continued on its way. London thought back to yesterday, when she'd kept looking for a moment to talk to Bryce about her search for her mother.

Should tell him now? she briefly wondered.

Then she remembered her keen disappointment at finding out the truth of that address, *65 Poppenhuisstraat*, the name *Reis Lust,* and the meaning of that phrase *"elke Europese taal"*—"Any European language."

The advertisement hadn't led to Mom at all—just to a brothel in the *Rosse Buurt.*

It's time to give up the search, she decided.

Mom didn't want to be found, and London had no leads at all, so there was no need to talk about it with Bryce, at least not right now. But her budding relationship with Bryce was still an open question that puzzled her.

She said cautiously, "Bryce, about you and me … Do we know where things are really going? With us, I mean?"

Bryce gently stroked her hair.

"Who says we have to *know* anything?" he said. "Us … you and me … we're not another mystery that has to be solved. Are we?"

He lifted her face to his, and they shared a soft, lingering kiss.

"No," London said, smiling into his eyes. "I don't suppose we are."

At that very moment the water taxi arrived at its destination. London, Bryce, and Sir Reggie paid the fare and stepped ashore and walked the rest of the way to the *Nachtmusik.* As they approached the gangway, they were faced with a distressing sight. A group of reporters with cameras had gathered there in wait for London. Somehow, word must have gotten out about London's recent adventure.

The reporters crowded around her and shouted out in Dutch …

"Is it true you caught the museum restorer's murderer?"

"What can you tell us about the case?"

"How many other murder cases have you solved?"

London was about to shout over the group, telling them that she really didn't know much more about the outcome of the case than she did. But suddenly she heard a gruff voice yelling in English.

"Get back from her! Leave her alone!"

Another voice called out sharply, "You heard what he said! Back off!"

The Dutch reporters stared stupefied as Bob Turner and Stanley Tedrow pushed them away from London and her companions.

"What's the matter with you guys?" Mr. Tedrow snarled. "Don't you understand English?"

London couldn't help but laugh. No, the reporters didn't understand English, and Bob and Mr. Tedrow didn't know any Dutch. In fact, Mr. Tedrow seemed barely to understand what country he was in. Even so, the two men successfully kept the reporters at bay while London, Bryce, and Sir Reggie climbed the gangway to get away from it all.

CHAPTER THIRTY SIX

Later that evening, the *Nachtmusik* surged up and down as it set out across the IJsselmeer, the large bay east of Amsterdam, on its way to the North Sea.

London was sitting alone at a table in the Amadeus Lounge, hoping that Sir Reggie wasn't troubled by the movement. When she had dried off and changed her clothes after returning from her adventure, her dog had curled up on her bed and gone to sleep.

She sighed with pleasure as she sipped her favorite drink, a Manhattan made from Elsie's special recipe. She knew that Bryce must be back working in the kitchen now, making sure that the late diners were being served excellent meals.

She remembered his words.

"Us ... you and me ... we're not another mystery that has to be solved. Are we?"

It felt good not to have to solve any kind of puzzle right now. She had decided to let go of the question about where Mom had gone and focus on her present.

And perhaps on my future, when I'm ready to think about that.

Gazing out through the wide windows, she realized that land was no longer in sight. This was the first time the *Nachtmusik* had sailed across open water since the beginning of its voyage back in Budapest. Until now it had been traveling along rivers and large canals.

She had forgotten how much she enjoyed voyaging over seas and oceans. In earlier years she had worked on huge cruise ships in the Caribbean area. But she noticed that some of the other customers in the lounge looked distinctly queasy.

One such passenger was Audrey Bolton, who clung fast to Cyrus Bannister as they came into the lounge and approached London's table.

Cyrus grinned at London as the two sat down with her.

"Audrey is feeling a bit under the weather," he said.

"It's all this *movement,"* Audrey complained, swaying in her chair. "I can't get used to it."

London produced a package of organic ginger gummies that she kept on hand for just such situations.

"Try some of these," she said to Audrey. "They sometimes help with seasickness."

Audrey obediently popped one of the candies into her mouth.

"I didn't expect this," she said. "And I don't understand it. What are we doing on the open sea, anyway?"

"We're on our way to Copenhagen," Cyrus said.

"But isn't this boat built only for river travel?" Audrey asked.

Before London could begin to explain the boat's special design, Cyrus started holding forth on the topic in his usual pedantic manner.

"Normally, a boat this size couldn't sail on such waters. But the *Nachtmusik* is equipped with a state-of-the-art, adaptable engine and ballast system, so it can handle both rivers and open waters."

London nodded and added, "We won't be sailing very far out to sea. I wouldn't want to cross the Pacific in a boat like this, but the *Nachtmusik* will definitely get us to Copenhagen."

And that's said to be an amazing city, London thought. She couldn't remember ever being there, even as a child. She was looking forward to visiting an exciting country that didn't remind her of Mom.

Audrey was still clinging to Cyrus's arm as if she were afraid that she might fall out of her chair.

Cyrus's expression clouded a little.

"Meanwhile," he said to London, "maybe you could tell us more about the murder case. I must admit I'm still trying to understand exactly what happened."

"So am I," London said, "but I think I'm starting to figure it out. Axel Meyer was in the stolen art business, and he paid Pier Dekker to create forgeries that wouldn't be detected. Recently Helga van den Heuvel caught on to what they were doing. Then she started blackmailing Dekker for a cut of the profits."

"But why did the *forgery* wind up in Meyer's gallery instead of the original?" Cyrus asked grumpily.

London said, "I'm pretty sure Dekker got worried about the part he was playing in the scheme, especially when Helga started blackmailing him. If she knew, who else was going to find out? So, he decided to double-cross both Meyer and Helga by switching the paintings again. He put the original back in its place in the museum and planted the fake in Meyer's gallery. Dekker thought he was safe then, but when Meyer figured this out, he went into a rage. He sneaked up on Dekker last night when he was getting into his rowboat to make a trip to the *Rosse Buurt*. He strangled his accomplice and set the boat adrift. Then he decided it would be smart to chain it up in Dekker's usual place in De Wallen."

London shuddered as she remembered what Meyer had said about the act of murder.

"It feels good."

Cyrus shook his head, looking genuinely uneasy.

"But that tulip petal!" he said. "It was such an obvious mistake!"

"Oh, I don't think it was a mistake at all," London said. "It was just an example of Dekker's pride and arrogance overcoming his caution. He couldn't resist putting some creative hint into his creative forgery—a sort of 'signature,' if you will. He wasn't content to be mere restorer, or a mere forger either. He *did* consider himself to be an artist, after all."

Audrey patted Cyrus's hand.

"So you see, dear, you *didn't* just imagine that thick paint being out of place."

Cyrus smiled, looking reassured that his observations hadn't been wrong.

"I would imagine," he said, "now that their attention is alerted, the so-called museum experts might discover other oddities among works in their collection."

"Maybe so," London agreed. "But I'd guess that most of the paintings they copied were less famous and less expensive works, probably from smaller museums or galleries."

Cyrus nodded and turned his attention to Audrey, who seemed to be feeling better now.

Meanwhile, London took notice of a couple of people she hadn't talked to since she'd come back aboard.

Uh-oh, she thought as Emil Waldmüller got up from his place at the bar and turned to leave. He nearly collided with Amy Blassingame who was walking across the lounge.

But instead of exchanging cross words or turning and fleeing, Emil and Amy simply nodded politely and walked on past each other.

London breathed a sigh of relief. Apparently, she had made the right call by shutting Amy and Emil up in the library and demanding that they stay there until they worked out their differences. And now it appeared that they were over whatever drama they'd had with each other and were ready to resume their professional lives.

But then London saw that Amy was holding something cupped in both hands. She held it carefully as she found a table and sat down, hunched over whatever she'd been carrying.

What is she up to? London wondered.

London got up and walked over to the table and said, "Hi, Amy."

Amy turned her head and saw London and let out a gasp of alarm. She quickly grabbed whatever she'd been holding and hid it in her hands again.

"Hi, London," Amy said, trying unsuccessfully to sound nonchalant.

London felt a tingle of apprehension.

"What have you got there, Amy?" she asked.

"Nothing," Amy said, holding it close to her chest.

But London caught a glimpse of something white and furry through Amy's fingers.

London stared with alarm.

"Amy, *please* don't tell me you've still got that baby fennec fox. I thought the zoo people picked it up."

"Oh, no, they did, it's not that," Amy babbled. "London It's not that at all."

"Then show me."

Amy opened her hands and revealed a live white mouse. The little creature just sniffed the air and made no attempt to run away."

"Isn't he adorable, London?" Amy said. "I named him Dewdrop too. I bought him in a pet store in Amsterdam."

London stifled a sigh.

"Amy, I don't know about this," she said. "I mean, I don't know what kinds of laws might be involved—"

Amy interrupted, clutching the mouse closely again.

"Surely you're not going to tell me I can't keep him. We can't very well sail back to Amsterdam just to return him, can we?"

"No, of course not, but—"

Amy looked alarmed, "But you can't throw him overboard. I won't let you."

"No, of course not," London repeated. "But—"

Before she could complete her thought or her objection, London's cellphone rang. Her heart began to pound as she saw that the caller was none other than Jeremy Lapham, the CEO of Epoch World Cruise

Lines.

The stowaway mouse would have to wait.

She stepped away from the table and took the call.

"Hello, London," Jeremy said. "I've got some news."

"What is it?" London asked.

"Well, I've consulted again with Alex, my astrologer, and he's updated his chart. He's taken another look at Eris, that dwarf planet that was discovered in 2005, and found that it has gone unexpectedly retrograde. Considering my own birth sign of Aries, I assume you know what that means."

"I'm afraid I don't," London said.

But she felt desperately afraid that it meant Mr. Lapham was going to cancel the voyage after all.

Instead, Mr. Lapham said, "It means that I've been much too casual about all these disasters aboard the *Nachtmusik.* It's time for me to take the ram—Aries, I mean—by the horns, so to speak. I'll be joining you in Copenhagen."

London felt as though the wind had been knocked out of her lungs.

"You'll … you'll … ?"

But she couldn't gasp out a whole question.

"I'll be seeing you soon," Mr. Lapham said. "Ta-ta for now, and toodle-oo."

He ended the call without another word, leaving London staring at her cellphone in disbelief. Feeling weak at the knees, London sat down in the nearest chair.

"He'll be joining us in Copenhagen!" she murmured aloud.

What could that mean? she wondered. Was the CEO coming to cancel the tour or to revise their schedule or … ?

There were too many possibilities to guess, but she was sure that life aboard the *Nachtmusik* was about to become much more complicated.

NOW AVAILABLE!

CALAMITY (AND A DANISH)
(A European Voyage Cozy Mystery—Book 5)

"When you think that life cannot get better, Blake Pierce comes up with another masterpiece of thriller and mystery! This book is full of twists, and the end brings a surprising revelation. Strongly recommended for the permanent library of any reader who enjoys a very well-written thriller."
--Books and Movie Reviews (re *Almost Gone*)

CALAMITY (AND A DANISH) is book #5 in a charming new cozy mystery series by #1 bestselling author Blake Pierce, whose *Once Gone* has over 1,500 five-star reviews. The series begins with MURDER (AND BAKLAVA)—BOOK #1.

When London Rose, 33, is proposed to by her long-time boyfriend, she realizes she is facing a stable, predictable, pre-determined (and passionless) life. She freaks out and runs the other way—accepting instead a job across the Atlantic, as a tour-guide on a high-end European cruise line that travels through a country a day. London is searching for a more romantic, unscripted and exciting life that she feels sure exists out there somewhere.

London is elated: the European river towns are small, historic and charming. She gets to see a new port every night, gets to sample an endless array of new cuisine and meet a stream of interesting people. It is a traveler's dream, and it is anything but predictable.

Book #5, CALAMITY (AND A DANISH), takes them to the stunning city of Copenhagen. London is thrilled to sail into the historic harbor of Nyhavn, with its colorful homes lining the harbor, and to visit a delicious pastry festival, where the country competes for the best Danish in Denmark. But when she has the bad fortune to discover a dead body, London's dreams turn into a

nightmare, leaving her little time to solve the crime herself—or else find herself imprisoned.

Laugh-out-loud funny, romantic, endearing, rife with new sights, culture and food, THE EUROPEAN VOYAGE cozy series offers a fun and suspenseful trip through the heart of Europe, anchored in an intriguing mystery that will keep you on the edge of your seat and guessing until the very last page.

Book #6 in the series—MAYHEM (AND HERRING)—is now also available!

Blake Pierce

Blake Pierce is the USA Today bestselling author of the RILEY PAGE mystery series, which includes seventeen books. Blake Pierce is also the author of the MACKENZIE WHITE mystery series, comprising fourteen books; of the AVERY BLACK mystery series, comprising six books; of the KERI LOCKE mystery series, comprising five books; of the MAKING OF RILEY PAIGE mystery series, comprising six books; of the KATE WISE mystery series, comprising seven books; of the CHLOE FINE psychological suspense mystery, comprising six books; of the JESSE HUNT psychological suspense thriller series, comprising nineteen books; of the AU PAIR psychological suspense thriller series, comprising three books; of the ZOE PRIME mystery series, comprising six books; of the ADELE SHARP mystery series, comprising thirteen books; of the EUROPEAN VOYAGE cozy mystery series, comprising six books (and counting); of the new LAURA FROST FBI suspense thriller, comprising three books (and counting); of the new ELLA DARK FBI suspense thriller, comprising six books (and counting); of the A YEAR IN EUROPE cozy mystery series, comprising nine books); of the AVA GOLD mystery series, comprising three books (and counting); and of the RACHEL GIFT mystery series, comprising three books (and counting).

An avid reader and lifelong fan of the mystery and thriller genres, Blake loves to hear from you, so please feel free to visit www.blakepierceauthor.com to learn more and stay in touch.

BOOKS BY BLAKE PIERCE

AVA GOLD MYSTERY SERIES
CITY OF PREY (Book #1)
CITY OF FEAR (Book #2)
CITY OF BONES (Book #3)

A YEAR IN EUROPE
A MURDER IN PARIS (Book #1)
DEATH IN FLORENCE (Book #2)
VENGEANCE IN VIENNA (Book #3)

ELLA DARK FBI SUSPENSE THRILLER
GIRL, ALONE (Book #1)
GIRL, TAKEN (Book #2)
GIRL, HUNTED (Book #3)
GIRL, SILENCED (Book #4)
GIRL, VANISHED (Book 5)
GIRL ERASED (Book #6)

LAURA FROST FBI SUSPENSE THRILLER
ALREADY GONE (Book #1)
ALREADY SEEN (Book #2)
ALREADY TRAPPED (Book #3)

EUROPEAN VOYAGE COZY MYSTERY SERIES
MURDER (AND BAKLAVA) (Book #1)
DEATH (AND APPLE STRUDEL) (Book #2)
CRIME (AND LAGER) (Book #3)
MISFORTUNE (AND GOUDA) (Book #4)
CALAMITY (AND A DANISH) (Book #5)
MAYHEM (AND HERRING) (Book #6)

ADELE SHARP MYSTERY SERIES
LEFT TO DIE (Book #1)
LEFT TO RUN (Book #2)
LEFT TO HIDE (Book #3)
LEFT TO KILL (Book #4)

LEFT TO MURDER (Book #5)
LEFT TO ENVY (Book #6)
LEFT TO LAPSE (Book #7)
LEFT TO VANISH (Book #8)
LEFT TO HUNT (Book #9)
LEFT TO FEAR (Book #10)

THE AU PAIR SERIES
ALMOST GONE (Book#1)
ALMOST LOST (Book #2)
ALMOST DEAD (Book #3)

ZOE PRIME MYSTERY SERIES
FACE OF DEATH (Book#1)
FACE OF MURDER (Book #2)
FACE OF FEAR (Book #3)
FACE OF MADNESS (Book #4)
FACE OF FURY (Book #5)
FACE OF DARKNESS (Book #6)

A JESSIE HUNT PSYCHOLOGICAL SUSPENSE SERIES
THE PERFECT WIFE (Book #1)
THE PERFECT BLOCK (Book #2)
THE PERFECT HOUSE (Book #3)
THE PERFECT SMILE (Book #4)
THE PERFECT LIE (Book #5)
THE PERFECT LOOK (Book #6)
THE PERFECT AFFAIR (Book #7)
THE PERFECT ALIBI (Book #8)
THE PERFECT NEIGHBOR (Book #9)
THE PERFECT DISGUISE (Book #10)
THE PERFECT SECRET (Book #11)
THE PERFECT FAÇADE (Book #12)
THE PERFECT IMPRESSION (Book #13)
THE PERFECT DECEIT (Book #14)
THE PERFECT MISTRESS (Book #15)

CHLOE FINE PSYCHOLOGICAL SUSPENSE SERIES
NEXT DOOR (Book #1)

A NEIGHBOR'S LIE (Book #2)
CUL DE SAC (Book #3)
SILENT NEIGHBOR (Book #4)
HOMECOMING (Book #5)
TINTED WINDOWS (Book #6)

KATE WISE MYSTERY SERIES
IF SHE KNEW (Book #1)
IF SHE SAW (Book #2)
IF SHE RAN (Book #3)
IF SHE HID (Book #4)
IF SHE FLED (Book #5)
IF SHE FEARED (Book #6)
IF SHE HEARD (Book #7)

THE MAKING OF RILEY PAIGE SERIES
WATCHING (Book #1)
WAITING (Book #2)
LURING (Book #3)
TAKING (Book #4)
STALKING (Book #5)
KILLING (Book #6)

RILEY PAIGE MYSTERY SERIES
ONCE GONE (Book #1)
ONCE TAKEN (Book #2)
ONCE CRAVED (Book #3)
ONCE LURED (Book #4)
ONCE HUNTED (Book #5)
ONCE PINED (Book #6)
ONCE FORSAKEN (Book #7)
ONCE COLD (Book #8)
ONCE STALKED (Book #9)
ONCE LOST (Book #10)
ONCE BURIED (Book #11)
ONCE BOUND (Book #12)
ONCE TRAPPED (Book #13)
ONCE DORMANT (Book #14)
ONCE SHUNNED (Book #15)

ONCE MISSED (Book #16)
ONCE CHOSEN (Book #17)

MACKENZIE WHITE MYSTERY SERIES
BEFORE HE KILLS (Book #1)
BEFORE HE SEES (Book #2)
BEFORE HE COVETS (Book #3)
BEFORE HE TAKES (Book #4)
BEFORE HE NEEDS (Book #5)
BEFORE HE FEELS (Book #6)
BEFORE HE SINS (Book #7)
BEFORE HE HUNTS (Book #8)
BEFORE HE PREYS (Book #9)
BEFORE HE LONGS (Book #10)
BEFORE HE LAPSES (Book #11)
BEFORE HE ENVIES (Book #12)
BEFORE HE STALKS (Book #13)
BEFORE HE HARMS (Book #14)

AVERY BLACK MYSTERY SERIES
CAUSE TO KILL (Book #1)
CAUSE TO RUN (Book #2)
CAUSE TO HIDE (Book #3)
CAUSE TO FEAR (Book #4)
CAUSE TO SAVE (Book #5)
CAUSE TO DREAD (Book #6)

KERI LOCKE MYSTERY SERIES
A TRACE OF DEATH (Book #1)
A TRACE OF MUDER (Book #2)
A TRACE OF VICE (Book #3)
A TRACE OF CRIME (Book #4)
A TRACE OF HOPE (Book #5)

www.ingramcontent.com/pod-product-compliance
Lightning Source LLC
Chambersburg PA
CBHW030619310726
48979CB00003B/785
9781094391083